T0322058

Glorious Exploits

'Bold and totally unexpected, I loved this book. A brilliant novel about friendship, the healing power of art and why we must fight for our dreams. I was hooked from the first page' Douglas Stuart, author of *Shuggie Bain*

'In *At Swims-Two-Birds*, Flann O'Brien gave us cowboys riding through Dublin. Now, Ferdia Lennon gives us modern-day Dubliners living among the ancient Greeks. This is a very special, very clever, very entertaining novel' Roddy Doyle, author of *Paddy Clarke Ha Ha Ha*

'As thrilling for me as the first time I picked up a Kevin Barry novel. *Glorious Exploits* is exuberant, funny, lyrical and profoundly moving. It is, quite simply, a rare beauty' Sarah Winman, author of *Still Life*

'With all the blunt humanity of Roddy Doyle, *Glorious Exploits* is a vividly conjured vision of the past. Madly ambitious, cathartic like all great tragedy, but shockingly funny too, Ferdia Lennon's outstandingly original debut is just glorious' Emma Donoghue, author of *Room*

'What a voice! What a story! A darkly funny double act from Lampo and Gelon, sandwiched in between the transformative experience of theatre and forgiving your enemies. I loved it from the first line' Claire Fuller, author of *Unsettled Ground*

'Sublime. Pitch-perfect dialogue, a fast-moving story that is both dark and lyrically beautiful, tragic and funny in equal measure. *Glorious Exploits* is an astonishingly original and gripping story of brotherhood, war and art. Ferdia Lennon is a fierce new talent' Rebecca Stott, author of *In the Days of Rain*

Glorious Exploits

FERDIA LENNON

FIG TREE
an imprint of
PENGUIN BOOKS

FIG TREE

UK | USA | Canada | Ireland | Australia
India | New Zealand | South Africa

Fig Tree is part of the Penguin Random House group of companies
whose addresses can be found at global.penguinrandomhouse.com.

First published 2024

011

Copyright © Ferdia Lennon, 2024

The moral right of the author has been asserted

Set in 12/14.75pt Dante MT Std
Typeset by Jouve (UK), Milton Keynes
Printed and bound in Great Britain by Clays Ltd, Elcograf S.p.A.

The authorized representative in the EEA is Penguin Random House Ireland,
Morrison Chambers, 32 Nassau Street, Dublin D02 YH68

A CIP catalogue record for this book is available from the British Library

HARDBACK ISBN: 978–0–241–61764–9
TRADE PAPERBACK ISBN: 978–0–241–66722–4

www.greenpenguin.co.uk

To Emma

That which is beyond us, which is greater than the human, the unattainably great, is for the mad, or for those who listen to the mad, and then believe them.

Euripides, *The Bacchae*

Death cannot be what Life is, Child; the cup
of Death is empty, and Life has always hope.

Euripides, *The Trojan Women*

Syracuse

412 BC

I.

So Gelon says to me, 'Let's go down and feed the Athenians. The weather's perfect for feeding Athenians.'

Gelon speaks the truth. 'Cause the sun is blazing all white and tiny in the sky, and you can feel a burn from the stones as you walk. Even the lizards are hiding, poking their heads out from under rocks and trees as if to say, Apollo, are you fucking joking? I picture the Athenians all crammed in, their eyes darting about for a bit of shade, and their tongues all dry and gasping.

'Gelon, you speak the truth.'

Gelon nods. We set out with six skins – four of water and two of wine – a pot of olives, and two blocks of that smelly cheese Ma makes. Ah, it's a beautiful island we have, and sometimes I think the factory closing is my chance to shake things up. That I might just leave Syracuse and find myself a little place by the sea, no more dark rooms, clay and red hands, but the sea and the sky, and when I come home with a fresh catch slung over my shoulder, she'll be there, whoever she may be, waiting for me and laughing. That laugh, I hear it now, and it sounds to me a soft and delicate thing.

'Why, Gelon, I feel so good today!'

Gelon looks at me. He's handsome, with eyes the colour of shallow sea when the sun shines through it. Not shit-brown like mine. He opens his mouth to speak, but nothing comes. He's often down, Gelon – sees the world as if it's filtered through smoke, no brightness to anything. We walk on. Even though the Athenians are crushed, their ships firewood, and their unburied dead food for our dogs, there are still hoplites on patrol. Just in case. Diocles gave a speech not yesterday about how you can never tell with these Athenians; a fresh batch could arrive any day. Maybe he's right. Most of the Spartans have left. Word is they're heading for Athens itself, all set to siege it up right and proper. End this war. But there are still a few about. Homesick and useless. In fact, four of them walk ahead of us now, their red cloaks trailing behind them like wounds.

'Morning!'

They look back. Only one of them salutes. Arrogant, these Spartans, but I'm feeling good.

'Down with Athens!'

Two of them salute now, but there's no life behind it. They look tired and sad, like Gelon.

'I say Pericles is a prick!'

'Pericles is dead, Lampo.'

'Aye, sure, Gelon, I know that. I say Pericles is a dead prick!'

This time two of the Spartans laugh, and all four salute. Ah, I feel so happy today. I can't explain it, but it's some feeling. Those are the best ones. The ones you can't explain, and we haven't even fed the Athenians.

'Which quarry shall it be today, Gelon?'

We stand at a fork in the road, and a decision must be made. Gelon hesitates.

'Laurium?' says Gelon, at last.

'Laurium?'

'Yes, I think so.'

'Laurium!'

We go left. Laurium is what the main quarry goes by these days. Someone thought it would be a laugh to call it after that silver mine in Attica that the Athenians used to fund this trip. The name stuck. It's a massive pit surrounded by a milky rock

4

face of limestone so high there's only need for a fence in one or two spots. At one of those is the gateway in; where a couple of guards are sitting on their arses playing dice. Gelon hands them a wineskin, and they wave us on. The path down is a windy ankle-breaker. A coiling brown serpent is what Gelon calls it when the muse is upon him. We can smell the Athenians before we see them. The way being all twisted blocks a full view, but the smell is something awful: thick and rotten, the air almost misty with stench. I have to stop for a moment as my eyes are watering.

'It seems worse than usual.'

'That will be the heat.'

'Aye.'

I pinch my nose, and we walk on. There are fewer than last time. At this rate, they'll be all gone by winter. Gets me thinking of the evening they surrendered. The debate went on for hours. Diocles pacing back and forth, roaring, 'Where do we put seven thousand of these bastards?' Silence. So he asks again. This time that Hermocrates prick mumbles about a treaty. Treaty, my arse, thinks I, and then Diocles says it. Not in those words, but he means the same. He says, 'Do you make a treaty with a corpse?' Laughter spreads, fingers wag, and Hermocrates sits down and shuts his beak. And through it all, Diocles keeps pacing, asking us what to do? Silence. Although now it's a throbbing silence. Ready to burst. Then he stops pacing; says he has something. Something new and strange. Something that will show the rest of Greece that we mean business. That we're Syracuse and here to stay. Do we want to hear about it? 'We do, Diocles!' But he shakes his head. Actually, it's too much. Too strange. Someone else should speak. But the time for that is long past. For we're Syracuse and here to stay, and we tell him as much. So he leans forward and whispers. No sound. Only his lips moving. 'We can't hear you,

Diocles!' So he says it. Still low but loud enough for us to hear: 'Put them in the quarries.' Then he shouts it: 'The quarries!' And soon, nearly the whole of Syracuse was shivering with those two words: the quarries.

Aye, and that's exactly what we did.

From a distance, they look like so many red ants swarming on the rocks, though these Athenians hardly swarm. They just lie about or crouch or crawl about, looking for a bit of shade. Still, to be fair, my eyesight's not the best, and some of those most stationary may, in fact, be dead.

'Morning!'

A few glance up, but none return my greeting. Now, as time goes by, some in the city feel we've made a mistake. That keeping them here in the pits is too much, that it goes beyond war. They say we should just kill them, make them slaves or send them home, but ah, I like the pits. It reminds us that all things must change. I recall the Athenians as they were a year ago: their armour flashing like waves when the moon is upon them, their war cries that kept you up at night, and set the dogs howling, and those ships, hundreds of ships gliding around our island, magnificent sharks ready to feast. The pits show us that nothing is permanent. That's what Diocles says. They show us that glory and power are shadows on a wall. Ah, and I like the way they smell. It's awful, but it's wonderful awful. They smell like victory and more. Every Syracusan feels it when they get that smell. Even the slaves feel it. Rich or poor, free or not, you get a whiff of those pits, and your life seems somehow richer than it did before, your blankets warmer, your food tastier. You're on the right track – or at the very least a better track than those Athenians.

'Morning!'

A poor bastard sees my club and raises his arms. A stream of words follow, most of which I can't understand, his voice being a faint croak, but I pick out 'Zeus', 'please' and 'children'.

'Fear not,' says I. 'We come not to punish, though you Athenian dogs deserve punishment. Gelon and I are merciful. We come –'

'Shut up.'

'What, Gelon? I speak the truth.'

'Just be quiet.'

I chuckle.

'Ah, you're in one of those moods, I see.'

He's already kneeling by the poor bastard, giving him water.

'Any Euripides?' says Gelon.

The man is sucking at the goatskin like it's Aphrodite's nipple, some of the water trickling down his beard. He's pink. Actually pink. Almost all of them are pink, though some are even red.

'Euripides, man, do you know any?'

The man nods and sucks some more. Other Athenians are coming forward now. Feet clanking with chains. There are more than I thought, though still fewer than last time.

'Water and cheese,' says Gelon, 'for anyone who knows lines of Euripides and can recite them! If it's from *Medea*, or *Telephus*, you'll get olives too.'

'What about Sophocles?' asks a tiny creature with no teeth. '*Oedipus Rex*?'

'Fuck Sophocles! Did Gelon mention Sophocles? You –'

'Shut up.'

'Ah, Gelon. I'm only saying.'

Gelon starts with the terms.

'No Sophocles, nor Aeschylus, nor any other Athenian poet. You can recite them if it pleases you, but water and cheese are only for Euripides. Now, my man. What have you got?'

The man who was drinking clears his throat and goes to

straighten up. It's a sorry sight. Try as he might, he can't do it. His neck flops, the head swaying from side to side, loose fruit blown by a gentle wind.

He says, ' "Eh, but we must learn to understand, King Priam . . ." '

He stops.

'Is that all?'

'Sorry, I knew more, but I can't seem to. My head, it's broken, see, I forget faces, and I can't remember my . . . I swear I knew more.'

The man puts his head in his hands. Gelon pats him on the shoulder and gives him one last sip. I think the Athenian's crying, but he still sucks away at the skin. Water pouring into him even as it pours out.

'Can anyone do better than that? A mouthful of olives for some *Medea*?'

Gelon's mad for Euripides. It's the main reason he comes. I think he would've been almost happy for the Athenians to have won if it meant Euripides would've popped over and put on some plays. He once spent a month's wages to pay an old actor to come to our factory and recite scenes while we shaped pots. The foreman said it was reducing productivity, and he threw the actor out. Gelon didn't give up, though. He had the actor shout the lines from across the street. You'd hear snatches of poetry through the blaze of the kiln, and though I think we made fewer pots that week, they were stranger, more beautiful. This was all before the war, and the actor's dead now, the factory gone. I look over at Gelon. His blue eyes wide and nervous. A block of cheese held over his head. Shouting about olives. Gelon's just mad. Never mind Euripides.

Many volunteer, but when it comes to it, most fumble and pause and complain about headaches and thirst, or just collapse on the ground so that we only get a line at a time. Two if we're lucky. One bluffer starts doing a scene where Medea is being wooed by Achilles, which even I know is a load of bollix. Medea was way before Achilles. She was with Jason.

' "But swift-footed Achilles it can never be! Oh Hellas, my father will never allow it. Achilles, what can . . ." '

Gelon raises his club, and the bluffer slinks away. Another takes his place. This one at least mentions Jason, but it's a bit Gelon already knows. Still, he gets a few olives for his troubles.

The day goes on in this way. The sun gets fatter, yolkier, and its heat less fierce. Pinks and reds bleed into the blue. I leave Gelon to it and take a stroll around the pits. Officially I'm scouting for actors. Gelon's taken a bold step and offered to return with a bag of grain if he can get five Athenians to do a scene from *Medea*. But he wants them to properly act it out. Like, perform it. He'll be lucky if he finds one. These poor bastards are just waiting to die. I imagine the worst spots of Hades are something similar. Hairy skeletons with a hint of skin. Apart from the hair, the only bit of variety to be found is in the eyes. Glassy gems made brighter by dying. Massive browns and blues peer out at me. I haven't found a leading man yet, but I'm looking.

Now, you watch these Athenians, and you feel like you're seeing their spirit float out through the nostrils and lips, one breath at a time. You feel like their skin withers and flakes in front of you, that if you only waited and watched one long enough, they'd disappear, and all that would be left is their teeth and a few slender branches of bone, white teeth and white bone sinking into the quarry, and maybe some day a house will be built with that very stone, your house, and you'll lie awake at night with the walls moaning, the ceiling weeping, a second sky dripping on your little head, and you'll hope it's nothing, the wind or the rain, and maybe it is, though maybe it's them Athenians twisting in your walls. These are strange thoughts. Hades thoughts, but the quarry is a strange place, and a man is not himself in here.

There's a scream in the distance. A lot of spirit lost in a scream. Must be serious. It comes again, just as loud. From a spot at the end of the quarry. Athenians seem to pour out and away from it so that instead of the usual wall of skin and rags, you can see the rock. I decide to take a closer peek. There's a huge man swinging a club. An Athenian rolled up like a wailing kitten at his feet. Actually, there are two Athenians at his feet. Though the other is clearly dead. The clubber's tunic is splattered with red. Is it Biton? Aye, it's Biton. Always Biton. His son was killed in the first battle with the Athenians. Well, not in the actual battle. He was captured and tortured to death. Biton comes here a lot. Even more than us.

'You're a terrible man, Biton.'

Biton turns around. I wink. He doesn't. There's a twitching in his cheeks. If possible, he looks worse than the poor bastard at his feet. The Athenian's face is a mass of gore, but there's strange hope in those green eyes. Shocking green they are. Lizard-green. They're bright, and he's already pulling himself away. Not ready to give up on life just yet.

'Gelon and I are up yonder. Collecting a bit of Euripides, would you believe.'

Biton doesn't answer. Just squeezes the handle of his club. The veins in his arm streak like lightning.

'Blinding heat we got this morning.'

Again nothing. The Athenian's still crawling away.

'You having a bit of sport? What did he do to deserve such attention?'

'Found them in the wall.'

'Wall?'

'They'd made a hole. Bastards.'

'They?'

Biton kicks the dead body at his feet.

'Asleep in the arms of this piece of shit. Fucking wrapped around each other. Like lovers.'

I nod. The Athenian's a decent bit away now. Crawling, a trail of red in his wake.

'There are fewer here than last time.'

'Bastards.'

'Aye, they're bastards. I give these Athenians two months at most. If Apollo keeps up this performance, maybe less. I think I'll miss them when they're gone. They break up the day somewhat.'

Biton puts his face in his hands.

'You're not the worst, Biton.'

The Athenian's still in view. He's not moving nearly fast enough. Go on, you bastard.

'Diocles says we ought to follow them back to Greece. Really finish the job. What say you? I, for one, wouldn't mind a stroll through their Acropolis. Maybe catch a show. They say it's stunning. Like nothing here in Sicily.'

Biton lowers his hands and takes a step away.

'That's some club you got there. Heracles massaged the Nemean lion with such a club, Biton. I salute you on account of that club.'

I salute Biton. The Athenian's moving tortoise-slow. I think, what's the point? Let it be, but ah, I don't want to see him die.

'Will you pop back with me and give your greetings to Gelon? He'd be delighted to see you.'

This is a lie.

'Too busy.'

'Aye, I can see you're a busy man. That's clear. The thing is, I fancy a bit of company as I stroll. The light's fading now, and it pains me to admit this, but I don't like this place in the dark.

The rats come out, and it frightens me. Now don't laugh, Biton. I know it's funny, but I say it plainly. It frightens me.'

Biton isn't laughing. He's walked off back towards the Athenian.

'Wait!'

He stops and turns to face me.

'Do you have your heart set on that poor fucker?'

Biton nods.

'I only ask on account of Gelon looking for a green-eyed actor for the role of Jason. Jason being well known to have especially green eyes. The eyes being a significant factor in what first attracted Medea, if the tales are true.'

Biton looks confused.

'I offer you this pouch of fine wine by way of compensation.'

He's still confused, but it's interested confusion. Since his son's death, Biton has become a devotee of Dionysus, but being skint, he gets to worship rarely.

'For me?'

'Aye, in exchange for the Athenian.'

His eyes widen. He looks ready to cry.

'Thanks.'

'Enjoy, Biton.'

He takes the goatskin and sucks at it mightily. The suction not being quite equal to Aphrodite's nipple, but surely that of a nymph or some lower goddess. I pat him on the shoulder and walk on ahead. It takes no more than a couple of strides for me to be level with the Athenian. He curls up in a ball, expecting more of the same. When the blows don't come, his fingers open up, and I see those green eyes staring out at me – lizard-green.

'Fear not, for I come not to torment, though you do deserve tormenting. I come to engage you in a theatrical performance!'

His fingers close, and he only rolls up the tighter.

'For fucksake! If I wanted to hurt you, I'd hurt you.'

The fingers part, and those green eyes return. I think he's saying something.

'Please, don't . . .'

'Enough snivelling! I may change my mind. Now tell me plainly, and no harm will come. Do you know Euripides?'

He doesn't answer.

'Speak! Do you know him? Euripides, a fine Athenian poet?'

'I do.'

'Would you be knowing any passages? I mean, could you say them when prompted? Be truthful.'

He nods.

'*Medea*? Do you know *Medea*?'

'Yes, I think so. I . . .'

'Think is no good to me, man. I'm considering you for the role of Jason. It's a key role. Now speak plainly.'

'I think, sorry, I'm sure, I remember quite a bit, please.'

I hand him a waterskin to clear his thoughts. He finishes half in one gulp. I squirt the rest on his face to wash away the gore. It's not as bad as it looks. A big gash on his cheek and another on his forehead. Nothing broken. I wouldn't call him handsome, but all things considered, he'll do. I offer him my arm, and he takes it. We walk. It all seems to be going fine till we get to the other Athenian. The one Biton killed. When we get to him, the green-eyed fella drops to the ground and starts crying, kissing the body and whispering to it.

'Enough, man. I'm in a rush.'

He ignores me, just keeps kissing and whispering so that his lips and face get all red and messy. I'll have to wash him again. That's a waste of water.

'Come on!'

Nothing. I raise my club as if to swing. It works, and he

moves away from the body right quick. His arms up to protect himself.

'Now stand!'

He goes to stand but stops, kneels back down, pulls a few bits of yellow hair from what's left of the head and squeezes them in his fist. Then he stands. I start walking, real slow, and he follows.

The moon's already out, a silver grin in the sky, but the sun is there too. Fat and red. In a little while it will be gone below the walls of the quarry and then below the sea and then, sure that's night-time. I imagine my friend will be delighted with night-time. The sun, it seems, being the principal cause of death in these here pits.

'You'll be happy to see the evening come, no?'

He doesn't respond.

'Answer me, friend.'

'Sorry?'

'I say you'll be happy now Apollo's making himself scarce.'

'It's not much better at night.'

'The rats?'

'No, the cold. It gets bitter. The change brings on fevers.'

'That why you and your mate were in the hole?'

He nods.

'Shows ingenuity. I respect that, but sure, Biton, the fella you met earlier, he hates Athenian ingenuity. Despises it. I reckon you pissed him off with that one. Having a kip in the shade when you should've been outside baking.'

The Athenian's crying again.

'Calm down, man. Have an olive.'

I hold out the cup. They're lovely olives: mixed with oil, salt, garlic and a secret ingredient. My ma makes them. Best in Syracuse. He hesitates but takes a few. He's still crying, but he's chewing too.

'What's your name, friend?'

'Paches.'

'Paches?'

He nods.

'I'm Polyphemus.'

I made that up. You can never tell with these Athenians. A name can be used for a curse or whatnot.

'Polyphemus, like the Cyclops?'

'Aye, the very one. Ma tells me my da had one eye. Poor bastard.'

'Oh.'

We walk on.

'You know, Paches. You Athenians brought this on yourselves. Sailing over here like sharks ready to eat us up. You're worse than the Persians. They're barbarians, but you're Greeks attacking Greeks. Aye, Diocles is right. You're scum.'

He doesn't answer, just limps on. Eyes watch us from the shadows.

'Still, my mate Gelon will be pleased to meet such a scholar of Euripides. He says he's finer than Homer. You'll meet him soon. Gelon, not Homer.'

I wink.

With the light falling, the rats come out. At first, there are only one or two, but pretty soon, the ground is full of them, the air heavy with their sounds. They look mad. Not like any rats you know: wet, red and very fat. They waddle over your feet, but if you don't step on them, they cause no trouble. Still, it makes me awful tentative as I walk. Paches doesn't seem to notice, yet he must, for he never steps on one. Gelon reckons there are over a thousand rats in these pits. He says if you listen carefully at night, you can hear their screeching from the city.

'The rats don't bother you, Paches?'

'No.'

'I think they would get to me worse than the hunger or the thirst.'

He looks at me as if to say I've no clue.

'Would you like some more water?'

He nods, and I hand him the skin.

'You miss Athens?'

He spits out the water. Coughs.

'Sorry, course you do. What I meant is, I hear it's really something. You know, we Syracusans looked up to you so. Sure, isn't our democracy taken after yours? Aye, I think I'd love to see it. The Parthenon. Gelon says it's more beautiful than anything, even in Egypt or Persia.'

'He's been?'

I go to pat my club, but don't.

'No. He's never been, but he's spoken to those who have.'

'It is.'

'What?'

'The most beautiful . . .'

He stops. I think tears are coming, but he masters himself.

'It is the most beautiful city in Greece by far. I've been to Egypt, and I think it equals anything there. I can't speak for Persia.'

'You've been to Egypt?'

'Yes.'

'The pyramids? Really?'

He nods.

'Would you like an olive?'

I hand him a few more.

'Thank you, Polyphemus.'

I spot Gelon in the distance. He's plopped on a rock – a couple of Athenians below him.

'Lampo,' I say quickly.

16

'Pardon?'

'My name. It's not really Polyphemus. It's Lampo. Sure, who'd be calling a child after a Cyclops?'

'Oh.'

I grin and nudge him forward.

'Brace yourself, Gelon. Here's your leading man!'

Gelon peers down.

'What?'

'Meet Jason. See those green eyes. Didn't you say Jason was green-eyed?'

Gelon takes in Paches. I don't think he's impressed, and in truth, the cuts Biton gave him are worse than I first thought. Paches looks a state.

'Green-eyed? What are you on about? Anyway, that poor bastard's dying.'

'You're a negative fucker, Gelon.' I put my arm around Paches. 'Show him, Paches. Jason's final speech, right, when he realizes his children are dead!'

Paches coughs.

' "You who are most despised by the gods, I –" '

'Wait!' says Gelon. 'If he's going to do it, at least do it as part of the scene. Medea, are you ready?'

'Think so.'

A very tall woman steps forward, but of course, there are no women in the pits. I look again. Isn't it only the poor bastard whose neck was swaying so, though his hair is much longer now and he's in a girl's chiton.

'That your sister's?'

Gelon nods.

'The hair?'

'From a horse.'

'You went all out.'

'Aye.'

17

Paches and Medea get in their positions. Gelon and I sit on a rock and wait. I think of what it would be like to see the real thing in Athens, and I feel an ache for I know I never will, but then I look around me: the quarry walls circling and the sky pressing down, thick with stars, or gods, and below equally thick with Athenians. Sure, isn't this quarry itself an amphitheatre?

A huge Athenian amphitheatre, with two little Syracusans watching.

They begin.

2.

The lantern of Dismas' sways like a stocious moon in the distance. We've had a few since leaving the quarry, and Gelon wants to finish up by the sea, and Dismas' is by the sea, precariously so. The path's littered with shells, crushed crabs, medusas of seaweed heaped in glistening bunches. I lob one at Gelon, and he kicks one at me. As we get closer, the waves blend with the clinking of cups and the crackling nonsense of a hundred voices together.

A handsome fella with one arm stands at the door, a fiery red horse branded into his forehead. This is Chabrias – an Argive war slave who Dismas picked up cheap on account of the paucity of limbs. Sober, Chabrias gives the impression of one experiencing a constant low level of pain – cheek and forehead muscles strained in a half-grimace – but late at night when the punters get generous, and a jug or two is brought to him, the cheeks loosen, the eyes brighten, and if you stay and listen, he'll regale you with stories of Argos: women loved, chariots raced, temples prayed in, sacred springs and verdant groves galore. Yes, a debauched and holy place is Argos. If only he could show you; and there's something in the way these tales are spun, their desperate urgency, that one feels poor Chabrias is trying to conjure it up as much for himself as for you. That he wants the ashes of his present to kindle and glow with Argos, till it all gets too much and he stops mid-sentence, looks at the sky, hums an odd tune and shows you the stump of his arm. I like Chabrias.

'Look who it is!' says I.

Chabrias bows, opens the door. The area around him decidedly jugless. We head in.

A blast of brine and fish scales fills the nostrils. Dismas' reeks more strongly of sea than the beach itself. Owing to its location, it's a favourite of fishermen, and packed in as they are, with the windows shut, the odours sit and settle. The air positively steams; tendrils of fishy fog rise from necks and soaking cloaks. The men crouch over their jugs, beards speckled purple as they boast or commiserate over the latest catch. Yet along with this human din, there are loads of other noises that the building makes. Over the years, the wind and rain have gnashed numerous tiny and not so tiny holes within the walls so that the structure seems to whistle, the ceiling beams and floor to creak and bend. Yet, this fragility only adds to your comfort. Your ears prepare your skin for an onslaught that never comes, and, as a man never cherishes something more intensely than in those moments he fears losing it, so too this constant expectation of elemental fury adds savour to your boozing.

Gelon heads straight for Homer's chair. A rickety piece of shit the blind bard is reported to have sat on during a visit to Syracuse a few hundred years back. It's stuck in the corner, a bronze inscription above that reads 'Homer's chair'. Is it Homer's chair? Well, there are many Homer's chairs scattered across Syracuse, and can they all be Homer's chair? Why not? The arse is capricious and does not wed for life, and so perhaps, yeah, it is Homer's chair.

A fella's already in it, and Gelon asks him to move. The fella says fuck off, and Gelon politely drags him by the scruff and sends him tumbling to the floor, apologizing as he does it. Heads turn, and many cheer and hoot, 'cause Gelon's well known in Dismas' and this ritual's often enacted when unsuspecting punters take his place.

I get the first one in. A new slave girl pours the wine. She's dark, almond-brown eyes and skin like freshly beaten copper. It fairly glows, that skin, and though she's only chattel, I find myself wincing when I see her eye my cloak, stained and tattered as it is. She hands me the jug, and I walk back to the table, do my best not to limp. Gelon's head's in his hands.

'Get that into you. We'll have no moping, alright?'

He looks up, tries to smile.

'We're having a jar!' says I. 'What are we having?'

'A jar.'

I fill our cups to the brim and raise my own.

'To Syracuse!' says I.

'To Homer.'

'Check out the new slave. She's stunning. Fucking hurts to look at her. I'm sore just looking at her.'

'Do you think he knew what he'd done?'

'What?'

'You think Homer knew when he'd written *The Iliad* that he'd written *The Iliad*? Do you?'

'Reckon so.'

Gelon nods.

'And Euripides. When he wrote *Medea*. You think he knew what he'd done?'

'Yeah.'

Gelon asks these questions every time he sits on Homer's chair.

'You know,' he says, 'I've a proposition for you. You'll probably think I'm mad, but still.'

'I already do.'

'What.'

'Think you're mad.'

He looks worried, but then I raise my cup, and we clink and down our drinks in one. Gelon goes to pour another, but the jug's empty.

'Fuck it. I'll get this one.'

He shuffles off, swerving on his way, and I sit and mull over what his proposition might be, but then the slave girl comes to my table and, before I know it, my hand extends, fingers grazing the spot on her arm where they branded her: the skin all puckered and raw.

'Where you from?'

No answer.

'Ah, tell me. You're new. Carthage? Egypt?'

She laughs. Part of her front tooth's broken off, so it looks like a fang, and her some gorgeous wolf.

'What's so funny?'

'Egypt?' she says. 'Are you mad?'

'You look like a pharaoh.'

She smiles and walks off. Her chiton swishing softly as she does. Fucking cracker. Gelon comes back, sets three sloshing jugs down.

'Three?'

'To Homer!' says Gelon.

'To Homer!' says I.

The door swings open, and several aristos burst in. They can't be more than sixteen. Silver bracelets glinting on their wrists, cloaks so white and fluffy, they seem like clouds as they float over the dirt floor and land at the table next to us. They stamp their feet and call for three jugs of the finest. Cragged faces look up from their drinks, curse. This has been happening loads since the war: beardless cunts such as these invading Dismas' and other quality boozers. They screech about democracy, try to stand you drinks, but you know they're only here for the bit of rough.

'Little shits,' says I. 'Not old enough to vote, but Dismas lets them in.'

Gelon's staring into the distance.

'Gelon?'

'Sorry?'

'Check out these fuckers. A testicle between them. Am I right?'

Gelon smiles, but his eyes are mournful.

'Lampo?'

'Yeah?'

'I saw Desma.'

'What?'

'She was in the wall painting over there. The one of Troy. She's one of the women being put on the ships at Troy.'

'Oh.'

Desma is Gelon's missus. No sight nor sound of her in three years. She ran off when their boy died. Word is that she hooked up with some fella in Italy. I'd be surprised, but Gelon sees Desma often and in the strangest of places. He's seen her in the shape of a join in a pot, a meaningless little crack, and he'll stare at it till you poke him. When you ask what he's been looking at, he'll whisper, 'Desma.' He sees her in a smudge of paint, a tree, a stretch of sky, and flowing water too. Gelon sees Desma everywhere. His face is in his hands again. This tends to happen on the fourth jug.

'We're having a sup, Gelon! What are we having?'

'A sup,' he says and takes a big glug of wine.

'And you're sitting in Homer's chair. Where are you sitting?'

'I can't sleep, Lampo. I lie in the –'

'Enough of that shite. Where are you sitting?'

'Homer's chair.'

'And what are we having?'

'A sup.'

I raise my cup for a toast. Gelon just stares into his.

'Hello, citizens!'

We turn around. It's one of the aristos from the table across. A slender thing, right hand on his hip, left clasped around a massive jug, more like a girl than a fella: hair shoulder-length, pretty face, long-lashed grey eyes and fleshy lips.

'Care to partake in a libation?'

Gelon mutters something, and I look away. The boy starts filling our cups all the same.

'To victory!' says pretty boy, eyeing Gelon.

We say nothing, just down our cups in one gulp. It's gorgeous wine, much better than the vinegar we've been drinking. A lovely smell off it too: citrus and honey. I'd heard talk of perfumed wine, but I wouldn't have thought the likes of Dismas' would be selling it. A drachma a jug at the very least.

'Good, isn't it?'

'Not sure,' says I. 'Need more exposure before delivering my verdict. Right, Gelon?'

'Right.'

Pretty boy laughs, slaps his leg. It wasn't that funny. Still, he pours us both another brimful, and we down it just the same.

'And now?' he asks, smiling.

'Being an empiricist,' says I, 'more research required. Feel the same, Gelon?'

Gelon feels the same, and pretty boy fills us up again. This continues till his jug's empty, but he doesn't care, just orders another and calls his mates over to join. Three shiny teens arrive and introduce themselves. I recognize the names of all their fathers, proper rich these fellas, but pretty boy wins the prize. His da's Hermocrates. Fucking Hermocrates. Pretty boy says he hates his da. That he's on our side and thinks the inequality in the city a disgrace. That it's workers like us that make Syracuse what it is. I scowl and say nothing, but this is a buzz. I tell them they don't know the half of it. How I had a duel with an Athenian at Epipolae, and it was Achilles and Hector stuff. Either him or me, and I jump up and act it out. They cheer, and I catch the slave girl looking at me. Fucking cracker.

'Another jug for Achilles!' shouts Hermocrates' son, and another jug is brought. The room's spinning now, not crazy spinning, but a gentle swoosh that gives the faces around me a dancing quality. Someone asks about my limp. Was it from the war? 'Yes,' says I, 'an Athenian archer got me from behind.' An arrow pierced my ankle. 'Like Achilles?' says one, and I burst out crying. The aristos huddle round. They tell me I'm a hero, that I've been wounded for Syracuse, and it's glorious. Soon we're all hugging. Hermocrates' son too. He clasps my hand, tells me his father would like to meet me. 'Like Achilles?' says I, and he says, 'Yeah, like Achilles.' Another jug is brought, and we swear brotherhood. I'm poor, and they're rich, but we're brothers. The tears are pouring out of me. Fuck knows why. I've had this limp all my life, no battles, no arrows, just a crooked foot, and I stare at it, on the filthy floor, twisted for all to see, and, for a brief moment, feel sacred.

Outside. A cluster of stars to light our path. The din of the city gets fainter and fainter till you hear nothing, only waves and the crunch of our steps. We stroll arm in arm, Gelon and I, and occasionally we sway into a bush, but mostly it's smooth going. I swiped one of the aristos' wineskins when we were swearing brotherhood, and we chug it as we walk. We've barely spoken since we left, and it's a shock when Gelon begins to sing. He has a lovely voice: low and liable to falter, but it's sweet and soft, and he gets strange feeling in it. He's singing a bit from *Medea*. The bit just after she's killed her children. Where the chorus chant about how it was bad form. He stops every so often when he forgets a word, then fairly shouts it when he remembers. It's clear now where we're headed: back to the quarry, and sure enough, not long passes before I get the smell, that rotten quarry smell, and Gelon stops.

'My proposition.'
'What?'
'My proposition. I never told you . . . Here it is.'
'I don't . . .'

'Directors.'

'What?'

'Me and you. We're going to be directors.'

He passes the wineskin. I take a swig.

'We are?'

'Aye.'

'What do they do?'

'They direct . . .' he hiccups. 'We're going to do Medea in the quarry. But not just bits and pieces. We're going to do the whole play. Full production with chorus, masks and shit.'

'Oh.'

A low moaning beside me. Gelon's crying.

'You alright?'

Nothing.

'Gelon?'

'Full production,' he says, voice shaking, 'with a chorus and music and masks. Costumes too, a proper play. Like they'd do in Athens. We start tomorrow morning.'

'Better let them know,' says I.

I stumble over as close to the edge as I dare.

'Wake up, Athenians! Wake up!'

It's hard to imagine that there are hundreds of them, perhaps a thousand, sleeping down there. You know it's true. That somewhere in the black they exist, but where and who, and what are they thinking, feeling? It makes my head spin and gives a kind of swirling beauty to the dark. I search for a stone on the ground, a little one, and when I find it, I throw it down. It flies through the air, a thunderbolt, and it lands below with a divine thud.

'Tomorrow morning! Full production! Chorus, masks and shit!' I turn around. 'Right, Gelon?'

'Right.'

I take a swig, reach for another stone.

3.

There was an old augur who lived at the end of Gelon's street. He was a poet too, but his prophecies were said to be better than his rhymes. You could see him before dawn and last thing at night, pacing with his arms behind his back, neck crooked up at the sky and eyes dizzy with starlight, muttering to himself. You could see him at the agora in the midday sun, knelt over, slicing up a lamb, a cat or a dog or whatever he could find; a fierce look of concentration on his face, arms soaked, as he sifted through stringy purples and pinks for a glimpse of what's to come.

Gelon was friendly with him, and one day he took the old fella aside. This was some years back, before the war and before Desma had run off, when their boy, Helios, was still alive, though barely. Anyway, Gelon asked if Helios would see the year out. Now the old fella looked thoughtful. After a long pause, he said if Gelon could get him an ox, he'd soon find out. Gelon, being poor, said he couldn't afford an ox. Okay, well, what about a sheep? Even a lamb would do? Gelon said he'd try. That night he stole a lamb from Alberus' farm, brought it to the prophet. The prophet told him to be at Dismas' the next evening, and he'd tell what he'd found. Then he bowed, took the lamb under his arm, and stumbled off into the night.

So the next day, they're in Dismas' and the old fella's drunk, 'cause he said the wine loosens up his interpretations, and all the while poor Gelon's pressing him: 'What did you see? Will Helios be okay?' At long last, he tells Gelon to lean in. Gelon leaned in. Then the old fella asked if Helios was the little boy

Gelon walked with often, the pale boy with the silly blue cap. Gelon said he was. At this, the old fella whispered that judging from the boy's appearance, he reckoned no. He'd be dead pretty soon. The boy looked sick, very sick, but in the end, he didn't really know, as there was no future, only what happened next, and he cut up the lambs and the cats and the dogs because what else was there? It was something, and a man needed something. Then he asked Gelon to get in another jug.

I mention him in passing because we pass him now as we walk to the quarry. He's beneath a tree, just past the Achradina, hanging from a rope, and in the red light of dawn, the rope seems a stem and he some dreadful flower. Gelon stops and says a prayer. I don't. For I've no time for a fucker who kills dogs.

We walk on.

4.

The directors arrive early – Gelon and Lampo, here for a casting. My head's killing me. I got sick twice on the way, yet here we are, and we're early. Why? Because it matters. That's what Gelon says. The relationship between an actor and a director is all about trust. Belief. I look at these Athenians before me – row upon row of chained skeletons – and belief seems an unlikely thing, performing a play impossible, but looks deceive. That's what Gelon says. He says Euripides' *Hippolytus* was put on during the plague at Athens. That though the city was ravaged, and bodies lay piled in the streets, and the sky was black with funeral smoke, the festival of Dionysia went on. Half the actors were dying. The audience too, yet the chorus sang; they danced. Gelon says this made it even better. That it gave the actors a frenzy most remarkable. In the same way, a soldier who's been dealt a fatal blow sometimes fights more fiercely than ever in those final moments. In just this way, those Athenians gave something special. Something beyond the normal run of tragedy. We're doing nothing but following their precedent. Carrying on where they left off all those years ago in Athens. That's what Gelon says. What he hopes.

We've chosen Laurium for our production: being sickle-shaped, with a bulge in the centre, it looks in many ways like an enormous amphitheatre. There's a spot at the quarry's edge where the limestone juts out to form a milky roof, below which is an abundance of shade. This we choose as our rehearsal space. Gelon sets out a couple of wineskins and a few loaves of bread. Already a gaggle of Athenians hover around us, their eyes zigzagging from the food to our clubs. In the midst of the crowd, I notice a pair of green eyes staring: lizard-green.

'Paches! How are you?'

Paches waves a splintery hand, and I walk over, embrace him. I can feel the veins in his arm: flowing twigs that move around the skin as I squeeze. I tell him we're doing a full production of *Medea* with a chorus, masks and shit. He nods. I tell him that on account of his eyes and his previous recital, he's our first choice for the role of Jason, and it will mean a full belly for at least a month. Sure, the prisoners get rations from the guards, but they're starvation rations: just enough to keep them alive, if even that, and at the mention of proper food Paches starts crying. It's fierce strange seeing water flow from a source so dry. I hand him a wineskin and a lump of bread. Now I've been hungry, and I've been thirsty, but never like this. With every bite and sip, his eyes gain light. Wisps of pink form around the cheeks, spread all across the face and neck. Paches wipes the tears from the green and stands a little straighter, asks me when we start and who we've chosen to play Medea. I give him more bread.

'Today it's just a casting,' says I. 'And so far we've only picked you. You're our first choice, Paches. This is a mighty honour. Don't let me down.'

Paches nods and chews. Athenians watch with anguished awe. They look from him to me and search for a reason. I put my arm around him.

'You may know this fellow as Paches, but from now on, he's Jason. I want him only referred to as Jason. Is that clear?'

The Athenians seem confused, but they nod all the same.

'You're Jason now, Paches.'

The bread's gone, but he still sucks away at the wineskin. You can almost see the swelling the liquid makes as it flows down his throat; hear a faint splash when it hits the stomach. To be honest, Gelon didn't want him as Jason, but I insisted. I rub his head affectionately, the way I've seen aristo mates do in the gymnasium. His hair's sparse, but what is left is mighty black. I imagine with the green eyes Paches was once something to look at. I stroke the hair, and it comes away in my hand, a light breeze lifts the strands up and scatters them all across the quarry.

'Who are you?'

He hands back the wineskin. It's empty.

'Thank you.'

'Who are you?'

'Paches.'

'No, you're Jason. Who are you?'

'Pa—Jason.'

'You hear that, lads? He's Jason!'

The Athenians stare at us, nod.

Paches says there's an Athenian in the quarry who's acted in a load of plays. Not the official ones in Athens, but small rural theatres around Attica. Still, a proper actor could be the making of this production, and we leave Gelon with the rest and set off to find him. Paches is real slow, and I keep having to stop and wait for him to catch up.

'Come on, Jason!' says I. 'How'd you ever get the fleece with that attitude?'

The quarry walls offer the best prospect of shade, but Paches and I stick to the centre. In the centre, there are tall rocks, and though I'm not the nimblest, I can climb them, higher and higher. So high the quarry opens up its secrets to me. Up here, I've seen it all. Their burials, their fights, the tree they prayed at. The only green thing in all the quarry, and how in the end they pulled it down and ate it. I've heard their chanting, their crying too. Some days I've sat on such a rock for hours, till my legs ached, but that wasn't it. It was only beginning then; I'd sit till the legs went numb, and I forgot them, and then something mad happened. With the numbness, it seemed that it wasn't a rock I sat on at all, but a cloud, and little great me a god watching all below.

Touring the quarry with Paches is humbling. I fancied myself a bit of an expert, but as we stroll, my ignorance is revealed in countless little ways. If you can imagine a crescent moon with silver roots spreading out into the sky, this is something of the quarry shape. The crescent being the open space, which by far makes up the greater share, but at its edges, there are passages that curve and twist deep into the rock. These are the roots I spoke of, and they're more numerous than I'd ever supposed. Paches knows them well. He explains that many of the Athenians spend the day in those tunnels to escape the sun and only come out at night. I ask if he'd been hiding in one when Biton killed his mate. He winces, turns away.

We find the actor in one such tunnel under a blanket of rocks, and I've to look twice before I see him. When I start to go in, he screams, and Paches has to calm him down. Apparently, he had a run-in with Biton a couple of days ago, escaped by crawling in deeper where Biton couldn't fit. He sits up, and pebbles and powder scatter off him like he's a mole popping up for air; I hand him some bread. His skin's white from the limestone, and his eyes massive and black. I turn from them to the lizard-green of Paches' and think what a shocking variety us creatures have when it comes to eyes.

'You think you could play Medea?' says I.

'I do.'

'All of it?'

He looks at the goatskin.

'Yes.'

'Opening scene?'

'Certainly.'

'Go for it so.'

'Now?'

'Aye.'

He looks at Paches.

'Do it, Numa.'

Numa coughs, asks for some water first. I pass it to him, and he takes a good swig, wipes his beard. Somewhere mid-wipe, his face starts to change, his posture too.

' "Oh, please, somebody look at me!" ' says Numa, in a woman's voice.

'Not bad.'

Numa blinks.

' "Oh, please, do you see what he's done? This man I loved, whose children I carried and fed, my milk and life down their throats, it was sweet with my love for him, and now do you see what he's done to me? I'm left alone, no warmth in my bed, and it's cold, so cold, I'm cold! Do you see it? Can you see what he's done to me?" ' He stops. 'Will I go on?'

'Aye.'

He goes on. Occasionally he pauses and forgets a word, mumbles, but overall it's the strangest thing. So different from anything else we've seen. Paches and I sit and listen to this starved bastard, half his body covered by rocks, and as we listen, something happens. The words and voice blend so that what he is blends, and he becomes two things at once, a starving Athenian, yes, but something else, hidden, then rising. He's Medea, poor princess Medea from Colchis, and as she lists her grievances against Jason: how she'd cast spells so he could get the Golden Fleece, murdered her brother, and betrayed her father, so he could regain his kingdom. How he'd sworn eternal love under starry skies, told her he'd never leave and then did, as soon as the opportunity arose, fucked off with a girl half his age, made a show of her, and now she's abandoned, now she has nothing to do but wander Greece a lonesome, wretched thing. When I hear all this, I ache at the injustice and turn to Paches and curse him. Tell him he's a fucker. That he hadn't a hope of getting the fleece without Medea. My voice is shaking.

'She loves you!' says I. 'She bore your children. You bastard!'

'What?'

It's Numa. No semblance of Medea left. He and Paches are staring at me. Both scared shitless.

'Sorry,' says I, 'was doing a bit of improv. That was brilliant, Numa. I'll have to confirm with Gelon, but I'm fairly sure the part's yours. Good work, Paches, too.'

I break off two big chunks of bread, pass one to Numa, one to Paches.

'Very impressed,' says I.

Back with Gelon, things have moved along nicely. We've a full chorus with fifteen Athenians, half of which say they've taken part in official productions back in Athens. Not as the main actors but in the chorus. To start, we do a bit from the middle, and Numa smashes it, even better than in the tunnel. As he speaks, I look at Gelon and his whole face shivers, each word from Numa revealing something new. When it ends, Gelon walks over and embraces him.

'Gelon, meet Medea,' says I. 'Medea, Gelon.'

'Thank you,' says Gelon.

I put my arm around Paches, rub his hair.

'Who are you?'

'Jason.'

I give him more bread. The chorus watch.

'Who is he?'

'Jason!' say the chorus, fifteen voices as one.

'You're Jason.'

Paches nods, chews.

5.

Six children at the side of the road with swords, helmets and white sticks. Seen nothing since leaving the quarry – a lonesome walk, with only our breath, the squawk of crows – and these little soldiers give the morning a weird splendour. They shout at us to put our hands up, or they'll gut us like fish. Gelon and I put our hands up, ask them not to gut us like fish. One of the boys steps forward. His helmet's too big, and the metal falls below his nose, but you can still see gaunt cheeks and grey eyes.

'Nice sword,' says I.

'Shut up,' says the kid. 'Want to be gutted?'

'No, thanks.'

'Do you?'

'Not at all,' says Gelon.

He walks from side to side, strokes his chin.

'What business have you in Syracuse?'

'We're Syracusan.'

'Lies.'

'Please,' says I. 'Have mercy.'

'They sound Athenian to me,' calls a child from behind.

The kid grins.

'You fellas from Athens?' He turns to Gelon. 'You fellas here to spy?'

'Never.'

''Cause you know what we do with spies, don't you?'

'Gut them like fish?'

The kid frowns, whisks his white stick past my chin across to Gelon's and, as he does, Gelon pulls away in disgust.

'A fucking bone.'

'What?'

'That's a bone he has.'

I look again: both ends of the stick are knobbly and yellow. In fact, on closer inspection, it does bear striking resemblance to a leg bone.

'That a bone?'

The kid nods. His mates cheer and wave their own bones.

'Where did you get that?' asks Gelon.

'Silence!'

He goes to flick it again, but Gelon takes his hand, kneels, looks him in the eye and, in a slow, calm voice, asks again.

'Where did you get it?'

'Silence –'

'I'm fucking serious now. Where did you get it?'

The boy mumbles something.

'I can't hear you.'

'Over there . . .' He points at some spot beyond his mates.

Gelon removes the helmet, pats him on the head. Fingers momentarily gilded with thick golden curls. He takes the bone.

'You shouldn't be playing with this.'

The kid nods as if he understands. Gelon has a way with children. If I'd said that, he would've probably hit me with the bone. Gelon throws it away. Somewhere in the grass, there's a whoosh.

'Now be a good little soldier and show me where exactly?'

The kid walks towards his mates, gestures for us to follow. The others look at us suspiciously, squeeze bones and swords, but none say a word. Instead, they march on, the kid in front. When we come to a fallen tree, he produces a bit of string tied to a twig, twirls it through the air, whispers. On we go, and this string is produced and twirled with greater frequency. Stones, bushes, piles of dust, leaves, and lizards, all caressed by it. When we ask him why he looks nervous, he says it doesn't matter. Gelon keeps at him, and he mutters about powerful enemies and how much is not what it seems. His eyes drift from Gelon to the ground, hope and embarrassment blending.

'Thank you for protecting us,' says Gelon.

The kid grins.

We come to some woods. The outer trees yellow and burnt, and the air smoky with singed bark. We follow deeper and deeper as the woods darken and a pleasant coolness takes hold. The kid stops.

'Look!'

Six armoured skeletons lie tangled on the ground beneath a willow tree, their bones twisting out from shields and leaves like pale roots. Their meat long since eaten away by wind, sun or teeth, but there's a funky tang to the air.

'Athenians,' says Gelon.

'Exactly,' says the kid.

He tugs at Gelon's cloak, leads him closer.

'Look, here. Engravings of owls on every single one, and see, there's Athena herself.'

'You boys shouldn't be playing with their bones,' says Gelon.

The kid nods, but then something passes over his face, and he looks from his mates to Gelon, frowns.

'Why the fuck not? They're our enemies.'

For ages, Gelon says nothing, just glances from the bones to the boys. The sun through the branches cracks the light on his face. Gelon's shocking handsome. But it's a desolate handsome, which only makes it better. Gelon has a face you'd imagine demands contentment, yet the briefest look at him dispels this. It's a cheeky reminder that beauty isn't everything. Look, it seems to say. Here's Gelon: godlike, broken Gelon. Look and remember beauty isn't all.

'It isn't right,' says Gelon, at last.

The kid strokes his chin as if considering the weight of these words.

'You really think so?'

Gelon nods.

I leave them to it and take a closer peek at the Athenians. No sign of a pyre, making a botched burial unlikely. Yet if we Syracusans had killed them, the armour would've been stripped and brought back as a trophy. Aye, it's mighty peculiar. I kneel and snatch a breastplate, have to pull hard as there's some gluey shit on the ribs – the armour's gorgeous; silver owls floating on bronze clouds. Craftsmanship is right. This will fetch proper coin back in the city. I peel off a set of greaves to go with it, wash away the glue with water from my goatskin, scrub it with a leaf. Only then do I throw them on. A bit loose but not bad, considering. The children have all the helmets, and it seems I'll have to nab one if I want a full set.

I stroll back to ask, but they're busy. The kid tells Gelon his name is Dares, and he and his troops will leave the bodies in peace. All bones will be put back. Dares asks if this is to our satisfaction, and Gelon shakes his head. He's been thinking and now feels the Athenians should have a funeral pyre; nothing big, just enough to blacken the bones and say a prayer. It's no more than any Greek deserves. Dares frowns. Make a pyre for the enemy? Say a prayer?

'You're only messing?'

'I'm not.'

Dares turns to his mates.

'What do you fellas reckon? We give these bastards a funeral?'

His mates say nothing. That is no words, but their faces scream with feeling. Even from under their helmets, you can see features twitch; eyes grow wild and blink in quick succession. Dares asks again. This time a boy steps forward. The boy's tiny. So small his mates almost appear men in comparison; the helmet on his head a cauldron. He can't be more than six or seven. Tiny boy's lips are moving, but I can't hear a thing.

'Louder, Strabo,' says Dares.

'No prayer,' tiny boy says; a trembling croak that barely rises above the wind in the trees.

Dares asks him to explain.

'They.' Tiny boy's hand stretches towards the heaps of branches and leaves. 'They killed my brother. No prayer!'

The words seem to echo, reverberating as they do around his cauldron helmet. He repeats them again and again. Mad that so much feeling is held in a figure so small. He rocks back and forth, points and scrapes the air. The other children look from him to the Athenians, and, for a moment, this tiny boy with the cracked voice is their leader. Many begin to tell a similar story. They shout about cousins lost at sea, butchered uncles, and fathers dumped in ditches miles from Syracuse. What pyre for them? What prayers for them? Dares calls for order, but it's no use. He rushes back and forth, stamps his feet, and waves his arms. Nothing. It seems he's lost whatever hold he has over them, but then he does something strange. He walks over to the tiny boy and kneels. The children shut up. Even to me, Dares kneeling appears unnatural, and I can tell from the expression of his mates, it's extraordinary. Dares takes the hand of tiny boy.

'Your brother was dear to you, Strabo?'

Tiny boy bites his thumb, looks at the ground.

'My da was too, and now he's down below with your brother. It's just me and my ma, and she's terrible strict. A nightmare, Strabo. But you know, still, I think we say a prayer for these Athenians.' Dares looks at Gelon. 'I think a prayer and a pyre aren't much. And I don't know. I think we can say the words not just for them, but for my da and your brother.' He turns to his mates. 'I think we can say it for all and have a pyre for all.'

Tiny boy looks up.

'A prayer for my brother?'

'Yeah, for your brother. What do you think? Will we do it? If you say no, we won't. Will we do it?'

All eyes are on tiny boy. Many debates I've seen in the assembly where the speakers roar about how it's a matter of the utmost importance. That Syracuse is drowning, and only our votes could pull it ashore, yes debates like that I've heard while my eyelids drooped and the assembly swayed to the breeze of yawns, but standing here awaiting the verdict of this armoured tot, is nearly too much for me. I can feel the blood in my throat and the trickle of sweat down my palms. What's it going to be, tiny boy?

His lips move, though I can't hear a word.

Dares smiles. 'Speak up.'

We all lean in.

'A prayer's okay.'

Dares lifts him, squeezes. Tiny boy looks in pain, but he doesn't protest. Instead, he hovers a few feet in the air, bites his thumb till Dares puts him down.

'You're brilliant, Strabo. Do you know that?'

Tiny boy says nothing, just shuffles over to his mates. Soon he's hidden behind a row of children twice his size. His consent won over, preparations begin. We set the pyre up three bodies wide and two deep. Each row is piled with a layer of branches, twigs and dried bark. To prevent the fire spreading, we circle the mound with stones and rocks. Dares has designated himself fire maker, and he steps forward with two sharp black stones, which he begins smashing together. In his eagerness he hits his knuckle and there's a glossy bead of blood but he doesn't cry out or stop, just keeps smashing. Fists dance with sparks, and soon a sliver of orange plays beneath his fingers – the layer of kindling withers as the branches spit and crackle. At first, there's more smoke than flame. The kids cough, but slowly, the smoke glows and pulses till the flames flick out like red tongues, lap at the bones. No one speaks, and for a long time, the only sound is breath and burning.

'We say a prayer?'

Through the smoke, I see tiny boy standing on one of the rocks. He holds a toy horse. Dares tells him to say whatever prayer he wants. The boy looks about him, then down at the toy horse in his hand. He coughs, starts, but his voice is weak as fuck, and we have to walk closer to hear him.

'So, Hades, I'm gonna tell you about my brother 'cause he's shy with strangers, and you may not notice him down there. He's got brown hair with bits of red in it, and he's big. Not like me. Proper big, and strong and fast, and he can do handstands and flips.' He stops, bites his thumb. 'He's a good worker too. Just ask Androcles, the carpenter. My brother worked in his shop, and Androcles said to Ma, that lad's a fine worker, that lad never stops. Ma said Androcles is awful mean about every-one else except my brother. I tell you, Hades, he's brilliant, and if you ask, he'll make you chairs and tables and anything you want down there. He made this.'

Tiny boy raises the toy horse in the air for all to see. In truth, it's a clumsy piece, and if it weren't for the enormous saddle carved on its back, it would look more like a dog than a horse. Tiny boy squeezes it.

'That's all I want to say. Thanks.'

The other children cheer, tell him the horse is wonderful. For the first time that morning, tiny boy smiles. His teeth are sparse and very crooked, like they were tossed into his gob. He shuffles in amongst his friends, croaks a thank you, looks down at his horse and bursts into tears.

★

The fire's gone. The wood burnt away, and what's left is smouldering bone and ash that smells oddly sweet. The kids bailed an hour ago for school, the armour stashed under branches and leaves. Gelon stands beside me as I prod at a glowing jaw with a stick.

'We can sell it,' says Gelon.

'What's that?'

'The swords, the helmets. We'll need money for the production. It's going to be proper, see. Masks and music. Like in Athens.'

I nod and walk over to the children's hiding place. It takes a while, but eventually I find a helmet that goes with my breastplate, put it on. Now, I've a full set.

'True,' says I. 'We will.'

6.

Konin's forge is at the edge of the city, past Victory Gate. It's a long walk from where we left the kids, and the sun is up – white and fat like a gluttonous star – and with the armour bagged up and tied to our backs, we're cooking. I take a sip from my wine-skin. The liquid's warm and crunchy. Sand creeps into everything out here, even the crack of your arse – though it's not just that. The city wind gets nastier as Syracuse grows. It's filled with broken pottery, crumbled walls and roofs. The wind often has a red aspect, especially in the evening. Hermocrates says we should be thankful for our red wind. That it shows Syracuse's prosperity, its growth, but Hermocrates is a cunt, and I remain sceptical.

We're at Victory Gate. They say it was beautiful once. Built to commemorate some battle against Carthage, full of bronze gods gleaming, but most of that is gone now, melted down or stolen, and all that's left are bits and pieces, green from the elements: arms, mouths and eyes in the ground, clutching or staring upwards.

'There's Konin.'

We can't see him yet, owing to the dust in the air, but we can smell the woodsmoke of the forge, hear the tinny clatter of his hammer. The proximity of the destination ups our spirits, and we walk faster, and soon we can see the slab of close-knitted muscle that is Konin.

'How are things, Konin!'

He stops hammering and peers out.

'Who is it?'

'Purveyors of quality merchandise.'

Before the Athenians came, Konin's forge was nothing more than a shack, but the war's been exceedingly good to him, and now it's two big buildings of bricks and mortar. The shack's become a stable – no mule for Konin. He's gone and bought himself a horse. I've always been fascinated by horses, the mad cost of them, and I set down the armour and walk over to the creature. It's a beauty; a chestnut coat with a pale star on its crown and moist brown eyes that look like they actually see you. I've no food on me, so I offer him a sip from my goatskin.

'Give that fucking horse wine, Lampo, and I swear I'll break your other leg, you limping git.'

I bite my lip and turn around with a grin.

'Wouldn't do him any harm. Sure, my uncle's horse loved a drop.'

'That was a donkey. None of your people ever had horses.'

I say nothing to this, but if he keeps it up, well, then we shall see.

'We've got armour to sell,' says Gelon, laying a helmet out on Konin's bench.

'I make armour. Why would I need to buy it?'

''Cause you're shit at your job.'

Konin curses, but it's Gelon's glance that shuts me up.

'Pulling your leg,' says I. 'No offence.'

'A lion doesn't get offended by the flea itching his balls. You're irritating, that's all.'

I go to say something, but Gelon shakes his head.

'You got me there, Konin. You're sharp.'

Konin spits a glob of luminous muck that lands pretty close.

'Too fucking sharp for you anyway.' He turns to Gelon. 'I'm not buying that armour.'

As if he doesn't hear, Gelon keeps laying the pieces out. A sword, a breastplate, a couple of greaves, until it's heaped on Konin's workbench.

'We're looking to get rid of all of it.'

'Are you fucking deaf or stupid?'

'What was that?'

'I said, are you deaf or stupid. I'm not interested.'

Gelon looks at Konin closely.

'Problem?' says Konin, but now there's doubt in his voice, and the two regard each other for a long fucking time. The hairs on my neck stand to attention, and the blood is pumping 'cause there's not just dust in the air now; there's violence too, and you can taste it. But then Konin looks down at his feet, hocks another phlegm and smiles with something that could pass for warmth.

'Ah, don't mind me, Gelon. My head's wrecked with this heat. I'm out of sorts, is all.'

Gelon nods and hands him a goatskin. Konin takes a bare sip and swallows hard.

'We need the money,' says Gelon. 'This is good craftsmanship. Athenian made. You can sell this on, easy.'

Konin looks at it now. It's way better than anything he could muster, but you wouldn't know it by his frown.

'It's alright,' he says at last. 'But I can't help you. I'd like to, Gelon, but truth is I don't need them. The demand is for Syracusan armour. Engraved with our symbols. Not fucking owls. I'd have to melt it down and rework it, and I've got too much bronze as is. I could only pay cost. I'd be robbing you.'

Gelon's stunned.

'Is there no one who'd be interested?'

Konin makes a show of thinking. Of course, he'll say no, yet suddenly his expression shifts and his teeth bare in a canine grin like a mutt scenting an unexpected treat.

'Actually, there is a fella. A foreign merchant arrived in the city a week ago. Apparently, he's a collector of stuff from the war. Doesn't care which side. He might take it off you.'

'Where can we find him?'

Konin shrugs.

'His ship's at the docks. At least, it was yesterday. It's easy to spot. The only merchant ship with a battering ram. An Athenian ram, no less – they say he had divers pull it up from a wreck in the great harbour.'

Gelon's eyes brighten somewhat.

'Thanks, Konin.'

We walk off, the sacks of armour on our backs, when Konin calls us from behind.

'Wait!'

Stopping in this heat is worse than walking, and I curse him under my breath.

'Don't clean it.'

'Sorry?'

'You might think it's a good idea to give it all a clean and polish, but don't. This fella's a bit particular. Apparently, he prefers the military stuff to be left as is.'

'You mean with the blood and other stains?' asks Gelon.

'Exactly,' says Konin.

'For fucksake,' says I. 'Who are you sending us to?'

Konin frowns.

'A rich buyer, that's who I'm sending you to.'

'Thanks, Konin,' says Gelon.

We're off. Dragging the stuff as the sweat rolls down our backs in salty abundance. When we hear the sea, Gelon stops and lays out the armour and blades on some rocks, curses. We cleaned and buffered every piece on the way. It seemed common sense that a gleaming breastplate would fetch more than a filthy one.

'Fuck,' says Gelon.

'Look at that.' I point at some amber gunk on the inside of one of the greaves. 'That's promising.'

46

Gelon inspects and shakes his head.

'Not enough.'

'How were we to know? Anyway, I don't much like the sound of this collector. It's creepy is what it is, and . . .'

The words die in my mouth. Gelon's taken a knife from his pocket or the pile, I can't tell, and he's making a cut along his left arm.

'Are you mad! Stop it, man.'

A bubble of dark blood forms then pops down onto the helmets, swords. More comes, falling faster till it's almost a flow, and the blades and other pieces seem to come to life under it, and they bloom redly.

'That's enough, man.'

I rip the sleeve off my chiton for a bandage, but he pushes me away. The air reeks of iron now, and Gelon looks pale. There's a splash that wets the sand, and he grabs the cloth off me, and I help him wrap the wound, wrap it tight.

'You'll kill yourself. No play's worth that.'

Gelon smiles. The first in a long while, and though I've had a scare, it lifts my spirits. Such conviction in it, like there's knowledge at the root of its feeling, and he grips my hand and squeezes. Strong bastard that he is, it hurts, but I won't say a thing. The pain is welcome; friendship's what I feel.

'It's poetry we're doing,' he whispers. 'It wouldn't mean a thing if it were easy.'

He passes me a wineskin, and we drink and wait for the blood to dry.

7.

The only real action I saw in the war was in this harbour. On account of my leg, I'm shite as a light trooper. But here, I played a part. Took a little fishing boat right up to an Athenian trireme and skewered a few rowers through the oar holes. It was a good buzz but weird. You couldn't see who you'd got, only feel the javelin sink into their meat, and watch the great oar twitch and slow, the life behind it ebbing away till it didn't move at all, and you knew the poor fucker was gone. Not much, you think? But great things are made up of a load of not much, and that battle was the greatest thing of all. That's what Diocles says. When the Athenians lost on land, their only hope was the sea. They tried to fight their way out through the harbour, but we were having none of it. Must have been five hundred ships on the sea that day and packed together so tight you saw soldiers marching from ship to ship like it was soil. If the Athenians broke through, they'd be back in Athens now, with their families, maybe even catching a play. Not rotting in the quarries. But they didn't.

The afternoon has cooled, and it's pleasant here. The sea-skin's a gentle swishing blue, and it's hard to imagine that whole forests of sunken ships lie underneath it, a second city. Gelon has stopped and is gaping at a slender dark-haired woman bent over a basket of fruit. A couple of wasps are trying to make a landing on the figs, and she looks up to swat them away. Gelon's face crumples. I suppose if you needed her to be, the woman's

49

hair and build were a fair pass for Desma, but the eyes are too small, the nose all wrong.

'Directors!' I chant in his ear, and he nods, though the greyish tinge to his cheeks shows his mind's elsewhere, and I have to lead him away almost like a child.

We're at the merchants' quarter of the docks now, and deckhands are unloading cargo. There are heaps of cloth dyed the loudest colours, tints and hues that make the wildest skies seem boring. It's dizzying. Your nose gets hammered by all the smells. Spices mixing with the sweaty tang of slavers' ships, and great quantities of food and booze leaking from badly sealed vats. This is just what Gelon needs. When we were boys, we'd come down here most days and stroll through the great harbour, arm in arm, our nostrils flaring and full with all the scents. If we were really going for it, we'd shut our eyes. Babylon burst to life inside our skulls, Memphis, Carthage, and lots more besides. Gelon would describe what he was seeing, and I'd do the same; we'd build those cities together, word by word. The merchants would go spare at us, 'cause blind as we were, we'd often knock into them, and sometimes we got a smack, but what was that to seeing the fucking pyramids? I put my arm around Gelon and close my eyes.

'We're in Egypt, man. The Sphinx is just ahead. Can you see it?'

He shakes me off. 'Will you ever cop on, Lampo?'

But I won't. If I'm honest, some days I still come here to sniff and stroll and lose myself in other worlds, and like when I was a kid, I wonder if the real places are anything like I'm imagining, and just like then, I wince, for something tells me I'll never know, but it's still a buzz.

'There,' says Gelon.

Near the end of the docks is a ship with a battering ram. It's no trireme, but a massive cargo ship, and the ram seems out of place. The bronze is crooked like a broken nose and all mottled and green with ropes of snottish seaweed dangling, but it's not just the ram that's a state. The wood of the hull is badly warped and curiously dark, like they had to throw on extra coats of pitch just to hold it together. If this fella has coin, he certainly isn't spending it on his ship. I look at Gelon and see he's having similar thoughts.

'Rich as Croesus, this fella is.'

'Shut up. I'm getting tired of all the negativity, Lampo.'

'Ah, that was a joke. You know I'm a positive person.'

Gelon doesn't answer. There are a few lads visible on the deck, none of them doing very much.

A ladder leads up to the deck, and Gelon climbs it. I follow, and we step onto the ship; right away, we're surrounded by crew, and they look agitated.

'What do you want?' squeaks a tall, sinewy fella with a jagged scar like a smile across his throat.

'We're merchants,' says I, 'and would like to discuss our wares with the captain of this ship.'

The fella with the scar looks us up and down.

'He's busy.'

'We've armour to sell,' says Gelon. 'Athenian armour from the war, never cleaned.'

The tall fella's eyes widen with something that might be interest.

'Show me,' he says. The words crackle in his fucked-up throat.

'We're serious merchants,' says I, 'and show our products only to those with authority to make a purchase.'

He lunges for the armour, and Gelon pushes him away. It all happens very fast. One moment, the tall fella looks like he's falling, and the next, he's spun around in the air, and he's got a

51

knife to Gelon's throat. I move forward but feel a blade pressing into my guts, and to take another step is to bleed.

'This is outrageous,' says I. 'The assembly shall hear of this.'

The fellas surround us now so that even if you were looking up from the docks, all you'd see is their backs.

'Let go of the bag.'

I've already let go, so he must be talking to Gelon. He is. The knife's still at Gelon's throat, but he grips the bag tight as ever, knuckles white.

'No.'

The tall fella seems a bit shocked at this, but he smirks.

'Not robbing you. Leave it with us and come back later. If the boss is interested, he'll pay. If he's not, you can pick it up.'

'Fuck off.'

The fella stops smirking, and there's a weary, almost resigned look on his face, and it's this more than anything that frightens me.

'Give it to him! Please, man!'

Gelon looks at me, surprised.

'We're directors, right?' I say. 'I can't direct it without you. Give it to him.'

He frowns but slowly lets go of the bag. A scarlet helmet tumbles onto the floor, and one of the crew picks it up.

'Look at that,' he says with a grin. 'The boss will love this.'

The blades are sheathed, and we're pushed towards the ladder, and it's everything I can do to walk in a straight line 'cause my legs feel bandy and insubstantial, but Gelon stops and calls over his shoulder.

'We'll return in the evening for our money or the armour.'

The crew laugh, and I feel a shit might be coming, as my guts flex. I pull him down with me, and soon we're back on solid ground, and people pass by, indifferent.

'They're mental,' I says, and walk fast as I can from the ship.

Gelon lags behind, and it's one of the first times in our lives that my pace exceeds his own.

'This way,' he says. 'We'll need a quote.'

'A quote?'

'For the costumes and masks. We need a price quote so we'll know what to negotiate for when we come back later.'

'Negotiate? You're fucking joking. You come back here, and you'll be on your own. Those men were dead behind the eyes. The sort that would cut your throat and play dice while you bleed out.'

He says nothing to this, just marches forward at a speed I can't match, to the maker of masks and costumes.

I follow.

8.

There's only one theatre shop in Syracuse. Not really open to the public, but Alekto, your one who owns it, lets us in on account of an old friendship with my ma. The shop was her husband's, and they ran it together until one day he disappeared. This was about twenty years ago, and I was just a kid at the time. There's been no sight or sound of him since. All sorts of rumours abound, but my favourite is that she killed him and used his skin to make props for the plays. And yet, this isn't even the strangest thing about Alekto. The strangest thing is that she kept the shop. There were three other costume makers in Syracuse when her husband disappeared, and the owner of each offered to buy Alekto out or, even better, marry her. She was a cracker in her day, but to both proposals, business and matrimonial, she said no thanks. It was her shop, and she'd run it, and besides, she believed her husband would return someday, and what then? Though I've heard that when she said this, there was a curious lilt in her voice. Anyway, she kept her shop and never remarried. Within a couple of years, Alekto's was seen as the best option when it came to fashioning all things theatrical. In ten, it was the only option. She'd driven the others out of business.

I knock a couple of times, but then Gelon pushes, and the door swings open. The house is a sprawler: four storeys, including the cellar, yet it seems even bigger on account of all the theatrical gear. You can't see the real walls 'cause they're covered with scene paintings from different plays. To my right must be Olympus – rolling clouds and gorgeous sunbeams thick and gold as honey. To the left are the battlements of some citadel, probably Troy, blood streaks on the limewashed brick, like gashes in pale skin, and tiny archers in the towers. It's so well done, I'm almost nervous walking past it, like if I don't leg it, I'll go the way of Achilles. Straight ahead is the best scene of all: Hades. The River Styx, to be exact, the water green and trembling, with faces and limbs rising. It reminds me of those statues at Victory Gate, but it's more beautiful than them. The light on the water is different from any I've ever seen in this world, yet it seems I know it. Gelon says that's what the best plays do. If they're true enough, you'll recognize it even if it all seems mad at first, and this is why we give a shit about Troy, though for all we know, it was just some dream of Homer's, and I walk towards this green soul river, and for a moment it's like I'm going home.

'Don't touch that. It's still drying.'

I look over and see Alekto's watching us. No clue where she came from, but I suppose it's her house.

'Good afternoon, fair maiden,' says I, bowing like an aristo and scratching some dirt from my chiton.

Alekto chuckles and shakes her head.

'Still a gobshite, I see.'

I say nothing to this.

'We're swamped today,' she says. 'Sorry, but I really can't have you distracting the lads with your gawping. Nothing personal.'

'It's not like that,' says Gelon quickly. 'Today's different.'

Alekto's wearing red robes that trail down to the floor, a scarlet thread glittering like something alive. It must be some costume she's trying on. There's a rumour that she acted once in a play, back when her husband was still around, and that he bet the head off her for it. They say she played the lead and did it on the sly, so that none of the audience knew, but they

56

screamed for more, and it was the best Clytemnestra they'd ever seen. Is this true? I don't know. It seems brazen even for her, but I often see her try on the gear, and she knows the words of all the old plays as well as anyone and will give you a speech from the best when the mood takes her.

'We're directors.' I straighten up, rock my shoulders back and in a voice that sounds eerily like the boss from our old factory, I let her have it. 'We come in a directorial capacity to survey the quality of your theatrical amenities for the purposes of –'

'Shut up.'

'Ah, Gelon.'

'Look,' says Alekto, 'I don't have time for this. What is it? And be quick.'

'We're putting on a play,' says Gelon.

Alekto bursts out laughing, but stops.

'Wait, you're serious?'

'Of course.'

She shakes her head then, more pityingly than anything.

'What play?'

'*Medea*,' says Gelon, so low it's a whisper.

'And where, may I ask, are you going to put on *Medea*?'

'The quarry.'

'Of course. A festering pit. A perfect location for entertainment. And who'll be in it? You two, I suppose.'

'The Athenians,' says I. 'We've already cast it and have proper actors too. Fellas who've done the real thing back home. Fucking pros. It will be good exposure for you, Alekto. Reckon a discount is only fair.'

Alekto says nothing for a long time. She always struck me as a person not easily surprised. One of those who see the different sides of things and so is rarely taken unawares, but I think we've shocked her now. She looks from one of us to the other, as if she's waiting for something that doesn't come, then she goes over to a cupboard and takes out a jug and three cups, fills them with red, passes one to each. I drink mine off, but Gelon just grips his, so tight I fear the clay will break.

'Look,' she says. 'I like you, boys.'

'Not a boy. I'm fucking thirty,' says I.

'That old? Sure, time flies is what it does. It seems like only yesterday your mother was putting you on my lap and asking me to sing to you. You were such a beautiful baby. You know that, Lampo?'

'I'm still gorgeous.' I wink. 'Anyway, stop stalling. We're directors alright and aren't here to reminisce but do business.'

Again, that pitying look.

'Yeah, well, see the thing is. You're not directors, really, are you? You're two unemployed potters with barely a few obols to scratch together. And those poor bastards in the quarries. They're not actors. Even if at some point in their lives they were, that's long gone for them now.'

'What are they, then?'

She hesitates.

'They're starving. Starving to death slowly because our assembly is demented, and in a few months, they'll be gone. They're doomed is what they are.'

That settles in the air, and we look at our feet, awkward. I pretend to sip, though my cup is empty.

'You're a tough negotiator,' says I.

'That's why we have to do it,' Gelon says with feeling. 'You're right, they're doomed, and in a few months, they'll be gone. With the war, it might be years before we ever see another Athenian play in Syracuse. Some people are saying when Athens falls, and it has to fall, the Spartans will just burn it to the ground. There might never be another Athenian play again!' The cup cracks in his hand, and the wine splashes on the ground. 'For all we know, those in the quarries are all that's left of Athenian theatre, at least as far as Syracuse is concerned.' He stops and looks down at his arm where he cut himself, scanning it intensely as if the words he needed might be found there. 'And it's not just *Medea*. The Athenians told me that before they left Athens, Euripides wrote a new play. A play about Troy. About the women at Troy after it's fallen. No one's seen it in Sicily. It's a whole new Euripides. And we're going to do them both. Do *Medea*, and *The Trojan Women*. See, we can't let them disappear. We have to –'

'Have to what?' says Alekto, her voice gentler.

'Keep them alive and put on the play.'

For Gelon, that's a long speech, and it's made him breathless, yet he stares at Alekto, defiant. This is the first I've heard of doing a second play, and it stings a bit that he kept it from me.

'Anything else?' says Alekto.

'No.'

She doesn't speak immediately, just nods to herself and gets Gelon a fresh cup, pours him another.

'Me as well.'

She looks over as if surprised to find me there. Fills my cup quickly.

'Alright,' she says at last.

'Alright, what?'

'I'll supply you with what you need.'

Gelon grabs her hand, presses it.

'But,' she says firmly. 'Don't look so pleased. I think your expression will change when you see my prices. Nothing here is cheap. I make the best.'

Gelon nods, eager.

'How are you going to pay for all of this?'

'Credit? Give you a stake of the profits?'

'Quiet, Lampo. We'll find the money. Just tell us how much, and I'll find it.'

She looks at him for a long time.

'I think you just might.'

They start getting into the technicalities of what's needed. The different clothes, how many masks, what wood and paint should be used in their making. Wigs? If so, which material? Goat hair being the cheapest, and human the most costly. I listen at the start but find my mind wandering and slyly remove the wine jug from the table and take a stroll into the other rooms: more robes and wooden swords and sceptres. A little ginger cat is licking at the gold paint on one of the fake crowns so that its tongue glints in its gob. The last room and the painted backdrops give way to wooden workbenches. There's sawdust on the floor and the grey glow of chisels and files. This is the masking room, and there are three fellas in it. The heart of the operation. Ma told me they're slaves from Libya that Alekto's husband bought cheap when they were kids. That was ages ago, and the Libyans are getting on themselves now, their hair grey. Gas that. Once they were children chiselling Agamemnons or Athenas, their whole life in front of them, and now they're old, still chiselling the same kings and gods, yet there can be but little life in front of them.

'Hope you boys aren't slacking off,' says I. 'Got a big commission coming.'

They look up, and only one of them nods. Cheeky bastards. This won't do.

'What materials do you use?'

Again, they look at me. No one says anything, and I feel my temper rising till one of them coughs.

'Ash, sir. Amongst other things. Linen too. It depends on the character.'

'Good choices,' says I.

They look like brothers. Tall and elegant when they stand, though they rarely stand, their backs sickle-shaped from bending over, because the delicate work of masking requires you to mostly sit on your arse, and their hands are soft. You can tell. Palms smooth and pink as a kitten's paw, not craggy like mine or Gelon's, but their eyes look red and flaming, sawdust and paint fumes itching the whites.

Usually, I don't say much to these boys, but seeing as today I come as a director, I feel it might be wise to learn a bit more about them before bestowing my coin. I ask if they're brothers, and the fella who answered first looks up, says he doesn't know.

'How can you not know if you're brothers?' says I.

'Well, we were sold so young,' he says, and the others look at him, as if in disapproval, but whether he doesn't notice or doesn't care, he keeps talking. 'You see, all the men in our village were killed, and they thought they'd get a better price if they sold us with our mothers. So they sent us to the nearest city to be sold, but the nearest city wasn't very near. We had to cross a desert, and somewhere along the way, the disaster happened.'

'What happened?'

'The disaster,' he says, indifferent to his mates' glaring. 'I can't remember exactly, but the man who was taking us ran into trouble. There was a sandstorm and men, violent men, bandits, I suppose. They took all our mothers, our fucking mothers. So that when we arrived at the city, we were half dead, dizzy with fever and thirst, and we'd forgotten who we were. We were all so young.'

'How many of you were there?'

'I'm not sure, lots, all the children of my village, maybe twenty?'

'Don't ask me,' says I, 'I haven't a clue.'

61

'Sorry, I'm just not sure.'

'What happened then?' I says.

'Oh, we were shipped to Sicily, and three of us were bought by Melissus. I don't know where my family are.'

'Melissus?'

He blinks.

'Alekto's departed husband.'

'Of course, so you know that some were your brothers?'

He looks a bit sad when I say this, doesn't answer for a while, puts down the mask he's painting.

'Can't say if they are, I really can't, but they could be. There was a girl who was sold at Catana. She was my sister. At least, she said it to me before they sold her. I don't remember much, but I remember her saying, "I'm your sister, Kalintha, and I love you. Never forget me."'

'Good stuff.'

I offer him a pull from the jug, but he shakes his head and gets back to work. I stand and watch them for a while until I feel a tap on my shoulder and see it's Gelon. Alekto beside him.

'Choose one,' says Alekto.

'I don't have the money yet,' says Gelon.

'I'll give you credit for one,' she says, 'Only one, so choose wisely.'

Gelon doesn't need to be told twice, and he's off looking at the masks. He spends ages, and some of them are splendid things, gorgeous really, and so it's a surprise when he settles on a little one.

'You don't want a queen's mask for Medea? A hero's for Jason?'

'This one,' says Gelon, holding it up.

'Interesting choice. That's for an actor playing a little boy. It's a tricky one to get right. It's much easier to do a monster or a god. Childhood is subtle.'

Gelon is silent, gazing down at the mask. He holds it gently as if afraid to damage the wood or scratch the paint.

'Helios,' he whispers.

I pretend not to hear that, and pass him the jug.

'Directors, man,' says I, 'that's what we are!'

'Yeah,' he says, but he doesn't take a sip, just stares at the mask, and I wait for the moment to pass.

9.

It starts to rain not long after we leave Alekto's. A drizzle that thickens and quickens till it becomes the mood of the city, and the sky takes on that mourning quality you get from weeping black clouds and shrieking winds that make the old buildings whistle and chatter like drunks in a tavern. The streets are tiny – twisted about each other snakily – and it gives me a fright when I feel a grip on my ankle.

'Fancy a song, lads?'

It's an old man with no legs. Ropes around his knees, and at the bottom of the ropes are tied bricks that I guess act as boots; keep the stumps in good nick.

'No thanks,' I says.

'Alright,' says Gelon, tossing him an obol.

The old man bows so that his hair dips in a puddle.

'I shall sing you a tale that will make the tears flow.'

'Have you not any happy ones?'

'Let him sing what he wants.'

'Thanks, son. This tale is a sad tale, but one that is more common than you'd ever suppose.'

The old man clears his throat, begins.

'*There was once a man born, and no one cared about him. There was once a man born, and no one cared about him! He felt so much and loved so much, but I tell you that no one cared about him!*'

'Ah, Gelon, he's shite.'

'Quiet.'

I pull Gelon's cloak, but he won't budge, so I say fuck it and settle in. Gelon's always had a weakness for anyone like this.

65

Even his Desma, beautiful as she was, had a broken nose. There's a tavern across the way, and you can hear music – proper music – and the lanterns at the entrance, well, the dancing flames and lively tunes sort of clash with the old man, who can't move so much, and I look down at him, and he's staring up at Gelon, singing his song.

Nothing for it but to listen. It's pouring now, and the water's rising, 'cause this quarter's kind of hilly, and we're at the bottom of that hill. It flows down and makes a pool where we stand so that your boots sink in and your ankles get slippery as the streets turn to mud. The old man is sinking too, his bricks going right down into the mud, and the end of his grey beard's getting dyed by it, bleeding thick colour along the hairs, giving him a filthy sort of youth as he screeches his song through the streets, and I'm starting to get into it. A few people have gathered round. At first, they're chuckling away, nudging and grinning, but as the song goes on, the chuckling stops, and I think the old man's won a few of them over.

It's clearly his own life story, though he never says this. Often these bastards just cackle out snatches of Homer or cobble together bits and pieces of famous poems, like those Athenians in the quarry, their minds slippery with hunger and madness, characters from random myths crashing together like waves in the sea. This is different. It's a story of the old man's life in song, and though it's no special life, he sings it for all to hear, gives it everything he has, and I admire that.

A rough childhood, to put it mildly. He says his ma was mental and used to choke him with a rope on the nights when his da, some rower, was away. And after these nights, his ma would cry and tell him it was just a game, don't tell Daddy, and she'd buy him sweets and toys. He still has the rope, the one wrapped around his left knee. I don't know if this is true, but everyone looks down at that left knee, and sure enough, the rope there is raggedy, worn away to a few greasy black threads, so much older than the one on the right.

He left home as soon as he could, and who could blame him? He thought he might become a rower like his da but was too young for the warships – got a job on a cheese galley that sent Syracuse's finest over to Italy and Greece. He sings of the sweat and stink of the hull, with great blocks of cheese over your head, and how the rats always seemed to burrow their way into those blocks, wouldn't show themselves till the ship was far out at sea. It got so bad that the helmsman traded a crate of their best for a massive tabby in Rhegium, that the rowers dubbed Ajax.

He sings a good three verses on Ajax, the tabby. All this stuff about individual duels with especially fearsome rats, and a real odd verse about Ajax climbing the mast and staring out at the horizon. Then he goes back to singing about himself.

He quits the sea and gets work as a stonemason. Has a knack for it and starts to prosper. He marries a lovely redhead from Corinth and has a daughter. The song gets almost jolly, and there's this lovely bit about him singing to his daughter so that she'll go to sleep. A song within a song, like, and it's beautiful. Of course, things take a turn. He hits the drink, and one night he comes to and finds himself standing over the cot with a rope wrapped around the child's throat. He hasn't tugged yet, so the girl's just sleeping peacefully, but the shame and horror of it course through him like venom and the next morning he legs it and never sees his family again. The song ends with him on a boat returning to Syracuse, flies buzzing about two arrow wounds on his legs, as he wonders if his daughter is okay. And then the strangest thing happens. The rope on his knee begins to glow and pulse like a coil of flame, and he understands that his pain, all that stuff with his ma, and what followed, they were part of the gods' plan, that even the worst of it was sacred, but then the rope darkens, and he looks up at the sky and sees it was just the moon and a cloud had passed over. He stops singing.

Cheers and silver follow and he bows, collects the gleaming coins from the mud, but as he's scooping, he lets out a cry. For in his hand, as well as muddy silver, is a gold piece.

'Who was so kind?'

'A fabulous song,' says someone behind me. 'Has anyone ever told you to go professional?'

'Sorry?'

'A man with your talents could be huge. Are you part of a troupe?'

'A troupe?' says the old man.

'Yes. Do you have a manager?'

The old fella looks at the gold in his hand.

'No.'

'Well, we really must change that. I'm staying at the house of Diocles. Do come down tomorrow morning and sing your song. I'm sure he'd be delighted to hear it. And then we can discuss your future in more detail. You're going to be a sensation.'

'Okay.'

I look back to see who the fuck this is. The speaker's a tall fella with a long hairy cloak lined with purple. 'Cause of the dark, I can't see his face clearly, just catch the glinting of rings in his ears and brilliant white teeth.

'Also, that rope you have tied around your leg. Did your mother really hang you from it?'

The old man says nothing, but from the wet shine in his eyes, you can tell she probably did.

'A fascinating piece. You know I would love to purchase it.'

'The rope?'

'Yes – I would, of course, remunerate you handsomely. How would five gold pieces sound?'

The old man's eyes are practically screaming now. Five gold pieces is mad money. Yet, what he says next surprises me.

'It's not for sale. Sorry.'

'Ten.'

'What?'

'Ten gold pieces.'

Ten's a fucking fortune. Ten will keep him in food and booze for a long time. He won't need to sing. Ten of those, and he'll be able to rent himself a nice little room in the centre for a year, with a roaring fire, and him all snug and protected from the elements, and you can see the calculations going on in the old man's eyes, his cheeks, his nails which are scratching the gold coin in his palms.

'I can't,' he says at last. 'I can't.'

People are laughing, but there's confusion in their laughter too. What the fuck? Ten gold pieces for that rope?

'So it really is priceless?'

No answer.

'Never mind. That is disappointing, but I'd still love to introduce you to some people in the business. Discuss your future. Be there tomorrow morning sharp. Big things are coming.'

'Thanks.'

The old man shuffles off down an alley on his bricks, and when I turn around, his patron is gone too.

'What was that?' says I.

Gelon shrugs, but I can tell his mind's on other things.

'We head for a sup?'

He shakes his head.

'I'm going back to the ship.'

'Not that shite again. Come on, man . . .'

'Listen,' he says. 'You don't have to come with me, but I'm going back. You heard Alekto. She'll make what we need, but it won't be cheap.'

I tell him the same as before. That it's suicide, and they'll only slit our throats and dump us overboard, but none of it makes any difference. He just shakes his head.

'Wait,' I says, feeling inspired. 'We'll rob that old fella. Take his rope and sell it to the rich bastard staying with Diocles.'

Gelon looks at me in a way that's hard to bear.

'What, man? I'm trying to find a solution here. Something that doesn't involve us dying.'

'You don't rob a man of his suffering,' says Gelon quietly. 'That's his.'

He shakes his head and walks off in the direction of the docks. I stay put. Maybe it's the fear of those bastards on the ship, but there's more to this than fear. It's the way he looked at me. Others have looked at me like that all my life but never Gelon. Like I was nothing. The only reason I suggested it was to save his skin, and he goes and looks at me like that. Well, fuck him. Ah, but those bastards will kill him. I take a step forward. Gelon's getting fainter now in the distance. I can just about see the queer tilt in the way he walks, head bowed, a kind of stamping rhythm to his gait, and then he's gone, swallowed by the dark, and I whisper it.

'Fuck you, Gelon.'

I walk away.

10.

A slow night in Dismas'. A fisherman is sitting on Homer's chair, cleaning a hook with a cloth. When he sees me, he scampers to another seat but goes back when he realizes Gelon's not with me. There's the smell of paint all around, and I notice a lot of the furniture is different: tables of polished wood, and a couple of chairs even have cushions. Odd, but at least the lovely slave girl is serving. Her hair's tied up in a ponytail with a big green ribbon, and I can see the scar on her arm that I want to touch.

'How are things?'

She looks over. There's something in her expression that makes me think she isn't altogether unhappy to see me, but she keeps wiping tables all the same.

'You're alone,' she says. 'I've never seen you here without your friend.'

'Ah, he's not my friend. He's just a prick I used to drink with.'

She arches an eyebrow at that.

'I was wondering,' I says, 'does Dismas ever let you out, or are you always working?'

'Working.'

'You like it?'

She shrugs.

'It's okay. Better than the fields.'

'You're way too stunning for the fields.'

She laughs at that. And I tell her I was thinking of opening a similar establishment myself, and if I did, I might need a girl like her. She glances at my cloak and my boots. Seems to find something funny in them.

'That scar, though. It does let you down a bit.'

She stops smiling.

'I mean, it's not the worst, but yeah. There's the teeth as well. I'm thinking now that maybe the fields would suit you better. Are you strong?'

No answer. She just keeps wiping the table, but she has one of those faces where the feeling pours out through every feature, and I want to kiss her scar and tell her it's beautiful, but I do nothing of the sort. Instead, I grab an arm, feel the muscle and say she looks strong, good for threshing wheat, and order a jug of the cheapest.

The wine is sour, and I wince as I drink, but the taste suits my mood. I picture Gelon with a knife to his throat and take a gulp. There are a few aristos in the corner, rolling dice and making too much noise. Their cloaks are the brightest things in the bar, and their perfume blends with the odours of fish and fresh paint, and the result is something weird and new. I don't like it. Sure, Dismas' was a kip, but it was our kip. Too much money's flooding into this city, and it's losing something, though perhaps that's just what a man feels when he can't see what he's won. Thirty years of age, and I live with my ma. Not what I'd planned for myself, but enough of this moping. I'm having a drink. I'm alive. Again, there's a flash of Gelon, this time bleeding out on the deck of the ship. I glance around. The slave girl is over at the table with the aristos, collecting empties. One of them grabs her arse, and they start hooting. She doesn't even push him off, just stands there with this faraway look in her eyes while the kid squeezes. I look away. Sure, it's none of my business. I set my attention back to the task at hand and refill my cup; a beetle plops out of the jug and starts doing the breast-stroke along the surface of my vintage. Its black legs paddle madly, and I think maybe I should give it a hand, blow it to the other side so it can climb out and live – bestow a deus ex, but that's not how life is. You're always alone, and the beetle needs to learn this. Gelon and I aren't mates. He's just a prick I used to drink with. There's more commotion in the corner, and I look up and see the aristo has a hold of her now, has pushed her down onto his lap. I stand and walk over, not really sure why.

'It's Achilles,' says one of the aristos. 'Join us for a libation!'

It must be one of the boys Gelon and I got pissed with, but I don't recognize him.

'You enjoying this?' I say to the slave girl.

She doesn't answer, just stares ahead as if she's somewhere else.

'Ah, easy there now,' says I. 'There's plenty of fun to be had tonight without mauling the staff. Right, lads?'

They look at me a bit confused. The kid who's grabbing her doesn't let go. He's a thick-looking fella, a frail blond moustache on his upper lip, and sweaty blue eyes.

'Come on, don't wreck the buzz, Achilles,' says the same aristo as before. 'Sit down and drink with us!'

I give him a proper look over and finally see it. The hair is much shorter, the same close cut as Gelon's, but the long lashes and grey eyes give it away; it's Hermocrates' son.

'Happy to have a drink, lads,' says I. 'Would be great if this fella here would just let her get back to her work, though.'

The groper with the moustache frowns and looks at his mates. The grip on her waist loosens but doesn't release.

'It's my birthday,' he says, staring. Moist eyes calculating as if to gauge what danger I pose, and then a grin spreads across his face, and he squeezes the slave's girl's tit so hard she lets out a little cry of pain.

'Ah, fuck off,' he says. 'She likes it.'

His mates laugh. Even Hermocrates' son is chuckling away, pouring himself a cup from a jug. I take the jug out of his hand and drink from it. They go quiet then.

'Delicious,' says I. 'Much better than the slop I was having. Ah, it's good sharing a libation with fellow citizens. I mean, I'm broke, and you boys are the quality. A mouthful of this is worth more than my clothes, but we're Syracusan. We're brothers, right, boys?'

Silence.

'Let's drink to democracy!' I drain it, some of the wine dripping down my chin, and then I go as if to pass the jug on, like in a proper libation, but I don't. Instead, I smash it into moustache's face, and he's howling on the ground. The slave girl scampers off and disappears somewhere behind the bar. The aristos are all on their feet now – look ready for murder – and I back away a little.

'We're going to fuck you up,' says a gangly fucker.

There are four of them, and if they make a move, I'm fucked. But I feel someone behind me. It's the fisherman who'd taken Homer's chair. He's got the hook in his hand, the sharp end glinting, and the aristos eye it.

'Go on,' growls the fisherman.

They look tempted, but then he slashes the air and they back away towards the door.

'Goodnight, citizens,' says I, winking. 'See you at the assembly!'

One of them says something about breaking my legs, another about having my house knocked down, but it's Hermocrates' son that unsettles me the most. He doesn't threaten or shout, he simply stares at me with his cold grey eyes, whispers to his mates, and they leave.

'Cheers for that,' says I.

The fisherman pockets his hook.

'I'll not have a local touched by them cunts,' he says.

Soon we're at his table drinking sour wine. The slave girl is behind the bar, and she's staring over at us. I can't read her expression, and I wonder what she'll make of all that. I'm not usually one for violence, and the shakes are on me now that it's passed. When I go to pour from the jug, more booze hits the table than our cups. I want to speak to her badly, and I hammer the wine down so I can go up again and order.

'And where was Gelon?' asks the fisherman. 'He's always good for a scrap.'

'Fuck Gelon. He's a snake, man. Don't ever trust him.'

The fisherman seems taken aback, and I force a grin and ask if I can sit in Homer's chair.

'Of course,' he says, getting up, 'you earned it.'

I sink into it slowly, enjoy the creaking of the wood as it takes my weight. 'If Gelon were here, I'd deck him, but he's probably dead. Ha!' I rub my hand along the bronze inscription that reads 'Homer's Chair'. I'm still grinning, but my stomach drops. When we were kids, there wasn't much theatre in Syracuse, at least not for the likes of us. Epic poetry was everything, especially to Gelon, and you could say if it weren't for Homer, we'd never have been mates. One day after school, he announced he would become a singer; all the other boys took the piss out of him except for me. I said, why not, that I quite fancied it too. The problem was we needed money. No singer was going to teach you poems for free, so we improvised. I sold my ma's loom and Gelon his da's trowel. Gelon got a beating, but my ma just started crying, and I told her not to worry, that I'd be a singer, and she could put her feet up from now on. Gelon had a memory like soil, everything absorbed. The singer offered to take him on as a real apprentice, but Gelon's da was having none of it. He was a potter's son, simple as.

I said, 'Don't worry, singer, you can have me.' The singer passed. That night Gelon and I paced the city, round and round we went, ten or eleven years old, and I asked him what we were going to do? And he smiled; his eyes were violet with bruises, his lip busted, and then he started into the first book of *The Odyssey*, and for a while, I didn't care that I was poor or that Ma and I were alone 'cause my da did a runner, and now I'd betrayed her. I didn't care about anything but the words he was saying. After that, we were inseparable. Even when he got married and had a son, he always had me around, made me part of his family. Yet here I am, drunk, crowing about what I did to some aristo pissant when my best mate could be bleeding to death. I get up and mutter some excuse. The fisherman looks confused, offended even. But fuck it. 'Cause right now Gelon is on that ship, and he's alone.

II.

Proper stormy outside. The waves smash along the beach, and when a cloud scoots off the moon, a thick yellow light slinks down, and some of those waves look like the lambent tails and faces of sea creatures. The collector's ship's in the distance, and if anything, it seems worse at night. The wood's all black and contorted, its sail full of holes and ragged edges that claw at the air like some wounded animal. Whether it's the rain or the fear, I start shivering. On the deck, lanterns swing from hooks, and shadowy figures move about – probably crew.

'Who goes there?' says a wrecked voice.

'It's me,' says I, trying to sound calm.

'And who the fuck are you?'

'A merchant. I came here earlier with armour . . .'

'He said you might come.'

'What's that?'

'Your friend. He's on the ship with our master.'

I stand there like a fool, neither going forward nor backwards until the same voice calls down to me.

'Coming up, or what?'

I say that I am, and go to the ladder. It's soaked, and the wooden rungs feel soggy in the rain, like they might come apart in my fingers. Still, I climb up and onto the deck. Just like last time, I'm immediately surrounded by the crew. The lamps swinging on hooks give an unsteady illumination to the faces, but I see knives, scars and eyes.

'Any weapons?'

'No, I've nothing.'

They pat me down all the same, and the bastards are rough and thorough. Still, it's true what I said. I've nothing on me, and, satisfied, the fella nods, goes to a hatch on the floor with an iron ring, and pulls it open.

'Down there,' he says. 'Your mate's down there. I'll show you.'

I feel sick but grin and follow the man down there. Straight away, there's a whiffy heft to the air. Sickly sweet, but with something sour beneath it. Your man walks on ahead through a corridor, past a few doors, and it's mad 'cause I've never seen a ship like this. I mean, with rooms like in a proper house, and you could almost forget you were on the water if it weren't for the pitching, the slight instability to the world as you step, and he halts at a door and knocks.

'Who is it?' says a familiar voice.

'I've got the other one,' says the guard.

He opens the door, and I peer into the room. It's dark, though a few lamps sputter in the corner. It takes a while for my eyes to adjust 'cause the air is smoky from the burning oil, but slowly my vision clears, and I take it in: scarlet carpets, two couches laid out, like the ones you sometimes glimpse through the windows of aristos' gaffs. Gelon is on one of those couches, a goblet in his hand. The goblet is made of fucking gold. Across from him, on another couch, reclining, is the fella who tried to buy the homeless bastard's rope. I can tell from the rings in his ears and the white teeth. So this is the collector. I step in and sink into a carpet so thick it rises above my ankles.

'You came,' says Gelon, frowning, but I can see in his eyes that he's pleased – relieved, even.

'Of course.'

The collector looks over at me and smiles. His teeth are ridiculously white and arrow-straight, yet there's an animal feel to them. Like they belong in the maw of something larger, in the woods, and not a merchant nibbling grapes.

'Take a seat,' he says.

I take a seat, and the cushions are so soft it's unsettling. Like my arse is on some thick cloud, and there's a sense that you're about to fall. The man seems to notice my discomfort, for he smiles.

'Wine?'

'Cheers.'

A door opens behind us, and this ancient servant hobbles out, holding a tray with another golden goblet and a jug. The old man wheezes as he pours and looks so frail I think he's going to keel over, but my cup is filled, and he retreats out the same door he came in.

'Is that fella alright?'

Again, that white smile.

'Agenor is younger than he looks.'

'Well, he looks about a hundred.'

'Exactly, he's ninety-two.'

I don't know whether he's joking or not, and I take a sip of the wine, examine my surroundings. There are paintings on the walls, but I don't see them clearly in the lamplight. I can only make out the details of the largest, and it looks to be of Heracles and the Hydra, though it can't be that, as in it Heracles is getting eaten.

'So,' says I, 'we have some fantastic examples of Attic armour to –'

'That's done,' interrupts Gelon. 'He bought it all.'

I look more closely at the collector. It's hard to place his age. The skin on the face is pale, barely lined, and the hair is dark, long and glossy, but there's something old about the eyes, the neck.

'The addition of fresh blood was quite a touch,' he says. 'No one has done that before.'

'Eh, that was from the war,' I says.

He grins. 'Of course it was. You fought in the war?'

Usually, I lie when people ask me this. Spin a tale of bringing

79

down Athenian hoplites with a slingshot, but something in the way this fella is looking at me tells me he'll know it's bullshit. And my lying will just amuse.

'Not really.'

He nods and takes a long sip of wine. I notice his cup is silver, not gold, and I tell him it's mighty generous to have Gelon and I drink from gold ones.

'Your praise is unnecessary. I prefer silver.'

'Bollix.'

He laughs at this, though it's a real quiet laugh, and I don't know if it's genuine.

'Where I come from, we believe that silver is the blood of the night. The stars are silver. The moon is silver. What is gold?'

'The sun,' says Gelon.

The man looks over at him and nods in agreement. The wine is sweet but thick and strong, and I can feel it go to my head. Usually, I'm happy to get pissed at a rich prick's expense, but I don't like it here, and if what Gelon says is true and we've sold the armour, I see no reason to stay.

'Getting late,' says I, looking at Gelon. 'Early start and all.'

The collector seems surprised.

'Leaving so soon? Surely you'll finish your drinks?'

'Of course we will,' says Gelon.

Your man smiles at this and raps at the wall behind him. The old servant hobbles back in with a fresh jug and proceeds to refill our cups to the brim.

'Where are you from?' I ask, more to break the silence than out of interest.

His eyes flit about in a way that implies he's thinking.

'You can't remember where you're from?'

More brilliant white teeth.

'Well, it's a tricky thing, isn't it? Asking someone where they're from. It can mean different things to different people.

80

For example, do you mean where was I born, or where do I call home? Sometimes they are the same, but often they're different.'

'You talk strange.'

He laughs, that quiet laugh, almost like he's holding it in his chest, and says this world is strange, and any talk that is to capture it is liable to strangeness and sometimes incomprehensibility.

I don't know what to say to this and settle for, 'Where were you born?'

'The less interesting question, but I'll answer it. I was born on the tin islands.'

'Never heard of them.'

'North,' says Gelon. 'It's where we used to get our tin to make bronze. Near Atlantis.'

'Atlantis? Yeah, of course.'

'A sceptic? I appreciate that. I think it's healthy to reserve judgement, but what your friend said is true, at least partly. I cannot speak for Atlantis, although that is the rumour. The tin islands are a long, long way from here. Far north and another world entirely. That rain outside, you think it's bad?'

'It's pissing.'

'Picture a land where it always rains. Storms like this every day. That's the tin islands, though it's greener than anything you can imagine too. You drop a stone in the ground, and it will grow into a tree in the land I come from.'

'Why'd you leave?'

He shuts his eyes tightly and then lets the lids unfurl all slow and languorous like petals in the morning sun.

'Oh, that is a sad story. It will only break your heart.'

He takes a long drink, and again there's silence. Gelon seems in one of his moods and is just staring into his cup. The collector appears content to watch us.

'What brings you to Syracuse?'

'Heraclitus said war is the father of all things, and my visit is certainly its progeny.'

'You're a slaver?'

His face scrunches in distaste, and for a moment, I think I've offended him, but then the cheeks relax, and there's a playful light in the dark eyes.

'Not anything so crude as that. Oh, certainly I buy things, and I sell things, and on occasion, some of those things are people, but I would never define myself by a rare and unpleasant activity. Really, it's the world that I'm interested in. The world in all its forms and all its denizens.'

I catch Gelon's eye and make a gesture to leave, but he doesn't seem to notice.

'Have you ever been to India?' says the collector.

'Can't say I have. Where's that?'

'Dionysus,' says Gelon, head bowed. 'It's where Dionysus travelled to, up past Persia.'

The collector nods eagerly.

'Correct again.' He turns to me. 'Your friend seems far more knowledgeable about the world than you.' Back to Gelon. 'Do you know it was the stories of Dionysus that drew me there? I wanted to recreate his journey.'

Something shifts in him, and he starts talking rapidly. A flow of words that rushes out almost like the rhythm of a poem. He says it was his dream to take Dionysus' route all the way into the heart of the Indus. Of all our gods, Dionysus was the only one he really cared for: the god of tragedy, wine, music and madness. The only god to die and be reborn. What might a man learn by following in such a god's path? He needed to know. It took years and cost a fortune, but he did it. All the way to the heart of India.

He's no longer reclining but on his feet, moving along the scarlet carpet and whispering of his voyage. He says it was obvious why Dionysus had gone there. Those people knew truths that will always be hidden from us. Just maybe, we might imagine them, in a dream or something, they'll flicker by like silver fish in a dark lake, glimpsed then gone, but it won't do us no good, this glimpsing, whereas those lads in India, they knew. He says there are snakes in India as long as ships, and they don't have fangs; they just swallow you whole, and he once saw a boy get eaten by one. It took ages, but the snake managed it, and for a very short while, you could hear the boy inside the snake. Mad brief moments were these, looking into the eyes of the snake and listening to the dying boy's voice, fainter and fainter and then nothing. We must visit India if we get the chance. We'd love it there. Gelon doesn't answer, just keeps drinking, head down. I say it sounds pretty good. The fella nods politely, but I can tell he doesn't give a shite what I think.

'Do you believe in the gods?' he asks suddenly, looking at Gelon.

Gelon seems a bit taken aback by the question, or perhaps he's just too drunk to understand.

'Are our lives governed by divine order, or is there only this?' He pinches a bit of the skin on his arm, takes up a piece of fruit and bites it, the juice dripping down his knuckles. 'What do you say?'

'I don't know,' says Gelon.

'Not good enough! Imagine your friend's life depended on it. Let's say he would die if you didn't give an answer. And that the answer needed to be the one you truly believed, what would you say?'

'Ah, here.'

'Quiet,' he says to me sharply. All trace of humour gone from his voice.

Gelon seems to be thinking. His eyes drift around the room, then settle on the mask Alekto gave him, which rests on his lap.

'There's a reason for everything,' he says quietly. 'Even if the gods don't know what they're doing. Something does.'

The collector smiles and turns to me.

'Your friend professes belief, yet I'm not convinced. What about you? Are the gods real?'

'They are real,' says I. 'And you're a prick.'

He seems to like this, for he laughs for a long time, that queer silent laugh, like a bird caught in his throat.

'You two are wonderful. I haven't shown this to anyone in Syracuse, but I think it's time.' He lowers his voice to a whisper, though there's no one else in the room but us. 'How would you like to see a god?'

Neither Gelon nor I answer, and he seems a bit taken aback. Like he'd expected excitement or shock, anything but silence.

'This isn't a ruse. You may have thought I asked you those questions in some idle fancy, like a regular sophist, but really they were a test, and you both passed. I tell you, I have a god on this ship, and if you wish to see it, say so now. Most profess belief in the gods, but few have ever seen one in real life, or if they have, they wouldn't know, for as the stories tell us, the gods love disguises, but here you have a rare opportunity. The rarest of them all. To see a real god in its divine form. Will you take it?'

Everything in me is screaming no, and I am about to say no, when Gelon's voice cuts me off.

'Yes,' he says. 'I want to see it.'

The collector raps on the wall behind us. The old man enters even more slowly than before, and the collector tells him that he is to show us the god at once, and the old man nods, hobbles to the wall just at the painting of the Hydra, pushes the head that's swallowing Heracles, and there's a click as it opens. He beckons us to follow, and we do.

12.

The room he leads us into is long, dark and narrow as fuck. It must be near the prow as it thins with every step we take. There are clay lanterns scattered about the floor, but most emit no light, maybe 'cause the floor is wet, and the rocking of the boat put them out. Only a few still burn, and their flames bend and twist like creatures in pain. The old man walks ahead, wheezing, and his slow tottering movements make an eerie counterpoint to those writhing flames and the boat rocking as the seawater at our feet sloshes. The room is jammed with wooden crates. Most sealed but one or two are open, and I trail a little behind Gelon and the old man so I can take a peek. It's more armour. A helmet cracked at the crown, with strands of brown hair poking out, shattered shields and stained blades.

Suddenly the air is full of smoke and sweet scent, and the old man starts coughing, even as he waves these sticks with orange embers at their end.

'What the fuck?'

'Incense,' says Gelon. 'For the god?'

The old man nods and drops the sticks to the floor; they hiss as their light goes out.

'This is an honour,' he wheezes.

At the end of the room is a crate bigger than all the rest. Much bigger, and it isn't square like the others but circular, so that it looks more like a bathtub, though there's a lid over it with metal bolts and a rusted chain that slinks down to the floor. The old man stops at this and tugs at the chain, panting; the lid of the crate creaks, moves a little, but not much, and Gelon offers to help. The old man seems conflicted and at first says no, but after a few more exhausted tugs, he gives the chain to Gelon, who pulls it easy, the lid sliding back like it's been oiled.

'Lampo, come on.'

I walk over and feel the blood thumping in my ears. The crate is full of murky water, coils of green seaweed.

'Sure, maybe he meant cod, not god,' says I.

The old man looks deeply offended, but he doesn't say anything. Instead, he leans over behind the crate and comes back with a long metal pole with a blunted hook at the end of it, and still wheezing, he stabs it into the water, and then there's this weird smell in the air. Not unpleasant but wild and strange. Everything feels suddenly altered now. It's like a rift's opened and a different world is seeping in, and the water starts to glow and pulse. The old man, still wheezing, stabs again, and the glowing intensifies, and I see a flash of something moving underneath the surface like rippling skin. The smell gets stronger, and the blood is hammering in my temples now. Everything in me is screaming to get the fuck out of here, and I turn to Gelon.

'Let's go!'

He doesn't answer, just stares at the shivering water, transfixed.

I pull at his cloak, but he's a block and won't be moved.

'Suit yourself, man. I'm gone!'

I turn around and bail. The collector is nowhere to be seen, and soon I'm legging it up the steps and back up on the deck. The crew are playing dice, and they look up when they see me. For a moment, I think they'll go for me, but they just nod. The fella with the scar on his throat even asks if I want to join them. I say no thanks and stand there, feeling suddenly foolish 'cause up here in the fresh sea air, with the wind on my face, the panic is gone, and so I just stand and watch the crew roll their knuckle-bones across the planks, their winnings and losses flashing in the moonlight, until I feel a grip on my shoulder and it's Gelon; patches of his cloak are dark and dripping.

'Time to go,' he says.

His face is pale as fuck, and if his voice doesn't shake, it certainly teeters.

'Alright,' says I.

The crew wish us goodnight, and we climb down the ladder and walk away from the ship quickly, but we've only taken a couple of steps when the collector's voice calls after us. I don't want to stop, but Gelon makes me.

'Goodnight!' says the collector. 'I can tell I am going to enjoy working with you both.'

The collector waves and Gelon does too, and then a strange thing happens. The crew stand up and wave at us, shout out goodnight like obedient children.

'What the fuck is going on, man?'

'Wave,' says Gelon.

We wave for a long time, and then we turn around and walk quickly away from the docks and back to the city proper, neither of us saying a thing. Only when we reach the Achradina crossroads does Gelon speak.

'Put out your hands.'

'Why?'

'Just do it.'

I put out my hands, and Gelon holds a pouch tied with a string. He can't get the string loose and so tears it with his teeth. Gold coins tumble into my hands until they're heaped and gleaming.

'Fuck,' says I. 'What does this mean?'

'A producer,' says Gelon, smiling. 'We have a producer.'

'Oh.'

Strange, I'm holding more money right now than I've ever held in my life. Years' worth of a potter's wages piled in my palm, but the only thing I can think of is what we left on the ship, and I ask Gelon if it's true. Was it a god?

His smile fades.

'Was it, man?'

He looks up at the sky, and his eyes get all silver with moonlight. They fucking glow, like he's gone divine on me, and I'm reminded of that old man and his song for then a cloud passes over the moon, and he's just as before.

'Yes,' he says softly. 'It was a god on that ship.'

13.

And like that, we're flush. It hits me, sudden, how foolish we've been. Directors without a producer are like a ship without a sail, the medium of wind to endeavours nautical being equivalent to coin in all theatrical, and till now we've had fuck all of that. Tuireann, for that's the queer-sounding name of our producer, thinks staging a play with the Athenians is genius. See, he's always been fascinated by the theatre but felt there was something too safe about the surface level of its pageantry that put him off investing. Now, at last, with us, he's found his kind of show. In fairness, I have my reservations about Tuireann, and his talk is most peculiar, but he's minted and understands talent, and that will do for now.

Gelon and I get down to the practicalities right away. Questions we'd been putting off for ages 'cause we knew we couldn't afford the answers are laid out quickly over a jug of Catanian red, and we state plainly what's needed to do this right.

Masks and costumes for the chorus and the main cast – twenty in total.

Sets – seeing as it's the quarry, a roof and stage are out of the question, as are benches, but there's certainly space for a backdrop or two that we could set up against the rocks.

Music – doesn't need to be a dithyramb or anything, but still. A tragedy without a tune is like a sun that doesn't give off heat: dead, and nothing will grow from it. When men go to war, they do it to music. When they set sail for better shores and row into the vast blue, they do it to music. Even our hearts beat to some rhythm, and the director who neglects it neglects what makes us men.

Food – the bottom of the list, but perhaps most important of all, we need to feed those Athenians if the play is even to happen. And this, in many ways, is the trickiest thing as it's not a once-off purchase but must be made several times, and what's more, transported down into the quarries under the eyes of the guards. Aye, looking at it now, it's the feeding of the Athenians that will prove most challenging, and sure enough, when we decide which task will go to each, Gelon insists he sort out the theatrical stuff with Alekto, and I use my contacts to arrange the grub.

'What contacts?'

'Your cousin works in the market, right?'

'He can't stand me.'

'Still your kin.'

That Gelon wants to go to Alekto's is no surprise, but I thought we'd go together at least, do each bit step by step, not cut up the tasks piecemeal, like some butcher. I'm about to say as much when he lobs a bulging pouch at me. I take a peek inside, and there's silver, yes, but a lot of it's gold.

'That's enough to buy food to feed twenty people for a few weeks,' says Gelon. 'Our actors will be well fed – none of that cheap barley. I want wheat and decent cheese. Alright?'

'No probs,' says I, feeling the pleasant drag of the pouch as I tie it to my belt. We agree to meet at the entrance to the quarry in a couple of hours, and then I set off.

There's something lovely in the way the pouch's weight pulls you down as you move when you know the truth is contrary. You're rising, up above your fellow men, even as your gait slows under the burden. The market's jammed. Not just the usual shoppers, 'cause these days we have tourists too. There are a group of Carthaginians over by the stone where they beheaded Nicias. The stone is stained as if with violet sap, and one of the Carthaginians touches it and then rips his hand away like it's scalding. They've a tour guide with them, and he's spouting on about how Nicias begged for mercy, which is bollix. I was there for it. Almost every Syracusan was there 'cause Nicias was the richest man in Athens, their greatest general, and yet on that day, we had him. Oh, it was mad. The executioner started cutting bits off Nicias' purple robes with a curved knife like he was shearing a flower till the chest was bare and pale, and Nicias started shivering. Still, the tour guide is full of shit. Nicias wasn't in the best of form, but he never begged. All he asked was that Athens forgive him. He said he'd never wanted to come here, but still, he'd done his best to win. Then he started whispering something over and over that I couldn't hear. The executioner, a decent chap who I stood drinks later in the bar, said it was 'Melisandra'. Just some mot's name. I'm about to curse the guide out for his lies, but then it hits me: the poor fucker is just earning a crust, and I watch him stuttering his fibs and feel something close to pity. This world's rough, and we can't all be directors.

I take the smallest silver coin from my pouch, an obol or something, and flick it at him, and he blinks and touches his face, immediately kneels in the mud to pick it up. The Carthaginians are frowning over at me now, annoyed that I'm interrupting their tour, but I just wink and stroll off. Pressing business.

I head straight for the millers' quarter of the market. The air shifts, and the scent here is rich and nutty with the crackle of woodsmoke. The different grains are heaped in pots, glinting like gold. My cousin is the wiry fella at the biggest stall, looking about him keen-eyed and eager, his lips cracked. He's from my aunt's litter, and she's been using his prosperity as a stick to beat my ma with these past few years.

'How are things, cuz?' says I.

He pretends he doesn't hear me, keeps scooping grains from one pot to the next, eyes narrowed with intensity as if it's sculpture he's doing.

'Wish I could natter,' says I, 'but here on business today. You know how it is?'

He cracks a smile at that.

'Sure, Lampo. Off to court for a bit of jury duty, is it?'

The court is just across from the market, and it's true that since our factory closed, I've sat jury duty for the few obols the state pays. Still, it's a nasty thing to bring up.

'Do you know what you are, Skiron?'

No answer.

'A fucking moron.'

He smiles and licks his lips.

'Is that what I am?' He looks around at his stall packed with customers, its pots brimming with grain, as if to say, is this stupidity?

'Aye, but it's worse than that. You're one of those rare idiots who's convinced he's a genius 'cause he got a little ahead, and for that, there's no cure. You're doomed, Skiron. King of the fucking cereal. You dumb cunt.'

The smile's gone, and a few of the customers are listening. I think I hear a muffled chuckle from one or two. Skiron nods to himself and sighs.

'Is there anything else?'

This is usually the moment where I ask for some meal on credit, and he licks his lips in expectation of the refusal. I unhook the pouch from my belt and toss it in the air, and man, the jingle of it hitting my palm, is the best tune I've heard in ages.

'There is, actually. I want two sacks of your finest wheat. None of that barley shite.'

'Yeah, good one, Lampo. I'm busy now.'

I take out a gold coin. They're gorgeous things. Not like any of the Greek tender you usually see. Persian, by the looks of it. The king at the back is an ugly prick with horns, but I wouldn't want to cross him.

'You'll be busier now,' says I. 'Make that three sacks of wheat. Chop chop. I'm a busy man.'

His eyes are fixed on the gold, which I spin on my knuckle. I can see the confusion in his face, and it's meat and drink to me. He wants to tell me to fuck off, accuse me of stealing it, but first and foremost, Skiron loves coin, and today I've got it. In the end, greed beats anger, and he clicks his heels.

'Well, Lampo, that's a big order. I don't have three sacks of wheat. I mean, I don't have all of that here with me.'

'Shame. Wanted to keep this in the family.'

I put the gold back in the pouch and make to seal it with the string.

'Wait!' he says. 'Give us an hour, and I can get it. If you're really pressed for time, I can give you some of it in barley?'

I grimace.

'Barley, man? It's the quality I'm feeding. Not donkeys.'

'Sorry, Lampo, of course. Wheat it is. I'll get it for you. Just give me an hour. Come back here in an hour, and I'll have it packed and ready to go.'

I make a show of considering, take the coin out again and spin it on my knuckle.

'Family,' says I with reluctance. 'The things we do.'

With that, I stroll off and, just for the buzz, head to the most expensive quarter of the market – where the aristos do their shopping. It's a different world here. It smells different; the sweat off the people is even different. Healthier and sweeter 'cause it's not mixed with dirt, and it leaks from the well fed.

The faces aren't as lined. People don't jostle one another as much. You've got room here. If someone knocks into you, they say pardon. Still, I notice I'm getting more bumps than most, and they're staring too. One glance at me says I'm different. The clothes, probably even my way of gaping about as if it's all new, give me away. The slaves here are better dressed than I am. I find myself at a stall of chitons, their colours loud and different: yolk-yellow, and forest-green, and even some flecked with the dusky purple of murex guts, but my favourite is a chiton the blue of lightning cutting evening sky. I've barely picked it up before I feel someone behind me.

'No touching.'

I turn, and it's a fat fella squeezed into a cloak fastened with a silver brooch. He looks me up and down to confirm his assessment was correct, then says it again.

'Don't touch.'

I unstring my pouch, let a few coins tumble onto my palm.

'Just back from Babylon,' says I. 'You take Persian?'

'Yes, sir,' he sputters, eyes like moons. 'Of course.'

I depart from the stall in the lightning-blue chiton with a magenta deerskin belt, a huge bronze buckle in its centre engraved with the words of a poem that the merchant said is early Homer. The pouch is lighter, but the weight of the buckle makes up for it so that it feels somewhat the same. People are looking at me differently now. I'm not quite one of them, but I'm not getting jostled quite so much, and whereas before the shopkeepers eyed me suspiciously, now they're crying their wares, but to it all, I'm imperturbable. That was a silly lapse – the money has a strict purpose. But on the other hand, looked at in a different light, could you not say the expense is justified? I'm a director now. Everyone knows the more you have, the more you get. These clothes will probably save us money when negotiating price, and this cheers me up as I stroll back towards

Skiron's stall, but then I stop. There's something awful on the ground. Like genuinely disturbing: my boots. The leather's scuffed to bits, and I can feel the pebbles cut through the soles. They didn't seem so bad before, but now with the new cloak, they clash. Like Zeus riding a donkey – just wrong. I stop off at a cobbler and ask for a decent pair.

He's slow to answer, so the gold comes out again, and I start on about the Hanging Gardens, and he becomes courteous as fuck, brings them out in batches for me to try on. I pick out a nice pair of solid brown leather, and the cobbler seems satisfied with my choice, then goes to say something but stops himself.

'What?' I ask.

He looks embarrassed, says never mind, it was a silly idea.

'Let me be the judge.'

'Well,' he says, 'there are a new set of boots just in from Egypt. And really, they're for the more discerning client. Cow leather is all well and good, but for a merchant who's been to Babylon, a man of your style, well, not to put too fine a point on it, it's not crocodile.'

'Crocodile?' says I.

The cobbler nods.

'Oh, yes. Durable yet astonishingly supple. Not to put too fine a point on it, this season it's all about crocodile.' He takes out a pair of the greenest boots I've ever seen. Little knobs all along them that catch the light of the sun like verdigris flames, and when I touch them, it's like rubbing something beautiful and deadly.

'How much?' I say, breathless.

He tells me the price, and it's ridiculous. More than I made in nearly a year as a potter. Of course, I'll tell him no, that I'll take the others, so it's as much a surprise to me as him when the words 'Bag them up' come out of my mouth.

The man nods, as if I've made the only sensible decision,

and starts to pack them away, but I stop him for I want to wear them now, and when I walk out of that stall, I stumble a little, 'cause the crocs have a mad heel on them, but then I get the hang of it, and it gives an alien feel to the world, almost like the ground itself has altered by being farther from it.

I'm in a barber's. An aristo barber's where they do the latest styles – five drachmae for a cut and a shave. Silly money. That's a week's rent in the city centre, and I shake my head and chuckle. Not a chance. But somehow, I'm in a cushioned chair and asking for that cut Diocles sports, slicked back with almond oil and shaved at the sides, and he says, of course, sir, of course.

I'm gliding through the market now, and even though I'm no longer in the posh part, it's the strangest thing. No one jostles me. It's like some invisible barrier has shot up around my person that can't be broken, and though the market's packed, it's spacious. A cart is parked up at my cousin's stall, and the driver is unloading pots of grain. That must be my wheat. Skiron notices me and waves me over, but I just turn around. Fuck him. He can wait. There's someone I need to see.

Dismas' is empty. Just a weather-beaten fisherman on a stool eating slop, and he looks up and hocks a phlegm in disgust when I enter. That yellow muck on the floor is more welcome than a warm embrace, for in it I see the resentment of a local for an aristo. I saunter to the bar. The slave girl's polishing the counter with a dirty cloth. There are dark circles under her eyes and an all-round languor to her movements, sweat patches on her grey smock, but regardless she looks stunning.

'Jug of the finest, my pharaoh.'

She glances over and there's a puzzled tautening to her features, like I'm a question that needs answering. The bar counter is polished bronze, and my reflection flickers back to me. My hair is no longer a scraggly bird's nest but a glossy work of art, each individual curl trimmed and oiled. I look fucking good.

'It's you!' she says, laughing, but there's no mockery in it: only surprise, and something else.

'Been very busy the last couple of days. A series of ventures that required my undivided attention. Cargo arriving and whatnot.'

'I thought you were a potter.'

This throws me, till I recall that I've told her nothing of my profession.

'So you've been asking about me?'

She blushes a little. It's hard to tell 'cause of her tan, but her cheeks are definitely pinker.

'Not really. Someone said your factory closed, and you were out of work.'

This someone sounds like a cock-block. She sets a jug down on the counter: Catanian red, and she pours me a cup. I tell her to get one for herself and flash the silver. She says she prefers white, so I say get a jug of that too.

'Aye. Not going to lie. For a while, it was rough, but in the end, it was a blessing in disguise.' I take a gulp. 'Needed to branch out, see. As Heraclitus said, war is the father of all things, and my fortune shall be its progeny.'

She takes a sip of her wine, dainty like, despite her being a slave, and there's the wet sheen of it on her lips.

'What are you doing now?'

'Oh, many different things. Importing spices, cloth, sl—' Was about to say slaves, but stop myself. 'You name it; I've probably some coin in it. The key is diversification. Put all your hopes in one ship, and it's the one that's liable to sink.'

She doesn't seem to credit much of what I've said, but she nods eagerly at the last bit.

'That's for sure . . . you can't depend on one thing.'

'I'll drink to that.'

I raise my cup for us to toast, and when we knock them together, our fingertips graze. Just a flickering contact, nothing really, but I shiver.

'You okay?'

'Ah, yeah, just thinking of the past.'

'Best not to do that too much,' she says, and seems to mean it.

'True. Now is where it's at. This city's changed more the last year than the previous twenty. People don't need to be what they once were, you know?'

Her eyes are bright and eager, and she takes another sip of the wine. I ask her where she's from, and she hesitates, but at last says, or rather whispers, 'Sardis, in Lydia.'

'That's Croesus' town, right?'

She nods, and there's a wistful sort of cast to her eye.

'You ever meet Croesus?'

Laughter and a shake of the head.

'Of course not. He's long dead. I saw his palace, though. The Persians burned most of it down, but even the little bit that's left is bigger than anything here.'

Her jaw tenses when she says this so that you can see the rise of muscle up by the ear, and there's a curious expression in her eyes. I think she's proud, and for some reason, this pride in some palace thousands of miles away that she'll never see again makes me sad, and yet I like her all the more for it.

'No doubt. Our city isn't much to look at, it's true, but that will change. You can't take two steps without some prick on a ladder screeching, "Watch out!" I think we'll catch up.'

I go to pay, but she shakes her head, and refuses the coin, doesn't even seem to notice the gold I flash at her.

'Those,' she hesitates, 'those people the other night. You shouldn't have done that, but thanks.'

'That was nothing. A bit of fun.'

An awkward silence follows.

I scour my mind for things to ask about Lydia, but nothing comes. Instead, I say, 'I didn't mean what I said last time.'

'What did you say?'

Her eyes tell me that she remembers well enough.

'Ah, nasty shit that I won't repeat. Everything I said, I meant the contrary, if that makes sense.'

'So I don't belong in the fields?'

'You don't belong here either.'

I let that linger for a while. She's looking at me intently now, her lips parted for a response.

'Is that Lampo? Tell him he's barred!'

A door swings open behind her, and a bald fella stamps out. It's Dismas. I haven't seen him in ages. There was a time when he did everything in the bar. Served the drinks, scrubbed the tables, cooked the soup and sang the songs. But that time has passed. He's opened up a fancy boozer in the centre, and the fella at the door only lets in aristos. Still, Dismas looks rough. He used to be fat in a jolly kind of way, but he served as a hoplite in the war, and those months baking in the armour drained the weight off him too quick. Now the skin on his face and neck hangs loose, almost like it's melting.

'Lampo?' he says as if he might have made a mistake.

There's a bewildered cast to his stare as he takes in the crocs, the lightning-blue chiton.

'Good to see you, Diz. Been too long.'

'Eh, you're barred,' he says, though there's still uncertainty in his voice.

'Am I?' I force a yawn. 'Barred from a place where I've bestowed my custom the last ten years?'

'You assaulted a customer.'

I've seen people cut open proper in Dismas'. Once so bad,

you could see the fella's guts hanging out like sausages, and he had to be sewn up by a tailor 'cause the doctor didn't have enough thread, yet the man who stabbed him was served the next day. I tell Dismas as much, but he shakes his head.

'We could've been closed down. Do you know who those lads were?'

'Don't know,' I lie, 'don't care.'

His cheeks are glowing now. They have that flushed look that was so common when he was at his peak weight, though this isn't due to food, but rage. I'll have to try a different tack.

'I'm sorry,' says I. 'I really am. Won't happen again.'

'I know it won't. That's what being barred means. It means you're done here. Now, will you leave or do I have to call Chabrias?'

I take out one of the gold coins and lay it on the counter hard so that it makes a clang, and sure enough, Dismas' eyes are pinned to it. I let it lie there for a while and then flick it over at him. He tries to catch but is too slow, and it bounces off his sagging throat and hits the floor. He kneels and picks it up, bites it.

'Back to your old ways,' says I. 'This fella's appetite was famous. Once saw him eat a whole calf by himself.'

The corners of her lips curl, but she stops the smile before it takes.

Dismas removes the coin from his gob. 'This is solid gold, Lampo. Where did you get it?'

I shrug and open up the pouch so he can see what's inside.

'This is its home,' I says. 'But it doesn't get along with the other coins. That is, except for its twin.' I remove another golden disc. 'I thought maybe your pocket could be a new home for them. Was I wrong to think that?'

The first coin has already disappeared, and now his eyes are on the second.

'Am I still barred?'

He shakes his head and laughs.

'Course not, Lampo. You know me. My blood was up, and I had to get it out. The boy's father made a stink, but it will pass. You and Gelon make this place.'

I flick the other coin over at him, and he catches.

'Look after those two,' I says. 'They're good kids.'

The gold disappears quick. Somewhere amid our little chat, the girl's gone too.

'What's her name?' I ask.

'Who?'

'Your one I was talking to.'

He hesitates as if he has to think about it.

'Lyra.'

'Lyra from Lydia. That has a nice flow to it.'

'What's that?'

'Lydia, that's where she's from? You fucking own the girl, do you know that at least?'

Dismas looks like he might be thinking about barring me again, but he just nods.

'Of course. Yeah, there were a lot of Lydians on sale when I got her. You don't see them so much any more. These things come in waves, I guess.'

'They do, of course.' I take out some silver and order another Catanian red and whatever Dismas is having. All animosity is gone now, and he starts chatting away to me about the headache he's having with the builders of his new place. Sleazy contractors are putting in dud bricks that are already cracking.

'They'll not cheat me,' he says, nursing his wine. 'I've worked too hard for this. It hasn't been easy, you know?'

'You've earned everything you've got. That's plain to see.' He frowns, but I can tell he's pleased. 'About the girl, though,' says I, casually. 'I mean, would you mind if I took her out one of the days. Like for a walk? I'd be happy to pay, man.'

Dismas gives me a big shit-eating grin.

'Ah, I knew it. If it's a go you want, I can tell her now. There's a room upstairs?'

I've been dreaming about this girl every night. And now all I have to say is yeah, throw him some coins, and go upstairs. It's that easy.

'No,' I says. 'Cheers, but no, man. I mean, maybe on the walk, but I like talking to her, you know. She's an interesting girl.'

Dismas chuckles and scoops a few olives from a jar on the counter, pops them into his mouth so that his fingers glisten with oil. Everything feels suddenly dirty now, like it's been rubbed with that grease, and I want to break something, but I don't. Instead, I look down at my crocs, the left crooked 'cause of my limp. They're too much, really. Like some costume from Alekto's, and I shut my eyes.

'What's wrong with you, man? If it's a walk you want, absolutely, go take her on a fucking hike for all I care. Will I call her now?'

'I can't go now. I'm busy.'

'When? Not at night, though. I need her for the evenings, see.'

'The afternoon. Day after tomorrow. I'll pick her up.'

'You do that, Lampo.'

He starts chortling again, and I think I might actually hit him.

'What is it?' I say, pleasant as anything.

'It's just funny. This war has changed so much, and I know I shouldn't be surprised by anything, but a minted Lampo. I have to say, I didn't see it coming.'

'Yeah,' says I, and I realize the girl is in the corner scrubbing tables. That she's probably been listening this whole time.

★

Back at the market. I don't know how long I spent in the bar, but I've had a few, and my head's got that fuzzy ache that comes from cutting short a midday booze. There's a sour taste to the air, but I have to move quick if I'm to get all this sorted. Skiron's stall is pretty quiet as the afternoon rush is over. When he sees me, he looks annoyed but checks himself and just waves. The wheat is there in pots piled high. It's the same colour as the waning sun: gold with a reddish tinge, and it smells lovely.

'Best grain you'll find in Syracuse,' he says, proud. 'It was a nightmare to get, but I told you I'd come through. What took you so long?'

'Business.'

He asks me what business I'm getting into, and my mind is wandering, so I don't even know what I say, but it must make sense, for he nods and asks how I want to move the grain.

'Have you got a cart or something?'

He does, but it will cost extra. No surprises there.

'The whole thing is forty drachmae,' he says.

I go to my pouch, and immediately I know something's wrong. It's still there, hooked firmly to the deerskin belt, but it's light as fuck, barely jingles as I lift it.

'How much was that you say?'

'Forty. I saw what you had earlier. That will cover it easy.'

There's barely eight left in the pouch. Where the fuck did it all go? Was I robbed or something? But I know I wasn't robbed. I fucked up badly here.

'Eh, that price is a little steep, cuz,' I says. 'Thought you'd sort me out.'

'That's not steep, Lampo. That's what the stuff costs. I told you this earlier. I mean, you have the money. I saw it.'

'I was robbed,' I say. 'This city is going to the dogs. Some little Carthaginian prick. Eight is all I can pay you, man. I swear.'

Skiron's practically foaming now. He starts shouting about how eight doesn't even cover the costs, that he'll be out of pocket, and it's not fair.

'Take it or leave it.'

It's a bit of a shock when he says he'll leave it, and now it's my turn to start sweating, 'cause Gelon will go fucking mental if I show up with nothing. I start jabbering about how we're family, and I need him to do this for me. Skiron cheers up. He's still out of pocket, and materially this is bad for him, but in a sense, balance has been restored. I'm asking a favour, and he licks his lips and nods to himself as if the world that had gone momentarily mad is back making sense.

'For eight, all I can give you is one of barley.'

I protest, but to be honest, I'm relieved. Barley is food, and food is life. Gelon will go spare, but at least Paches and his mates will eat. There's no chance of Skiron giving me a cart now, though, and I'm left with a single sack of barley, and I start heaving it along the ground, and people are staring, 'cause I'm dressed like an aristo and doing the work of a slave.

'See you later, cuz!' calls Skiron after me.

I keep heaving the sack out of the market and down through the streets, and the movement causes the dust to rise into my face, but fuck it. On I go till I'm out on the dirt road that leads to the Laurium pit, moving tortoise-slow, and doing fierce damage to the crocs, and then I see him, waiting at the turn-off is Gelon. But he's not alone. There are six kids around him. Dares I recognize at once.

'Why did you do it?' says Gelon, taking in the lone sack, my boots and all the rest.

I tell him I was robbed in the market, a fucking pickpocket got me, and this was all I could afford. I brace myself for a blow that never comes. He just shakes his head, more sorrowful than angry, and this disappointment hurts more than any punch. He points at the sun, which is huge and red and rolling across the sky like the head of Nicias in the square all those months ago.

'They'll not eat tonight because of you.'

'Can't we go down now?'

'Too late. The rats will be out, and it won't be safe for them.'

He gestures to the kids. Dares and his mates protest, but Gelon's already walking off, back towards the city, and the children follow.

I don't.

Instead, I sit on the sack and watch the red sun sink below into the pits and whisper a promise I hope I'll keep.

14.

Two sacks of barley grain
Eight blocks of soft cheese
Ten skins of wine
Twelve skins of water
Four pots of olives
Cups and spoons

The kids are waiting for us at the market. They hover about giddily as we buy what's on the list, and at some point, I notice they've started carrying our stuff. One kid has a bowl, another a block of cheese, and another a wineskin, as they whistle and laugh. I'm about to curse them out when Gelon breaks the news: they're going to be a permanent part of the production. He says every proper play needs assistants, and these boys will be perfect. Besides, their school has just closed for building works and it will keep them out of trouble. Dares nods at every word. I say nothing. It strikes me as a pretty bad idea, but when Gelon's mind is set on something, he won't be swayed, and these kids are now the production assistants, whether I like it or not. It's an eerie walk this morning. The moon is still up, a slender blade that's larger and crisper than the frail sun. Theros is long gone. The leaves don't so much fall as rip from the trees. All of them are red, and they skitter along the roads like bleeding stars under that knife of moon. The children are boisterous, chatting and singing songs, but as we approach the quarry, a heaviness settles over them. Only Dares remains the same. He's glued to Gelon's side and asking endless questions about all things theatrical.

Suddenly, music pierces the quiet. Lovely music rising just over the crest of the hill, and our pace quickens. Me and the kids almost race up that hill, but when we reach the crest, the music stops, and there's nothing but the cawing of crows and an old man with a large straw hat sitting on a rock. There's a wheelbarrow beside him and a tan dog on a rope wagging its tail.

'Was that you playing?' I ask.

The old man looks at me as if he doesn't understand the question. Gelon takes out the purse and gives the codger some coin, and little Strabo starts patting the dog while the other kids move the food into the wheelbarrow, cover it with a cloth, and we go on. Not a word was spoken between the old man and Gelon, and I almost wonder if the music was in my head. I ask Gelon who the fuck was that, and he just mutters something about a man selling a wheelbarrow. We've reached the pit now. The guard at the entrance arches an eyebrow when he sees the kids, the wheelbarrow, but the silver Gelon passes him calms his nerves.

'We'll be coming down most days now.'

'Right, so,' says the guard, pocketing the coin.

'Some days, you might hear music, but don't let that bother you. It's just part of the production.'

'Right, eh, what?'

Gelon's voice turns gentle and lowers to a whisper. He tells the guard that it's nothing to worry about. It's important work we're doing. The guard looks spooked, but Gelon keeps whispering, tells him that it's theatre. We're saving the last known play of Euripides, man, and you can be a part of this. The guard seems uncertain, but Gelon's tone reassures, as do the extra pieces of silver and the bloated wineskin I hand him, and when we go on, he wishes us luck.

There was a time when being a quarry guard was a nice little money-spinner. People wanted to go down and see the great Athenians in chains, but the months have passed, and the Athenians are no longer a top attraction. Visitors are rarer and rarer now, and to be a guard at the quarry is not what it once was. I think we overpaid him.

A decent few Athenians must have died since last time. As we move the food, we often have to weave the barrow around stone heaps. These are the makeshift graves they put up when one of them dies. In fact, there's a burial going on now. A few Athenians carry stones, grunting under the weight of stones no bigger than fists. They have to hold them with two hands, press them to their chest like mothers cradling babies. The kids stare at them dumbly. Dares, as usual, is the first to speak.

'The Athenians?' he says, incredulous.

Gelon nods, and the kids eye one another uncertainly. It's clear this is not at all what they expected. The mighty invaders, butchers of their fathers, brothers and uncles. Can it really be these ragged skellos hugging rocks?

'Hunger,' says I. 'Even the gods need to eat.'

Dares nods as if he understands, and I think he does, but the other kids are still gaping. Strabo, the tiny boy who said a prayer for his brother, is most perplexed of all. He wanders out from our troupe almost like a sleepwalker, hands stretched in front of him, as if he wants to test they're real, but one of his mates takes him by the hand and pulls him in.

'We must stick together in here,' says Gelon. 'Any one of you who can't do that is gone, that clear?'

Dares nods eagerly and turns to his mates.

'You get that?'

The five other children shout that they get it, and we walk on. I push the wheelbarrow, and the kids march alongside it so that it almost looks like we're part of the Athenians' funeral procession. If they knew what was in that wheelbarrow, what would they do? They look too weak for violence, but anything can happen; that's why we covered the food. All they see is a ragged cloth, and it seems odd to me that as they cradle their funeral rocks, life wheels past them, weeks or even months of life rolling past, but they don't know. Sometimes, it's better, I think, not to know.

We find Numa in the same tunnel as before. Paches arrives soon after. Last time we were here, we left them with a small bag of boiled oats, and they both look better.

'Been rehearsing?'

No answer.

They're staring at the kids. The kids are staring at them.

'Boys, this here is Paches and Numa. Two of the finest actors you'll ever find. Paches and Numa, meet the boys.'

'They'll be production assistants,' says Gelon.

The assistants and our actors continue to regard one another warily.

Then Dares pulls the cloth from the wheelbarrow.

'You both must be very hungry,' he says, and cuts them each a thick wedge of cheese.

Hunger, what an odd thing it is. Is the source of all love a lacking? Is that what creates emotion? Not a presence but an absence. Do you need to be emptied to be filled? I'm no philosopher, but this is what I think when Numa's and Paches' eyes widen and glisten, and they claw at the cheese. Even Dares' composure is rattled by the way they attack the food. When the cheese is gone, I give them each some wine and a few cups of barley, which they hide under rocks in the tunnel.

'Good thinking,' I says.

The chorus arrive soon after. We feed them before rehearsal. The kids distribute the drink and food, as Gelon explains that these fellas are production assistants and will be joining us from now on. Some of the chorus seem puzzled but most just nod and tuck in. I tell Dares to make sure that each of them gets a little extra so they can save some for later. Cheese, wine and olives are handed out. The food sprinkles over them like nectar or faith, and their legs and features seem close to lively, so that when I ask if they're ready for a go at scene two, they sound almost excited.

A cough behind us.

Gelon stands on top of the wheelbarrow and says that before we begin, he'd like to say a few words. This is what he says.

15.

'I first saw a play when I was seven or eight. It wasn't Euripides. It was Sophocles. It was *Oedipus Rex*. That was it for me. I was a boy and sat on my da's knees, and I looked at the doomed king trying to find out who killed his da, and I felt awful for him. I imagined what that must be like, and I squeezed my own da's hand and told him I'd never kill him. My da said to be quiet.' Gelon laughs strangely.

'I felt awful that night. I cried and had a fever. Why had the gods let Oedipus kill his da and marry his ma, and blind himself? Why let that happen when it was clear he was a good man? Could they not stop it? Were the gods weak? Did they not care? I cried and didn't understand, but you know what? I remembered that Oedipus was good. That even though he'd done and suffered all those horrible things, he was still good; whether the gods cared didn't matter. And I remember as a kid feeling that this was awfully sad and beautiful. There was dignity even in the worst that could happen under this sky, and I felt less alone. I think most of all, I was a very lonely kid.' He takes a sip of wine, coughs.

'I love Athens. I think I'll always love the city that wrote that play. I prefer Euripides now, but I've told you of *Oedipus* because it was the first one that got me. I don't hate you. How could I? Even though I know you came to make us slaves. I can't hate you. I believe any city that gave us those plays has something worth saving. That's why I'm here.' Gelon looks around him. 'I think.'

The Athenians stare. It's the most I've heard Gelon say in

one go since his boy died. He's never told me that story before. The Athenians look strange. I don't think they've understood all he said, but they get the essence of it. This fellow on the wheelbarrow loves their theatre. Is hopelessly in love with it, and in some small way, he loves them because of it, and that, more than anything else, is why we're here.

Broken down and starving as they are, you'd imagine they wouldn't give a shite if some Syracusan loved Athenian theatre, but they do. You only need the quickest scan of their faces, and you see it. Something that I haven't glimpsed since I stared across at these Athenians two years previous, in battle, when they were gleaming in armour. That very same thing is in their eyes now, though in a much, much frailer form: pride. These fellas are proud to be Athenian. It doesn't last long, but while it's there, it's unmistakable and kind of beautiful and foolish.

When Gelon hops off the wheelbarrow, they shuffle up to him. Their backs are a little straighter. One Athenian, an older fella with long silvery hair and beard, asks which scene they should start with. Gelon says it's up to them, a thing that strikes me as odd at first, but then it hits me that he's building up their confidence. They choose one of the agons. The scene where Medea first tells the chorus that she plans to kill her children and the chorus tell her she's a terrible mother. And I recall the night Gelon told me he wanted to do this. He sang a song from Medea's chorus. It was a bit a few scenes later, when the kids are dead, and it gives a weird sense of time merging, and for a moment, I have the feeling that the future and the past aren't separate at all, just different snatches of a single song, always sung, given consequence when heard. I take a swig from the wine and pass it to Paches, but he barely sips. I ask what's the matter, and he says he wants to keep a clear head for the scene. Yes, things are getting peculiar. Numa is struggling with his wig, which is tangled to fuck, and Gelon has to rip it open for him.

'We'll be getting proper stuff soon,' says Gelon. 'I've commissioned it from Alekto's. It's the best shop in Syracuse for everything theatrical.'

Numa nods and fixes the wig on his head as best he can. Just like before, he starts to transform, subtle at first, a tilt to the head, and the cast of eye, but by the end, even his way of breathing has altered so that he hasn't even said a word before one of the kids lets out a little yelp of fear. I look over and see that it's Strabo. One of his mates throws a hand over his mouth and pulls him close. Numa's gone, and only Medea remains. She tells the chorus that there's no question of the children living. That would leave Jason with something. If a man has something, it can always be built upon. It's like a farmer whose crops fail, he can always plant new seeds, but if you take everything away, if you poison the soil so that nothing can ever grow again, well, then he's thoroughly done for. And yet, as the words are spoken, you get that prickly feeling that Medea's on about herself as much as anything: bearing witness to what's been done to her, even more than what she'll do.

It's the chorus's turn. And we all look to them to see how they'll respond. They have no wigs. No costumes. They're meant to be wealthy noblewomen of Corinth, but between what they're meant to be and what they are lies a distance only the man who fancies a messy death would jump. The chains on their ankles jingle when they shuffle their feet in what seems like an attempt to dance. I feel for them. They've no music, and a chorus more than any other part needs music to come alive.

'We're working on it, boys,' says I, 'have no fear. You'll have proper tunes soon. Ones so raucous, you'll make a dithyramb seem like a lullaby. This is just practice.'

The chorus nods and still shuffle their feet in a semblance of a jig. Gelon starts to hum what must be the music from the scene 'cause, for a moment, Numa breaks character and smiles, eager, then he disappears and Medea's back, staring at the chorus, defiant. Gelon hums louder. It's not the same as real musicians with instruments, but it's something, and a rhythm is building. I can feel it. The silver-haired fella is the best of them. He's really going for it, slapping his knee and urging the others on. Some of his vitality seems to be catching, for the chorus start to move their feet more quickly and the chains writhe like grey serpents at their feet, and it might be my imagination, but it feels like the clinking of those chains corresponds to the tune Gelon is humming.

' "You cannot do this," ' sing the chorus. ' "They are your children. It is against the law of the gods." '

' "The gods?" ' shrieks Medea, pointing at the sky. ' "Am I not the granddaughter of the sun god whose very light shines upon you now? Do not speak to me about the law of the gods! Look at the sun. It shines down on all deeds, just the same." ' Medea spins in the air and bows.

The chorus howl that this is against nature. That even the wolves in the woods protect their young. ' "It cannot be. Perhaps the sun shines upon all things, but that is so the gods can better see our deeds and judge." '

Gelon hums louder, and I notice that his voice is not alone. Dares has joined him, hesitant at first but growing in confidence, and seeing Dares do it, some of the other kids join in too. They don't all have his sense of rhythm or quickness for picking up the tune, and so, in many ways, the music is worse, but the boys' voices create this odd effect that is unspoken, but I'm sure that everyone feels. Like it's the voices of Medea's children, their music, pleading with their mother along with the chorus to spare their lives. It's unsettling, and I feel my hairs stand on end, and the debate continues back and forth: the chorus against Medea. Yet though they outnumber her fifteen to one, it's her will that dominates, and the chorus's arguments wither, while the hum of the children rises higher and higher, and near the end, a curious note is added. I look over and see that it's Strabo, the tiniest of them all, yet his shrill croak seems to rise above the rest, and I think to myself, we might actually have something. This could be a proper theatre. We're fucking directors. But then the singing stops suddenly and the chorus scamper away in fright.

'What the fuck is this?' roars someone from behind.

There's a big fella walking towards us. A club slung over his shoulder and a demented look in his eyes. It's Biton.

'Evening, Biton,' says I, forcing a grin. 'How are things?'

He doesn't answer, just stares about him. Takes in the scene as if through a red mist: Numa in his wig, the chorus cowering in the distance, and the wheelbarrow of food. Yet, the rage dilutes somewhat and blends with bewilderment when he sees the children.

'What's going on?' says Biton.

I go to speak, but Gelon cuts me off and steps out in front.

'It's none of your business, Biton. No need for any trouble.'

Biton looks at Gelon. There was a time that they got on well enough. Biton's son worked in our factory, and sometimes we'd go fishing together.

'You're feeding these bastards?'

Gelon tells Biton about how they might be all that's left of Athenian theatre. That we're putting on a show to keep Euripides alive, 'cause Athens might very well burn if the Spartans besiege it.

A savage light goes off in Biton's eyes at the mention of Athens burning, but it dies immediately, replaced by something else.

'You're giving food to these bastards. That's Anchises' son over there.' He points at the blond child holding cheese. 'The

Athenians killed his father. And little Strabo over there. His brother was speared from behind after he'd surrendered. I saw it happen. You're bringing these kids down here to fucking feed their families' killers? Is that what you're doing, man?'

Biton's weakness has always been the grape, and I take out one of the wineskins.

'You look parched, Biton,' says I. 'Get that down you.'

He knocks it out of my hand and stands on it, crushing it under his boots till it bursts and the wine leaves a scarlet spray on our knees. Then he grabs my throat and actually lifts me in the air.

'You offer me wine again, and I'll break your fucking skull, Lampo.'

Gelon steps forward, and Biton lets me go. I fall, gasping, into the dust.

The two of them are squaring up to each other now. Gelon is tall and wiry, strong, but Biton is huge and built like a fucking ox as well. There's not many people I'd favour over Gelon in a fight, but one of them would be Biton.

'Leave it!' says Dares.

He hurls himself between them, a brave little bastard.

Biton looks down at the boy. There's spittle on his lips, and I'm not sure if he even sees Dares.

'My father and your son served together,' says Dares, reaching up and touching Biton's arm. 'They were good friends.'

There's a shivering in Biton's cheeks, and his fist is clenched, and I think, oh, no, he's going to hit the boy, but he doesn't. He just backs away slowly.

'This won't stand, Gelon, you hear me? Next time, children or not, it's happening.'

'Whenever you want to, Biton. Just ask.'

Biton nods.

'I'll find you. You're convinced you're hard, but I don't

fucking think so. I know it's an act. I knew you when you were a kid, and oh, you were a weak one. Always crying and singing your songs like a fucking girl. You're soft, Gelon, and I'll show the world how soft you really are.'

Biton twitches, and there's absence in his eyes – a black sea under an eclipse. There's nothing he won't do. The soil is rotten, and no seed will grow again – our very own Medea.

'See you, Gelon.'

He swings the club back over his shoulder and walks away. I pity any prisoner who crosses his path tonight. Even Gelon looks shaken, and some of the kids seem on the verge of tears. Strabo is holding his toy horse for comfort. The cast takes a while to return, but at last, they do. Paches is the first one back, followed by Numa, and the silver-haired Athenian. Finally, the rest of the chorus shuffle over in dribs and drabs. Though they're jittery as fuck, and the cawing of a crow nearly sends them dashing into a tunnel.

'Don't worry about Biton,' says I. 'It's just that he's more into Sophocles.'

No one laughs, although Gelon looks over at me as if he's glad I said it. He nods his head and starts to hum the music from the scene. For a while he's alone, until Dares joins him. The chorus start to shuffle their feet to its rhythm, and their clinking chains blend with the rhythm, make it more intense. Numa paces in front of them. He's not quite Medea yet, but he's something different than himself. Finally, Strabo starts to hum too, his wooden horse pressed to his lips as if it were some musical instrument that he's playing. They start the scene again, and perhaps Biton's arrival instilled the necessary energy and terror that the piece required, for it's even better than before, wilder, sadder, more desperate, and I think to myself, this is real.

We're directors.

16.

I tell Gelon straight what I need the money for. It doesn't sound great: give me gold, so Dismas will let me walk his slave girl along the beach for an hour or so. He's going to say fuck off. No question, but I had to ask.

'Alright.'

'What's that?'

Gelon takes out a pouch and hands over a fistful of coin.

'There's a spot,' he says softly. 'A little cove about a mile past the Achradina Gate.'

'Yeah.'

'Me and Desma would head down there when we first started going out. The sea is awfully still, and you can watch the lights of the city in the evening, but you're on your own. There are dolphins too. It's so beautiful, Lampo.'

I want to hug him and tell him I'll never forget this, but I don't. I pocket the coin and say I'll be back later for rehearsal and that he should bring a weapon, as Biton will keep his word.

'So will I.'

'Course, man. You'd take him too, but it's best to be safe.'

Gelon frowns, and I think he knows I don't mean it, but he says nothing and we part.

I don't go directly to Dismas'. First, I stop off at home and change into my lightning-blue chiton and the crocs. There's an amphora on the table with some olive oil in it, and I dollop it on my palms and rub it into my hair and beard, twirling the strands as best I can. There's no mirror to check the effect, but it will have to do. Ma has a little patch of soil in the back. Not really a proper garden, just enough to grow some veg for the stews, and flowers for the window. There are barely any flowers this year, on account of the drought, and I don't like to take them as she's been growing these bastards for months, walking miles each day to the city well for their water, but fuck it. She wants grandchildren. I pull the scant few that have bloomed up from the roots, and pop back in to rub a little more oil into the curls and beard.

Now I'm ready.

It's still hours before the evening rush, and Dismas' is sleepy. The man himself is up at the counter, polishing cups.

'Looking good, Lampo,' he says. 'She's upstairs getting ready. Will you have a drink?'

'No thanks,' says I.

'Lyra!' he shouts. 'Get a move on. He's here.'

Dismas turns back, all smiles.

'That will be three drachmae. Just make sure to get her back for the evening. The place is heaving after sundown, and I won't be here.'

I hand over the coin.

'Much obliged.'

It isn't even a hot day, but beads of sweat are rolling down my cheeks. I wipe them away, and my hand is greasy from all the oil, and it shakes.

'Actually, make it a quick one.'

'Catanian red?'

'You got anything stronger?'

Dismas takes out a dark bottle with orange chips in the clay like flames and barely fills the cup.

'That all?'

'Trust me. Just try it.'

I knock it back and immediately start retching.

'Fuck,' I sputter, 'what was that?'

'From Scythia. Mostly I use it for cleaning, but you looked like you needed it.'

Truly foul. It's searing my throat and chest, yet along with the pain, there's a loosening. The nerves are there still, but they're no longer snakes writhing in my belly, just the usual worms, and I remind myself she's only a slave. Lampo, you've got this. She's a fucking slave.

'Here she is.'

The door opens behind the bar, and Lyra steps out, tentative, even bashful. She's wearing a green smock, the fabric so thin it's almost translucent. Her hair isn't tied up like when she's working but down around her shoulders, in thick dark lustrous curls, and I actually flinch as if from a blow. She looks too fucking good.

'For you,' I says, handing over the flowers.

'What do you say?' says Dismas.

'Thank you, they're lovely.'

She presses them to her nose.

'Make sure to be back by sundown.'

Dismas walks us out to the door of the bar, almost like he's the girl's father. And I imagine that's what's happening. She's a Syracusan girl, and I'm courting her in the traditional way, and her da approves of the match. It seems to work, and I can feel my spirits rise, until Dismas leans in and whispers in her ear:

'Look after him. Whatever he wants, till your shift starts.'

She nods and sniffs the flowers again, as if to cover her face, and we step out together.

There's been a reddish tinge to the sky these past few days, and with all the building works bringing up dust, the air in the streets is misty, the few feet in front of you obscure, and I'm afraid sometimes I might lose her in the crowds, but she sticks close. I can feel her fingers graze my own, and on instinct, I grip her hand, and she presses it back, and I'm beaming, but then I hear the words of Dismas, anything he wants, and let go. She asks me where we're headed, and I say that's up to her. 'Wherever you would like,' she responds, and for a while, it goes round in circles, just as we, too, are going round in circles, 'cause it's our second lap of the market when I remember the cove Gelon spoke of and think, fuck it.

'The sea,' I say. 'Let's go to the sea, but first, I'll get supplies.'

Skiron's in his usual spot, licking his lips and screeching the price of grain. I contemplate strutting over with Lyra on my arm to ruin his buzz, but I don't. It would only get back to Ma in the worst possible way. Also, we don't need wheat or barley, just booze. I fancy some Catanian, but I know Lyra doesn't like red, so I also grab an Italian white the vintner says is 'causing quite the stir'. It certainly causes a stir in my pockets, for a great deal of coin leaps up and out of them at purchase. For a bite, I get a loaf of freshly baked rye bread, still warm to the touch and flecked with chunks of black olives. Some soft cheeses that Lyra picks out, and we're off towards the cove.

It's a fair walk. The beach here is mostly sharp stones, and she has to stop once or twice to take one out of her shoe. I ask her for one of the stones, and though she seems confused at the request, she hands one over. It's round and deep yellow, smoothed out by the sea, and I tell her this stone is worth a fortune.

'Is it?' she asks, vaguely interested.

'Yeah,' says I. 'They say the goddess Lyra got it stuck in her shoe once, a long, long time ago.'

This is lame, but it will have to do. She shakes her head and looks out at the sea. Above is clouded, and the surface of the water's more like melted iron than its usual blue. There are still swimmers out, heads bobbing up amid the metal waves, with an occasional pale hand or a foot rising.

'You swim?'

She's looking at me as if she has to think.

'Don't know if you can swim?'

'I could when I was a kid. But I haven't done it in years.'

'Ah, it's something you always remember.'

I let that hang in the air, and we walk on. There's a shrine to Proteus a bit ahead. It was pretty busy during the war, as anyone who had to serve on a ship would come down and make an offering, but things have quietened a lot. The priest who looks after the shrine is sitting on the steps, playing with a tabby. He dangles a bit of loose thread from his cloak and lifts it up and down, always just out of the cat's reach, grinning like he's just outsmarted Hermes when the cat leaps and misses.

'Fucking eejit,' says I. 'No wonder people are losing their faith.'

'Is it much farther?'

It's another mile or so, but I don't say that. I say, 'You tired?'

'No. No, I'm liking the walk. It's just these shoes. They're terrible. I've another sacred stone, if you're interested?'

'Pass it on.'

She hands me a more jagged piece this time. The same grey as the sky, but I pocket it anyway. We don't say much more for the next mile, and walk in silence. But this isn't the silence that comes from comfort, no, it's that strained silence, where you can feel the throb of the other's thoughts; stillborn sentences that die on the lips before they're spoken. I want to speak, but nothing right is coming, and so I just ask her if she's got another stone in her shoe.

'Don't think so,' she says. 'I'll let you know when I do.'

We're coming up to Gelon's cove now. There are caves in the cliffs that you can see when the tide is a little lower. Some people say this is where Odysseus was imprisoned by the Cyclops. I reckon that's why Gelon first brought Desma here. It's beautiful, certainly, but Gelon always needed something else. Most people believe in the myths 'cause we attach them to real places, and it adds to what's already there, but with Gelon, it's the contrary. He believes in what's right in front of him through the stories we tell.

'They say Odysseus blinded the Cyclops in that cave.'

'Oh.'

'You can't actually see it now, on account of the tide.'

She nods politely, but I can tell her mind is wandering. The slave is getting bored.

'You reckon you'll ever see Lydia again?'

She starts at that and looks at me, eyes suddenly awake.

'I don't know,' she says.

'Odds must be slim –' I stop. 'Let's set up here.'

That flush is in her cheeks, stretching from her ear down along her jaw. I'd forgotten to pack a blanket, so we have to sit down on the damp rocks, and I lay out the spread. The clasp on one of the wineskins came loose, and the top of the loaf is soggy mush. I tear it off and chuck it, and almost immediately, there's a flurry of feathers as gulls come swooping down. Maybe they'll get drunk.

'I don't think I'll ever go back.'

She's staring ahead of her, across the wine-dark sea. There's a pricking of conscience, and yet something in me whispers: keep up the good work.

'A realist,' says I. 'Reckon you're right.'

'There was a time I was sure of it. Something would happen. My father would come to get me. Dismas would fall in love with me and set me free. The war . . .' She laughs. 'I can't tell you how much I wanted Athens to win. Remember the pamphlets they launched into the city?'

'You can read?' says I, surprised.

She nods and takes a sip of wine.

'They teach women to read in Lydia. I used to read a lot, but the best thing I ever read was those pamphlets. *Athens is here to free you.* It was probably lies, but any dream will do.'

'That's great, though. That you can read. Fair play.'

She shakes her head.

'Greek is easy. Persian is the tricky one.'

My head is spinning now.

'Clever bitch.'

She smiles. The first genuine one since our walk started, and she takes a long pull of the white and passes it over. The wine is cool, fruity, and something else I can't describe. I imagine that something else is her.

'My father taught me,' she says. 'He worked in the government.'

'So were you an aristo?'

She looks confused at the question, so I rephrase it.

'You were rich?'

A scrunch of distaste, as if to be rich was somehow a petty thing. And she starts talking about her da. He wasn't rich but could have been if it were money he wanted, but that was too easy, too vulgar. He wanted knowledge, and about all sorts of things. The tides, the wingspan of a fly, why leaves were green, and the movements of the stars. There wasn't a subject that didn't interest her da, and he could even predict the eclipses. A right prize of a da, he was, and I grin so hard my teeth hurt.

She's animated now in a way that I've never seen in the bar and starts explaining how a lunar eclipse works. She picks up a white stone she says is the moon, and then goes off on one, about axis and rotations, and how the gods aren't needed to explain such events. Her hands are moving through the air, her eyes very alive. I reach over to the arm that holds the rock and swat at the part of the skin withered from the branding.

'Sorry,' I say. 'Saw a wasp.'

She goes all stiff, and looks unsure of whether to continue.

'Go on.'

She goes on, hesitant at first, but it soon builds up to its previous speed and intensity. The wind blows her dark hair over her eyes, and she brushes it away, leaving grains of sand on her eyebrows.

'He could predict eclipses,' says I. 'Yet didn't know his daughter would be a slave. Some soothsayer.'

It's like I've hit her – a livid streak cuts across the skin of her jaw.

'I never said he was a soothsayer. That's the opposite of what he was.'

'No need to get annoyed. Just buzzing with you! Have an olive.' I pass her one, but she doesn't take it. Just stares up at the sky. The clouds are dark and thin; they move about like insects.

'Finish what you were saying about eclipses.'

She shakes her head.

'I don't want to.'

'Remember what Dismas said, though. Whatever I want, you're to give me. I want to hear about eclipses.'

Ma's flowers are in her lap, and I pick one up and jam it in her hair.

'Go on.'

'No,' she says. 'You can have me, but I'll not talk about that again.'

I can't think of a response. We just sit there and stew. A good twenty feet away from us, in the sea itself, a pale rock protrudes. The rock is slender, almost like a hand. A nereid's hand. I pick up a stone, and it comes to me like a revelation.

If I hit this hand, then it will all work out with Lyra. If not, my life is fucked. I aim as carefully as I can and throw. It's going wide, and my insides twist, but then whether it's the wind or something else, the stone swerves mid-air and lands with a soft slap against the pale rock, the sound more akin to hitting skin than stone. My heart pounds in my chest: she's the one.

'You're gorgeous.'

A sigh almost of resignation, and she turns her face towards me, closes her eyes as if expecting a kiss.

'Not so fast,' says I. 'I think we've got off on the wrong foot here.'

'We haven't. I understand you perfectly.'

'But you don't. You really don't. See, the thing is, I like listening to you. All the things you've been saying about eclipses and the harmony of numbers, I like listening to all of it, but there's another part of me, and it's fucking poisonous, and it whispers in my ear as you're talking. She thinks she's better than you, Lampo. She thinks you're a jobless cunt with a club foot, and she'll walk with you on this beach. A snail-paced walk on account of your limping. She'll mooch along 'cause you've paid her master, but really she knows that she's quality and you're dirt, slave or not, and I hear all this in my skull, and I want to scream, but I don't. I say words that I hope will give you some of the pain I feel. I'm fucking scum.'

She's taken aback at this outburst but nods at the end. Whether to show that she understands, or in agreement with me being scum, I'm not sure. I tear a piece of bread. More for something to do than any hunger, and put it in my mouth, pretend to chew.

'I wanted to come out here today,' she says, not looking at me.

'What's that?'

'I wanted to come and walk with you. I was looking forward to it.'

'You had no choice.'

'No,' she says. 'I had no choice about coming, but whether I wanted to or not is my own business. Dismas can't touch that.'

That little stretch of blush along the jaw intensifies, and she looks up at me, then away.

'I can't read,' I says.

'What?'

'Can't read. My da fucked off when I was two. Ma did her best, but in the end she had to take me out of school early so I could start the trade. My mate taught himself to read, and he's tried a few times with me, but it didn't take. I reckon it might take with you, though.'

She seems to be considering it.

'Dismas wouldn't let me.'

'He lets you come out here.'

'This makes sense to him. I don't think me teaching you to read would.'

'The coin would make sense.'

She takes the wine and sips it, dainty, then leans over and picks up a stone. The same white one she used to represent the moon. She looks about the ground, then stands up.

'Come here.'

I follow her, and we walk over towards the sea and stop at a stretch of wet sand. She starts to carve something into it, slow and methodical.

'See?'

I look at the symbols, and I know it's Greek, but that's about it.

'What's it say?'

'*Lampo*. See, there is the L and then A. You must know . . .'

I peer down, and it looks weird and wild. I've never seen it written before. You see names on statues, ostraka, temple

130

doors, but they're of the rich and famous. They're carved in stone. Yet perhaps it's right that my name should be written in sand, and before she can explain the last letters, a wave comes crashing in, soaking our feet, and when it recedes, the letters are gone.

'I love you,' I say, and the words startle me.

'What?'

She seems frightened now.

'I said, I love you. What do you make of that?'

'It doesn't make any sense. We're strangers.'

I look out at the sea, and there are no answers there, nor in the sky. It's all empty, suddenly really empty. Not even a bird flying, and there's a rattle of thunder.

'That's a sign. Zeus thinks we should be together.'

The faintest crack of a smile and a shake of the head.

'That's just moisture building up in the clouds. When they meet each other, it's like a collision. Think of a chariot race where they crash into one another, and it causes the sound. Father wrote a treatise about it.'

'It can be a sign, too, though. Sure, why can't it be both?' A few drops of cold rain on my face. Another crackle of thunder – closer this time. We should probably get going, but not yet. 'What if I bought you?'

She's about to say something, but the words die on her lips.

'I don't have enough coin now, but I'm telling you, this city is changing, quick. I could make money if I had a reason. I know I could. What if I bought you and set you free? How would that sound?'

It sounded good. You just had to look in her eyes, which just then were practically dark moons of hope, but just as soon, they've turned to slits of suspicion. As if she fears it's all just some joke.

'I can't trust you.'

What to say to this? She's right. She can't trust me. I don't trust myself. I've screwed me and others over too many times for that, but if ever there was something I believed in, that I wanted the way Gelon wants a thing, so intensely that it just has to be. If ever there was something, it's now, and it's her.

'You can't trust me. That's true.'

She didn't expect that.

'Exactly,' she says, as if that settles it, yet there's a trace of disappointment.

'But, trust or not, what if it happens?'

'I don't get you.'

'You've no reason to trust me. But let's say somehow I got the money, and Dismas agreed to sell you. Would you have me?'

The wind is howling now. The sea, an endless pack of grey wolves tearing at the shore, and we have to walk back a bit to avoid being soaked. I see her lips move, but I can't hear the words clearly and have to ask her to repeat them. I lean in so that we're very close, and I can smell her above the salt.

'I would have no choice. If you bought me, you would own me.'

For fucksake. I want to shake her. Could she not lie to me at least?

'But if I gave you a choice? What then? Is it back to Lydia, or could we get something going?'

I can see her thinking. The thoughts flickering behind her dark eyes, and the movement in the muscles of her throat as she goes to speak, but she swallows the words and still considers. Only now do I cop the obvious. Regardless of the truth, she'll tell me yes, 'cause what else has she? A few more years in Dismas' getting groped while she has her looks. And after that, who knows? Dismas doesn't strike me as the sentimental type. He'll sell her on, and what I said that night will come true.

She'll be threshing wheat in the fields. Perhaps she sees something of this in my face, 'cause she frowns and shakes her head.

'What?'

'My life isn't as bad as you think. It might not seem like much to you, but it's mine, and it could be worse. How do I know it wouldn't be worse with you?'

'Fucksake. Am I that bad?'

'I'm honest. I don't know if you are, but I'm honest. This is me.'

This wasn't how I pictured this going. But there's a voice in the back of my head that's whispering: her reluctance is good. It's smiles and eagerness you need to be wary of, and so I don't curse her out like I want to. I take her hand, and she flinches a little but doesn't pull away. Its warmth clashes with the cold rain falling down from above. I push my fingers about her wrist, and there's the pulse of her blood.

'It's you,' I says. 'I see that, and I hope you can see me. I'm not much, that's true, and if you were free, perhaps you wouldn't think twice, but let's look at things plain. I don't have the money now, but I will work for it like a madman to get the coin to buy your freedom. Then it's up to you. If you want to fuck off, fuck off. If you stick with me, you see this is it. A potter with a crooked foot, but I think if you were with me, I might be something more. I think I've never had anything to work for, nothing to believe in, really, and a man needs that, more than anything. I'd throw in my lot with you and work till the skin came off my fingers if it were for us, and not just me.' I try to straighten out my foot so that it doesn't slant, but it's no use.

'Fuck it. That's my piece. I've said it.'

I can't face looking at her. She's there, though, I can hear her breathing, even amongst the wind, and it's rapid and uneven.

'I will,' she says, almost to herself.

'What?' I lean in. 'What will you do?'

'If you keep your word, and I am free. Then I'll stay here with you and try my best.'

'Are you serious?'

She nods, and there are tears in her eyes, though I can't tell if they're of joy or grief. They roll down her cheeks and join with the rain fresh from the sky, and I think that's the closest we'll ever get to the heavens.

'It's us now. You'll never be alone again.'

She looks away, and together we walk back to Dismas'.

17.

The cock hasn't crowed before I'm up and out of bed, moving barefoot across the cold stone floor by touch, softly as I can, so that my steps don't wake Ma. I put the box in the crook of my arm and slip out the door and onto the silver streets. Silver, owing to the quarter-moon, which is small, cloud-wrapped but oddly bright. A dog on a chain pisses against a wall, growls when I go past, but something in the eerie stillness welcomes me. Like I can do no wrong. I walk back over, guided by the light of the moon shimmering off the chain and the glinting spittle on the dog's fangs. Its eyes bulge with fear and fury, yet I stretch out my hand, slow, pat it on the head, and though it still growls, that growl lowers till it's a gentle hum.

'Ah the boy,' says I.

The tail wags merrily now, beats the air, and I rub behind its ears, and it licks my palm. That was a buzz, and I walk on feeling pretty good about the world and my place in it. It's so fucking early. No one is up but me and that dog, and a couple of birds singing into the night. It's cold. I mean really cold, and I shiver as I walk, sniff the air until I catch the first whiff of the salt, and hear the waves. It's brighter here, owing to all the star- and moonlight reflecting off the sea-skin, and I stroll over to the shore and splash a fistful of stars on my cheeks for good luck. The water's warmer than the air, but it's still bracing. In the distance is the sprawling silhouette of Dismas', stark against the moon. Course it's long closed, but I'm not here for a drink. The guard dog is at the doorstep and seems to be sleeping.

At the crunch of my steps, it stirs, neck crooked up, and the right ear twitches. It only strikes me now that the reason I petted that dog on the way was in preparation for this. Dismas' dog is huge and mean – kept locked up when the bar is open, but at night he lets it loose. Every couple of weeks, some poor bastard gets bitten, but most know enough to avoid the place after a certain hour, and this is well past that hour. I've no bone with me, only some stale bread in my pocket, and I fling it over at him. The hound sniffs it a couple of times, but that's all. Its eyes never leave me.

'Easy there, boy.'

It starts snarling, and I think of turning back. There's no real reason to do this now. But then I open up the box and peer inside, and I think no. I'm not going to dash a hope 'cause of a little difficulty. Odd, but the fear passes, and as it does, the countenance of the mutt changes. Nothing drastic. It doesn't suddenly start bounding about and wagging its tail, but it's not snarling any more. Lampo, tamer of beasts. I'm fucking Heracles. I walk over to it, not even bothering to slow down, 'cause I got this, and I pat its head.

'Ah the boy,' says I. 'How are things?'

It bites me. Like really sinks its teeth in, and I let out a muffled cry of pain and shock.

'For fucksake!'

It releases its grip and seems about to leap at me, really go for the throat, but for some reason, it doesn't. I don't know why, nor do I stay and ponder. I just leg it quickly past and feel the wet heat of the blood in the crook of my arm. Hubris, methinks. The gods have brought me low, just like Heracles, yet thinking this raises my spirits some and though it hurts like a bastard, putting a spin on the pain makes it my own. At the back of Dismas', on the ground floor, lie the servants' quarters. Dismas used to sleep on the second, but Lyra told me that most nights now, he stays in the city centre at the new place.

She said her room's the one on the left with the green shutters. I can see the one on the left, but in the darkness, whether it's green or not, I've no clue. I walk to it and rub along the wood. There are cracks in the paint, and I peel some flecks off with my thumbnail and taste. It tastes green. Can colours have a taste? They can, I decide, if you care enough, and this tastes green. I knock on the shutter, loud so that she'll hear, but not so loud as to wake the others. Nothing. I knock again, and the only noise is my knuckles, and the soft trickle of blood down my arm.

'Fuck,' says I.

The hound is behind me now. Not growling, just watching, and I don't fancy another bite, so I ready my knuckles for what I decide will be the final knock when the shutters open, and I see her.

'Who is it?' she says, frightened.

'It's me. It's Lampo.'

No response, and I stand there feeling suddenly foolish and unsure.

'What are you doing here?'

'I wanted to see you.'

But it's too dark to see her. All I can see are her teeth when she speaks and the general shape of her. Still, I can smell her: the night sweat, and the hair. Maybe I came to smell her. Can you do that? It sounds daft, and I reach out to touch. I feel her smock and the warm heat of her body underneath.

'Is this what you want?'

It is, but not like this. What if the dog bites my arse? Or if I sneak in the window, and some other servant tells, and she's beaten. I don't want her as a thief in the night.

'This,' I give her the box. 'This is for you.'

'A gift?' Her voice is curious.

'In Syracuse, this is how we court. You bring the girl gifts. Is it the same in Lydia?'

'It is,' she says, real quiet like.

'Good. Well, that's all we're doing.'

I turn and walk away, though slow enough that I can hear her open the box and catch the little laugh of pleasure as she takes out what's inside, and I'm off. The mutt gives chase, and it might be my imagination, but for a while, as he snaps at my heels, I don't even seem to limp. She's cured me, I think, and even when I'm a long way away from her and the dog, and the jerky arc of my foot returns, twisting through the sand, I can't stop grinning.

I'm to meet Gelon and the kids at the quarry in a couple of hours. Before that, I go to the market. Though it's still dark, some of the vendors are already here setting up shop. I offer my services. Just a couple of obols and I'll help move their crates, unload the cargo. Dogsbody work, but the kind they need, 'cause pretty much all over the city business is booming, and several vendors take me up on it. I spend the next few hours sweating and heaving crates and amphorae until my muscles ache and the skin on my fingers looks like curdled milk. The pain is real, but the silver they pay me is realer. It's not much. Barely enough for a few jugs in Dismas', but I won't spend it on booze.

Later, walking the lonely road to the quarry, I listen to the sound the coins make in my pocket – much fainter than the din from the pouch Gelon gave me, yet its music is all the sweeter, 'cause it's mine, and it's hers, and I know in time we can make it a song.

Gelon and Dares stand at the crossroads with the wheelbarrow, both of them laughing. I haven't heard Gelon laugh in so long that it jolts me out of my reverie.

'Morning, Lampo!' he says with a smile.

'Morning, Lampo,' echoes Dares, then with interest, 'your hand. It's bleeding.'

'Wolf,' says I, 'made Cerberus look like a puppy, but don't worry. I fought it off.'

Dares looks doubtful and I change the subject; ask them where the others are. At this Dares frowns, and stands a bit straighter.

'Very sorry. It's not good enough, I know, but they're young and immature, and timekeeping is not their strength. Don't worry, though. I'll give them a talking-to.'

Now it's my turn to smile.

'You're a hard taskmaster, Dares,' says I. 'Reckon you'll make a good soldier.'

'General,' he says, seriously. 'Strategy interests me immensely.'

I nod and grab some nuts out of a bag in the wheelbarrow, pop a few in my mouth. We stand around a while, Dares doing most of the talking. Ideas he has for the play. He wants to know if there's a sword fight at any point? Gelon tells him there are no sword fights in *Medea*, nor the new Euripides, as far as he knows, but Dares keeps at it. He says Medea could always fight her way out of Corinth – and isn't the new Euripides set in Troy? Gelon tousles his hair and says he'll have a think about it.

Laughter in the distance, the shuffling of small feet. The other children are arriving, and you feel the change they make to the air. Like their chatter is filling up the lonesome road with some of that excitement for life and, as if in sympathy, even the sun seems to be emitting a bit more heat.

'You're late!' says Dares.

The kids slow their pace and look at one another, hesitant. Little Strabo is trailing a fair bit behind them, running to catch up, and he's so pleased they've slowed; he doesn't stop to ask why but, laughing, overtakes his mates and runs straight into Dares with a crash.

'You're late, Strabo,' says Dares fiercely.

'It's alright,' says Gelon. 'He arrived when he was meant to arrive.' Gelon reaches into the wheelbarrow and starts handing out figs to the children, and though Dares looks unhappy that lateness is being rewarded, he says nothing.

There's a different guard outside Laurium today. A stocky fella with a busted lip. He seems hung-over and half asleep, and before Gelon goes to his pouch for silver, I intercept him and give the guard some booze, which he takes and waves us on, no questions.

'No point wasting coin,' says I.

Gelon nods and puts the cloth over the food, and we roll the wheelbarrow down into the pits. There must have been a leaf-storm in the night, 'cause the quarry is awash with the red and gold skins of Carpo. There are even leaves on some of the prisoners' heads, lambent as crowns, and the prisoners stare at us like chained kings as we roll by.

There are more graves again, the stones heaped in piles about the height of Strabo, and I give a silent prayer that none of our cast are beneath those rocks. The smell has eased too. Perhaps it's the weather, the coolness taking the edge off the rot, but whatever it is, the quarry's scent has altered. Paches spots us before we do him, and I'm pleased to see that there's more improvement. He still looks awful, but the black hair has thickened about his scalp, and the skin is tauter. He grips my hand and smiles, says that the others have been rehearsing. The chorus are up by the quarry walls, and he leads the way. I can't see them at first. Paches explains that they're hiding in the tunnels, and then I notice their eyes peering out wetly from the dark.

'Been hearing good things from Paches,' says I. 'You boys are making me proud.'

The eyes blink, and slowly Athenians start to crawl out on

their bellies, their faces white as ivory gods from the powdered limestone. Gelon goes over and offers his hand to help one up and, observing, Dares rushes over to do the same. Pretty soon, all the kids are doing it, skipping over to the walls and helping the pale creatures on the ground to their feet. Strabo is so tiny he stumbles when a prisoner takes his hand, but he persists, and soon the prisoner is up, and Strabo, grinning proudly, walks the fella over towards the wheelbarrow, and from a certain angle, you could be forgiven for thinking you were just seeing a man with his son, and something in the way the Athenians take the boys' hands and the way the kids' expressions change makes me wonder if, unbeknownst to them, that's what these poor bastards are doing, performing fatherhood and childhood for each other, 'cause surely a lot of these men have kids back home that they'll never see again, and I feel like I should look away, like I've caught an intimacy, and so I turn around and count the cheeses in the wheelbarrow.

Rehearsal takes a while to get going this morning. The Athenians really tucked into the food, and their energy is flat to start with, but that seems to be a pattern. The first hour after they've eaten, there's a languor to all they do, but it's the only way, as without the food, they're utter shite. That's not the real issue. The issue now is how we go about joining *Medea* and this new play, *The Trojan Women*. I'm not sure how I feel about sticking two plays together. I reckon we should just do one or the other but Gelon's having none of that. He says we've already put too much time into *Medea* to abandon it, and as far as he's concerned, it's Euripides' best. No, *Medea* stays, but *The Trojan Women* stays too. It's the new Euripides, his latest, and for all we know the last he'll ever write. We've got to do it, to keep it alive – and what's more, we've got to get as many people to see it as we can.

'We do?'

'Aye.'

This is a shock. I always thought the play was just for us, probably Tuireann and his crew, and maybe now the kids. But to actually bring an audience down to the quarry, to put it on like a proper play. It's too strange. They'll probably arrest us.

I say as much, and Gelon's cheeks flush, and I'm sure he's about to curse me out, but in the end, he just sighs and, in a calm voice, says, 'Are we playing at directors or doing it proper?'

'Doing it proper.'

'Then that's all that needs to be said. A play has an audience, or else it's just rehearsal.'

He turns to the Athenians. Many of them clutch their stomachs after eating too much.

'What do you think? Audience or not?'

It might be in my head, but I feel like I can read their thoughts plainly as they shiver across the gaunt faces. They don't want an audience of Syracusans any more than I do, but they understand this is Gelon's show. I'm here, but I don't run things. The food comes from Gelon, as does everything else. I see all this in their eyes, and before their lips move, I sense the answer.

'An audience,' says one of them. It's Antikles: the Athenian with the silver beard. He's stroking it now, or near tugging it in agitation, and he turns to the others. 'Isn't that right? What do we want?'

'An audience!' they chant, fifteen voices as one trembling chorus.

Only Paches doesn't speak.

'Grand,' says I, 'just don't expect an ovation.'

'Let's start.'

Slowly the Athenians get to their feet. After a brief discussion, it's decided that today will be given over to *The Trojan Women*. I don't know much about it. Only that it's set at Troy, and it's another unpleasant surprise when Numa starts describing the plot. Well, the thing is, there is none. It's just Hecuba, Cassandra and a chorus of Trojan women having a terrible fucking time. It's after the war, and Troy has been razed to the ground, and the Greeks are divvying up the spoils. It's not like the usual tragedy where things start out well enough and take a dip. Things start at the bottom, or what you think is the bottom, and then the Fates wink and the earth begins to shake and crack, and Hecuba and her crew realize that what they thought was the bottom was nothing close. Their lives are going to get a whole lot worse. It's the strangest bit of darkness I've ever heard, and I can see even Gelon is taken aback when he listens to the details. Evidently, they'd been teasing him just with little hints, and this is the first time he's heard the plot in full.

'That's too grim, man,' says I, when Numa's finished.

'It's an amazing play,' says Numa, undaunted.

I turn to Paches. For he's the only one of them I trust.

'What do you make of it, Paches? Tell me, straight.'

Paches looks at his mates and then the walls of the quarry. He scratches his head in thought, and a couple of hairs come away in his fingers, though not so much as usual.

'It's like nothing I've ever seen before,' he says, at last.

'Did you like it?'

Paches shakes his head.

'No, I didn't, but I'll never forget it. They say Euripides thinks it his best.'

'He does?' says Gelon, and at that, I know we're fucked. *The Trojan Women* it is, then.

The main role in *The Trojan Women* is Hecuba, and there isn't even really a discussion about who gets it. Numa's the best we have and is eager, so it's his. After that, the key one is Cassandra and then Helen. The blokes in this play don't do much but be pricks. Menelaus pops in near the end, but he has scant to say. No, the question now is who will play Cassandra and who will play Helen. Cassandra's mental at this point but still gorgeous, and Agamemnon's mad for her – wants to bring her back to Argos. The fucking eejit thinks his wife will welcome them with open arms, husband and mistress, but Cassandra knows that to go to Greece is to die. Yet she goes. It's a good role and one I'd like Paches to have, but Gelon's not so sure. He wants to see some others from the chorus give it a shot, and I guess that's fair, but fuck it. I want Paches.

'There's a symmetry to it.'

'Lampo, I'm busy.'

Fuck that. I'm a director too, and I say as much.

Gelon sighs and looks at me.

'Say your piece.'

'Think about it, man. We're joining two plays. The audience is going to notice that it's the same actors, and though that's often a weakness, we can make it a strength. Play off their expectations, you know?'

'Go on.' Gelon's not quite interested, but he's not just humouring me any more, either.

'Well, Medea is a woman who killed her children, and Hecuba's a woman whose life is over 'cause her children are killed. There's a pattern there, right? One destroys everything, and the other endures everything. It's got rhythm, and you were spot on to pick Numa for the role. But think of Jason and Cassandra. What's their link?' I put my arm around Paches. 'Jason is the ultimate philanderer. Right? His faithlessness is the cause of all the ruin. If he just kept his promise to Medea, they'd be grand, but he can't do that. He needs a bright young thing to sink his chops into, and 'cause of that, it all burns. And here we have Cassandra –' I tighten my grip on Paches – 'Agamemnon's going back home, and just like Jason, he's won. Though his prize isn't some fucking fleece but Troy itself. He could be sitting pretty in Argos, drinking wines of the best, his wife cooing in his ear, but he has to have the bright young thing, and his wife won't stand for that. She cuts him up, and that sets the blood feud in place. 'Cause after he's dead, the children kill their mother in revenge. Do you not see it, man, they're broken mirrors of one another. It's perfect!'

I'm breathless now and pacing. Everyone is listening to me, their eyes fixed. Even the children seem keen, and they look over at Gelon, eager to hear his response.

'There's something to what you say, but it's not that simple. Clytemnestra hates Agamemnon anyway. He sacrificed their daughter just to change the winds.' He stops as if struck by an idea. 'There's a counterpoint in that. I mean, if Agamemnon were in the play, I could see that for Paches, but he's not.' He turns to Numa. 'Right?'

'Right,' says Numa, 'Agamemnon's just referred to.'

This is a blow, but I don't give up yet. The main cast get dibs on food, and I'll not have Paches on chorus rations.

'Fair enough. Still, you're missing the point. It's a cracked mirror we want, not the same thing. It needs to be altered yet recognizable. Besides, look at him. Cassandra's a role he was born to play. Right, Paches?'

'Yeah,' says Paches, with less conviction than I'd hoped.

Gelon asks the kids, who don't seem sure one way or the other. Then he asks the chorus, which is stupid as, of course, they'll want auditions, 'cause it gives them a chance to get a proper role and the perks that come with it.

There's a flattish stone that resembles a podium, and Gelon dubs it the casting rock. He tells those who are interested to line up, and each will get a chance to deliver Cassandra's monologue. To my surprise, a few don't even audition. I ask one why this is, and he mutters something about stage fright. However, these timid fellas are in the minority, and most give it a shot. One by one, they step onto that rock and do Cassandra. It's a messy business. Thank fuck we have Numa. His memory is insane, and he seems to know Cassandra's words, as well as Medea's – whispers prompts to those who need it, which is pretty much everyone.

The scene we're doing is where Cassandra's about to be carted off to Agamemnon's ship and then to Greece for mistresshood. These are the last words she'll utter in Troy, and with them, she delivers her prophecy for the future. A proper wreck-the-buzz is Cassandra. It's rivers of blood with a hole in the boat, and you can't swim. Bleak stuff, yet clearly with some power if done right. None seem able to do it right – reminds me of those first few days when we came down to the quarry. It's as if the casting stone is darkening with every attempt, taking a little piece of their spirit so that each Athenian has less confidence than the last. Paches is up next, and I'm fierce nervous but grin.

'Show them how it's done, Paches.'

Paches nearly trips when he steps onto that rock, but he adjusts quickly and finds his balance. He looks about and takes a deep breath, nods to himself and goes for it. I mean, he really goes for it. It's better than anything he's done as Jason, and when he's finished, I look over at Gelon and see he's impressed. Numa stands up and clasps Paches' hand.

'Brilliant.'

'Gelon, meet Cassandra. Cassandra, Gelon.'

There's a cough behind us. I look around, and there's one last Athenian making his way onto the rock. He's slender and barefaced and can't be more than nineteen or twenty. His skin is dry and pale as the rest, but there are barely any lines, and his eyes are hazel, with long dark lashes, and weirdly expressive. He looks like a doe or some other woodland creature, and that's the impression he makes as he stands on the rock, unsteady on spindly legs, skittish as a deer, his whole body seeming to tremble with suppressed emotion, and I get a sinking feeling.

'I'd like to try,' he says in a shrill voice.

'Hard luck,' says I. 'Auditions are over. Right, Gelon?'

Gelon shakes his head, his eyes locked on the young fella.

'What's your name?'

'Linar,' he says.

'Go on, Linar. Whenever you're ready.'

Linar nods and looks about, raises his long arms towards the sky and scratches as if trying to claw out the sun.

' "His mistress," ' he says in a feminine voice, but still clearly his own. ' "The man who destroyed all I love is to share my bed. His mistress," ' he fairly hisses the words. ' "I who gave my life to Apollo will be his mistress. Has the god abandoned me? Was it all in my head?" '

On he goes, and he's fucking fantastic. I don't know if he's better than Numa, but he's just as good, only different. With Numa, you can see him transform into the characters, but with this fella, it's the opposite. He's not transforming but sinking. Sinking into a thing that's there already, deep inside him, a hole that's Cassandra-shaped. He fairly screams his prophecy down at us, and it sucks the light out of you and makes the hairs on my neck thicken. You can't look away, but you want to. I glance over at Strabo, and he's whimpering; even Dares is unsettled. On Linar goes, shivering on his podium, manic, his hands twisting in the air like strange flowers in a storm. Finished, he looks spent and fairly collapses off the rock, and one of the chorus have to catch him. No one claps or cheers. They just stare ahead, dumbfounded. Gelon looks over at me, and there's an apology in his eyes, but no doubt what needs to be done. That's Cassandra.

'Sorry, Paches,' I says. 'You did real good.'

He nods, but he's clearly gutted. He gave that audition all he had, and still it was nowhere close.

Everyone is a bit subdued after Linar, and we move around, unsure of how to proceed. Scenes are mentioned, but which one to start with? Well, that seems a path covered in mist. Gelon calls for a quick break. They're already stuffed, so food is out of the question, but there's plenty of wine, and each gets a cup. It does the trick, and their spirits seem to enliven with every sip. So much so that it's Antikles who suggests we get back into it; he's up and eager, fondling his silver beard and explaining to the others that it's all about practice.

Another cough.

Linar again. He looks ghastly. A sheen of sweat on his grey face, and he's clutching his cup in trembling fingers.

'What about Helen?' he says, breathlessly. 'Who will play her?'

This mention of another casting finishes the work the wine had started, and now the chorus are positively lively. What about Helen, they say? It's a key role. Even the children get excited at this. For everyone knows and hates Helen of Troy. Cassandra was strange and obscure, but the villainy of that Spartan is something they understand well enough.

'Yes,' says Dares. 'It seems that before we move on, this part must be cast.'

I lean over and whisper to Paches, 'You want to play Helen?'

He nods, but it's clear the fight has gone out of him, and I wouldn't put my money on him in another audition just now. Fuck it.

'No need,' says I. 'Paches is Helen.'

They all look in my direction. I can't lose another one, or it's a joke I'll be.

'Maybe,' says Gelon. 'If his audition is the best.'

'No audition.'

'What?'

I fancy I hear some chuckles from the chorus.

'Think about it, man. This is Helen of fucking Troy. The most beautiful woman in the world. She doesn't audition for the role. She just is. You make these fellas dance and perform to see who'll be Helen, it's like they're begging for scraps, and Helen doesn't beg. She just is.'

This is a good point, and I'm pleased with myself for making it. Helen just is. I look over at Paches, and there's a smile on his face; his back's a little straighter. I got this.

'She begs in the play, though,' says someone in the chorus.

'Yeah,' says another. 'Isn't that the whole point of their scene, that she's trying to persuade Menelaus not to kill her?'

There are murmurs of agreement, and I'm wondering how the fuck did we get here. How am I debating with these pricks in chains?

'Sorry to break it to you, fellas, but you're a long way from the assembly in Athens. You don't have a vote.'

'Listen,' says Gelon, annoyed. 'Don't speak to them like that.'

More murmurs of approval, and it seems that an audition for the role of Helen is inevitable. And sure, why don't I let that happen? Paches already has the role of Jason, and if it's rations he needs I can give him extra. What is it that's bothering me so? I need to win this. Either I'm a director like Gelon, or I'm moral support. I don't mind being the second director, but a director nonetheless. I'll be that or nothing.

'I'll walk so.'

'What?' Gelon looks shocked.

'You heard me, man. The way I see it, I haven't asked for much. I thought it was the two of us in this. Maybe I'm wrong, and if so, no worries. I know the way back to town.'

A quiet takes hold, and Gelon and I have become the show.

The Athenians, hungry and broken though they are, want to see what will happen next. Who will win this? The tall, handsome bastard or the limping git who follows him? I can tell from their stares who their pick is, but they still want to know, and the lines must be said, the roles played. They wait and watch.

'This is that important to you?'

'It is.'

'Why?'

'It's a role he's born to play.'

Gelon holds my gaze for a long time, then shakes his head and mutters, 'At least he's got the eyes.'

'The eyes?'

'Aye, didn't they say Helen had emerald-green eyes?'

Is it my imagination, or does Gelon wink at me? The Athenians whisper to each other, and soon it passes around the chorus and amongst the children, that perhaps I'm right. One Athenian recalls the mention of Helen's wondrous green eyes. More follow him, and suddenly it's true. All agree that Paches should play the role, and yet I know it's a load of bollix. Helen's eyes were no more green than Jason's. Gelon made it up 'cause he didn't want to lose me, and I clasp his hand and feel awkward, break away and head over to the wheelbarrow, take out a jar of olives and hand them to Paches.

'You need to plump up. Helen has a cracking figure.'

'Thank you,' he says, voice shaking. 'But why?'

'We're mates,' says I, surprised that it's true.

Paches wipes his eyes.

I go over to fetch more bread.

18.

A few hours later, and we're in Dismas'. It was my idea. Gelon wanted to go straight home, but I needed to talk to her or even just see her. She's not at the bar tonight or serving tables. She's onstage. Or rather, next to a stage that is really a few boxes roped together. Dismas stands beside her and grins; his hair is slicked back and glistening with oil. He coughs and asks for quiet, and though it's a long time coming, eventually the punters settle down, and he says that as Carpo creeps in and the trees wither, the clouds pissing down upon our heads, a bit of music is needed to keep the spirits up, and we're in luck. He's just discovered that this girl he bought is not just a beauty. No, she has some lungs on her. He heard her singing this morning for the first time ever. Singing to herself, all delighted as anything, and he thinks, why should he be the only one to enjoy her tunes when his hard-working patrons could listen as they sip their drop of red? Lyra looks mortified. Like she'd rather be anywhere else, but Dismas tells her to get on the box, and she does. When her eyes settle on me, something loosens, and though she still seems nervous, the desperation's passed.

'This is a song from my home,' she says. 'I've translated the words into Greek, so –'

'Get on with it!' shouts a fella behind me.

I turn on him.

'Shut the fuck up.'

The fella stands, but Gelon does too, and he sits down right quick.

Lyra goes on. She says it's a simple song her maid used to

sing her when she was a child. Everyone here knows she's a slave, and you can feel their discomfort at these references to another time and world, and someone else mutters that they're here for a tune, not her life story, and she starts singing.

The voice isn't beautiful, and at first, I'm disappointed, yet as the words tumble out, I feel a tingling on my skin because there's a wildness to it – an uncommon thirst for life and other things – and I see that I don't know this woman at all, only wish to. The song is clearly foreign. Putting it in Greek only makes it stranger. It's about a young shepherd who falls in love with a girl he sees bathing in a lake, but he's too afraid to say anything to her, because poor and plain as he is, what could he offer? So, he decides he will trick her into loving him. He climbs a very tall and leafy tree that grows above the lake, and on that night, there's a full moon, a huge yellow moon, and the shepherd decides that if he were to speak as the moon, convince the girl that he was not a shepherd at all, perhaps she might consider him worthy, and so he climbs the tree and in his best moon-voice tells the girl he's the moon and has got it bad. As you'd expect, the girl is sceptical at first, but listening to the moon boast of its exploits – how the seas are beholden to it, how wolves and waves and all things of the night fall under its sway, and that its home is in the sky, in proper luxury, waited on by thousands of servants, stars you'd call them, thousands upon thousands of silver flames that have no other purpose but to do its bidding – listening to this, the young girl believes, is entranced. She had hoped for a handsome husband. A steady job, some land, maybe even a few cows, but to marry the moon and be served by stars. Her folks would love it. Her mates would be so jealous. And she says as much, and the shepherd laughs, says it's only what she deserves, yet the more he speaks of his night kingdom and his servants in the sky, the less sure he is. He takes a closer look at the girl staring up at him, her eyes weak with longing, and she doesn't seem as lovely as before. Her teeth are a bit crooked. Her left ear sticks out. Without saying a word, he decides he might be rushing into things, and so he climbs down and silently departs. The girl, alone, stands there pleading with the moon to say something, anything. The shepherd walks the hills, no longer really a boy, but now the moon, and if he sees someone who takes his fancy, he'll hide and speak to them in his new voice, and all who hear it fall in love, and many a heart is broken, and that is why we call those who are mad with longing lunatics. It's not the moon moving them, but the mad shepherd who's forgotten who he is.

People clap, but it's like they're rubbing their hands together for warmth, and none are on their feet. Actually, this is not strictly true. There is one fella on his feet, and he cheers. A solitary voice with a peculiar ring to it, and when I turn around, I see Tuireann, our producer, a few tables behind us, standing up and grinning.

'The man himself,' I whisper to Gelon.

Gelon nods, hand tensing about his cup.

'Let's go,' he says.

I don't fancy a chat with him either, but I haven't even spoken to Lyra yet and so shake my head.

'Ah, we'll stay a bit longer. The night's just getting going.'

'How are my directors?'

Tuireann sits down at our table and asks us what we're drinking. When we tell him, he shakes his head as if that won't do and calls for a wine I've never heard of. It arrives at our table in great ceremony, the jug sealed and covered in dust. The wine he pours from it is dark and viscous, almost like sap.

'Dismas serves this?'

Tuireann shakes his head and smiles.

153

'Of course not. I had him order it in. There are only about ten of these in all of Sicily.'

I say nothing, just look down uncertainly at the black liquid and take a sip. It's so thick it's chewy, and the taste is salty and sour. My first impulse is to spit it out, but then it hits you softly, a gentle heat spreading across your chest, like the stroke of a woman's hands, and I take another sip, look down at the cup, confused.

'You'll always remember your first drink of Babylon Black.'

'This is from Babylon?'

'A vineyard just outside, to be exact.'

'Mad. You've been to Babylon?'

'Of course.' He looks about him. 'Where's that singer? I believe a tip is in order. She really was marvellous. I must admit I'm surprised to hear songs like that in Sicily. I didn't think you had it in you.'

I'm about to tell him she's from Lydia, but something holds me back, and so I say, 'The play is nearly ready.'

'Is this true?'

He doesn't look at me but at Gelon.

'Almost done,' says Gelon. 'Just need another week or so, and we're good to go.'

'And this new Euripides you spoke of? Have you decided to go ahead with it?'

Gelon starts describing *The Trojan Women* and how we're going to do it. Tuireann listens, rapt, as if he's never heard a better story in all his life, and I see this is as good a time as any to make myself scarce and find her.

'Just have to check something.'

Neither look up, and I slip away. The place is heaving. The sweat of the bodies causing a kind of mist so that the walls are obscured, and the room feels larger. I have to squeeze and jostle my way over to the bar, and a few punters curse me out, and I curse them back, but they know me, and nothing comes of it. At last, I'm beside her. She's running back and forth, and her body seems red and rattling, she holds so many jugs and cups, bowls of stew. Her smock is filthy, her hair lank with sweat, but there's one item of clothing that's new and mostly unstained: a pair of yellow shoes. The first gift I bought her, and it's a foolish happiness I feel, seeing them on her feet.

'I'm the moon,' I says, 'can I cop a feel?'

She looks up from her task and smiles.

'Not a chance.'

'That's no way to talk to his celestial majesty.'

She laughs and nearly drops the bowl of stew.

'Just let me finish this. Alright?'

'Of course.'

I have to wait quite a bit, but at last, all the plates and bowls are deposited, and she slips into a nook with me so we can talk.

'You were class,' I says, taking her hand.

She shakes her head, but I can see she's glad to hear it.

'I didn't want to do it at all, but Dismas made me.'

'There won't be much more of that, my pharaoh.'

She smiles, but I can see she's sceptical, and I squeeze her hand tighter, almost like I'm trying to merge my finger bones with hers, so they're indistinguishable, and I ask if she could step outside, 'cause betwixt the reek of sweat and fish guts is no place to court such a beauty. Lyra seems reluctant, but I keep at her, and, at last, she says just for a moment, and we sneak out the back. The fresh sea air is so intense after the fog of Dismas' that I'm gasping, and I put my arm around her, feel the damp heat of her skin beneath the smock. She tenses a little but doesn't push me away.

'Have you other songs?'

She nods.

'Will you sing them to me? I want to hear all your songs. Every song you know, I want to hear.'

The wind blows her hair over her eyes and into her mouth so that her words are muffled, but I think she's saying yes, that she'll teach me. I feel a rough hand on my shoulder. The first thought I have is that it's one of those aristos, and it's a beating I'm getting, but when I turn, all I see is the short, gaunt figure of Dismas staring up at me.

'There's going to be a fucking riot if you don't get your ass in there now and start pouring,' he says to Lyra, barely even looking at her.

She apologizes and runs back in, and I think I might deck Dismas right here. He must see the thought in my eyes, for he takes a couple of steps back, and when he speaks, his voice is conciliatory.

'It's jammed in there, Lampo. You saw it. You want to talk to her, that's fine. You know me. I'm a reasonable man, but you don't mess up my business.'

Strange. The plan, of course, is to buy Lyra's freedom off Dismas and marry her. I've discussed it with Lyra. I even confided in Paches during a meal break this evening. Yet, I haven't said it to the one person who needs to know for it to be real, and this is Dismas. Why haven't I said it? Was I only playing, or is this real? I grin and spread my arms out.

'Dismas, you absolute legend. Give us a hug.'

He backs away again, wary of this sudden friendliness.

'What is it?'

I take out a pouch of silver. My savings from the morning shifts lugging boxes and crates. Not much, but the moon is shining just now, and its light makes the glow off the coins more intense, and I shake them loudly.

'I want to buy Lyra.'

A grin spreads across his lips, but whether in expectation or mockery, I can't be sure. He says nothing.

'You hear me, man? I said I want to buy the girl.'

'I heard you, but do I want to sell her? That's the question, isn't it?'

The idea that he might not want to sell her had never occurred to me.

'Of course you want to sell her. You're a businessman. You follow the coin and not your heart, and that's why you win.'

Dismas nods at this, seemingly pleased, but then he shakes his head sorrowfully.

'That girl is very dear to me, though. Almost like a daughter.'

A twinkle in his eye that I don't want to consider too closely. I take a deep breath and smile all the wider.

'What's your number, man? We can get this done.'

'Three hundred drachmae.'

Take my worst fears and double them. That's what three hundred drachmae is: silly money.

Dismas knows this, for he says, 'That includes emotional damages, though. Can't put a price on that.'

'You just fucking did, man. You'd get two slaves for three hundred.'

'But not two of her,' he almost whispers the words. 'Only one of her, Lampo, right?'

I'm fucked. It's not only more money than I have. It's more than I could ever hope to have. I cover my hands with my face, and there's still the scent of her skin on my fingers. Am I losing faith too easily? Aren't there a load of things that have happened to me this last while that would've seemed nuts? I'm a director, and our play will be performed soon. I saw a god. I know this isn't strictly true, as I legged it before it broke the surface of the water, but I felt its presence. I've become mates with an Athenian. Three things that I would have told you couldn't happen have happened, and that's not to mention the world that, this past year, has been turned inside out and on its head. Athens on the point of destruction. Syracuse a great power. Lampo a director, and a god in a crate on a ship. Anything is possible, and it always has been. For the world was once just a dream in a god's eye, and the man who gives up on himself makes that very same god look away.

'I'll get the money,' says I. 'I don't have it now, but I'll get it.'

Dismas is speechless. He'd expected me to haggle. He'd expected me to tell him to fuck off or plead. Whatever he'd expected, it wasn't this, and I look him in the eye and clasp his hand and say it again.

'I will get that money. I promise you that. Will you promise that she'll be mine when I do?'

Dismas stares at me now as if seeing me for the first time.

'I promise. For three hundred drachmae, the girl is yours.'

'She's mine, then,' says I, and I turn and walk back into the bar.

Gelon is at the table alone. His lips are stained black from Tuireann's booze, and I wonder if mine are too, so I wipe them hard with my cloak.

'What did he say?' I ask.

Gelon opens his mouth, then shuts it, tries to pour more wine into his cup, but the jug's empty.

'What's wrong?'

'Do you think we've made the right decision?'

'Of course. Eh, what do you mean?'

'In taking his money. Like why is he helping us, really, Lampo? The things he says. I don't know if we should have taken it.'

'What do you mean why? That's obvious, man. He appreciates talent. He knows he's on to something with us. Right?'

Gelon says nothing. This is a blow. Gelon has never shown hesitation before. I've always had my doubts, but it was his certainty that kept me going; something has shifted in him. There's less melancholy and more fear, and he orders another jug, and we sit there and drink in silence. Each of us is afraid. It's there in the way we hold our cups. It's in the way we look about us, squinting into the misty nooks of the bar to see what's hidden. This skittishness gives an altogether different quality to our boozing. Tonight we're not drinking to forget, but to remember and dream. It's hope that makes us afraid, and I remind myself that a man should be grateful for his fears, 'cause it means he has something to lose and to win.

19.

It's all a bit of a haze, to tell the truth. Most nights, I don't sleep more than a couple of hours, and some nights I don't sleep at all. These are the strangest. I reckon your mind needs to dream, 'cause on the days where I haven't had a wink, things happen that I can't rightly credit. The sky often takes on that wild vermilion of the sea in the great harbour during the final battle. At night the moon seems constantly full, and the bats whirling about it are the size of ravens, and yet I know the bats in Syracuse are tiny. It all makes me wonder if exhaustion has torn the firmament in my mind and let them loose. But I think I'm happy. I know I am. Sometimes I feel like crying, but I reckon that's 'cause at last things are happening, and I care how they unfold.

Each morning I get up while it's still dark, and with a bone for Dismas' dog and a gift for Lyra, I set out. Sometimes her window is already open, and she's there waiting. Those are the best mornings. Other times she's still asleep, and I have to knock, and she'll open the window, drowsy, yawning, and those are pretty good too. This hour or so, before the sun rises, is the only time we have alone. I ask her about Sardis and what her life was like before they took her. Even in the dark, you can see her liven at the mention of home, all breath-hungry as she launches into a description of the city and its streets, the bakeries, and temples, her father's hands, and the orange hill behind their house that burned like a torch in the morning. We take it in turns – me speaking of what I'll do and her speaking of what she's done and seen. It gets so intense that I can believe in the great city of Sardis, and I can believe in the splendour of our future, yet it's the here and now, the two of us standing a few feet apart, that seems incredible, and often I need to reach out and touch her, prod her warmth to be satisfied she's real.

I leave these meetings faintly dizzy, stumbling to the market to begin the morning shift. The foremen know me now, and I've got a regular gig hauling crates. The boxes seem lighter. What a few weeks ago made me gasp and grunt and flail about, I manage with ease. I can feel the cord-like sinews in my arms, and though I'm no Gelon, I'm stronger than I've ever been. The work done, I nip back home with some breakfast for Ma, stash my wages in a boot under the bed, and set out for the quarry.

When I reach the crossroads, the sun is just beginning to creep up over Epipolae, but I've already a day's work behind me. Sometimes I'm the first one there. Other days I'm last and hear laughter before I see them: the kids chasing about the wheelbarrow. Dares yapping to Gelon as Gelon listens with a contented grin, and I wonder, is it Euripides we're saving at all? Yet, the show is coming together. Each morning the food is distributed, and we get straight into a scene; the meatier, the better. We still don't have the music sorted, which makes no sense, given the money we've spent on everything else. Instead, we have Gelon humming the tunes, with the children joining him, almost like a second chorus, but the strange thing is it works. Dares must have made them practise 'cause the kids' harmonies are way better than before – as good as those choruses of aristo children you sometimes see in the festivals – and it's not just the kids who are getting better, all the cast are rising to it.

The extra bit of food we're giving them has started to take effect. A stranger could tell which Athenians are the actors by the fullness of their cheeks, the straightness of their backs. As our cast fill out, the other prisoners wither all the more. They seem desiccated and cracked as the leaves that blow in from the trees above the quarry. We wheel past them, the food covered by cloaks, but of course, they know what's going on. It seems mad that we ever believed we could do it in secret – probably we only pretended to believe. Still, what the fuck can these fellas do but keep their distance? Gelon and I carry our clubs, but these Athenians are so weak the kids could probably fight them off. Still, more than the physical, it's their spirits that are broken. They've nothing left, and they're no longer even really afraid. It's like they've gone past the point of fear and desire. Sure, if we gave them some food, they'd eat it, but I wouldn't even say they want it now. Whatever is in them is a dying ember that one would have to take great pains to make burn, and we don't.

There's been no sign of Biton, and the greatest disruption to rehearsals these days is the weather, which has taken a sharp turn. It often pisses rain, and Gelon doesn't like the kids getting wet. His own boy, Helios, was very prone to all sorts of coughs and aches, and I want to tell him that these kids aren't Helios; they're healthy and tough, and we can just push on through, but something holds me back. Regardless of the constant stops and starts, the play takes shape. Slowly, like an ant carrying stones twice its size, we progress – putting snatches of scenes together – and though we're directors, the Athenians have their say, as do the children, and it's hard to tell if this is what we think it is, 'cause it's altogether dreamlike, and I haven't slept much, but I often cry listening to their speeches, especially in The Trojan Women, and half the time my face is covered in a scrap of cloak or hidden behind a loaf of bread so the kids won't see me. There's always more to do; some aspect that we haven't thought of, some linking scene we've left out, or a snatch of dialogue that even Numa can't remember so that we must fashion it ourselves, discuss and debate what the words will be. There's always something.

Until there isn't. Until one day, when the sun is setting, bathing the chorus in a wounding light, the children humming their musical accompaniment, the first quarry rats emerging into the dying evening, and Hecuba stares up at the sky and roars her final lines.

Gelon and I both look at each other and smile, for the play is ready.

It's an audience we need.

20.

Alekto beckons us in, and the Libyans lay their work out on wooden benches for us to inspect. I frown and peer closely at each piece, stroking my chin, but to be honest, it's all fucking brilliant. There's masks and costumes here for each of the cast, even the chorus. The most striking bit of kit is for Helen. It's a luminous piece of finery, a flowing purple robe with butterflies and roses embroidered in golden thread, the cost beyond imagining if the dye is real.

'That Tyrian purple?'

Alekto laughs and shakes her head.

'Indistinguishable, right?' She takes up a glistening violet clump like a heart. 'It's beetroot and a secret ingredient.'

The mask for Helen is something too: scarlet lips and ivory cheekbones. I asked Alekto to make the eyeholes especially wide on account of the actor having green eyes just like Helen, and though she looked at me like I was an idiot, those eyeholes are chasms. You'll be able to see Paches' lizard-green blinking out easy, and I think the effect will be good.

It's some assortment. We have the rags of *The Trojan Women* next to the fancy robes of the Corinthian nobles in *Medea*. The gold crown of Corinth's king on a pile of gleaming armour, and wooden weapons, and it's odd seeing these pieces all fashioned to denote character, lying there empty, hollow, and tomorrow they'll join with the Athenians for a brief moment and fizz with life. Nothing here is alive yet, but it throbs with expectation; the robes, and crowns, twitching almost like spring flowers just before the bees rock up.

'It's just wood,' says Gelon, lifting up a sword.

'What age are you? You think actors use real swords? We paint it, see.'

She points at a bucket of shimmering liquid.

'Of course. I'm just impressed.'

'Sensible fellow,' says Alekto, beaming.

She ushers us into the next room to check out the backdrops. Gelon wanted there to be a painted backdrop for each of the plays. The *Medea* backdrop shows a luxurious bedroom, all rugs and cushions, and I like that there are paintings on the walls of the room in the painting. I take a closer peek and see that one's a painting of a child, and I point this out to Gelon, and he nods intently.

'That was his idea.' Alekto gestures to one of the Libyans. The fella who told me about the journey through the desert where he lost his ma. He looks nervous now. As if he's afraid to be credited for anything.

Gelon walks over, takes a coin out of his pouch, gives it to the Libyan, who bows, and thanks him profusely. Something tells me it's the compliment more than the coin that moves him so. That child's face in the painting above the bed is a masterful touch. You might miss it. You could watch the whole play and not know it's there, but I think you'll feel somehow that it is, and if you do spot it out of the corner of your eye, well, I think you're not likely to forget.

The backdrop for *The Trojan Women* is familiar. It's the gleaming walls of some citadel, with the blood streaks on the tower, but Alekto has adapted it for our purposes. There are holes in the wall now, cracks that split down through the towers, and flames like red ivy curl around the battlements. I never thought you could give such vitality to buildings, but the way those walls are twisted makes them seem like a writhing creature on the point of death. Troy is burning, bleeding and ending. Just looking at it makes you shiver, and I glance over at Gelon and see that he's back fumbling in his purse for more coins. Alekto is chuckling to herself, delighted at the desolate looks on our faces, 'cause it's better than we could ever have hoped, but I don't feel good. No, I feel pretty unsettled right now, and I look away and ask the Libyan to start packing. It's time to get out of here. For, now that the gear is done, we've a play to promote.

Gelon settles up with Alekto. She says the Libyan will take the cart and drive us and the stuff over. Sound, but not surprising, 'cause it's taking up a load of space, and I'm sure she wants it off her hands.

'Wait!' she says.

We're already in the courtyard, and I'm just about to hop into the cart with the gear. The Libyan's fixing the harness onto the mule, and Gelon takes something green from his pocket, an apple or some other bit of veg, and he's feeding the mule and rubbing its ears.

'Are you really going to put this on?'

'Of course.'

'With an audience?'

'Aye.'

'In the fucking quarry?'

'We've told you this,' says I. 'Alekto getting senile? Say it ain't so.'

'It's madness. You know that?'

'Bye, Alekto!'

It's the Libyan who's got the reins though, and we don't budge.

'Lampo, shut up,' says Gelon.

I look back at Alekto, and I see that he's right. She's not just trying to talk us out of it. There's more going on here.

'That's some of my best work,' she says. 'Good as what they do in Athens. Make no mistake.'

'We know that. Thank you.'

She shakes her head, exasperated almost – with herself or us.

'The quarry! No one will come, you know that?'

'They will,' says Gelon, with odd certainty, and Alekto peers at him, then at the cart heaped with her creations.

'What time does it start?'

We tell her, and she nods to herself, turns on her heels and walks away.

'Cheeky bitch,' says I.

The Libyan slave gives me daggers, tugs at the reins, and we're off, rolling through Syracuse.

'How do we promote this?'

'We tell people.'

'Grand so.'

And like that, we get stuck into promotion. On the way to Gelon's, we shout at passers-by. Scream that the most amazing show is in town, the last Euripides, and it's here for one time only in the Laurium quarry. People stare, confused. I can imagine we don't make the best impression: two broke fellas on a cart pulled by a mule, roaring their heads off. The Libyan seems pissed off. Hasn't said a word since we left. I shouldn't have called Alekto a bitch, but the directing game is stressful, and sometimes tempers are flared – I tell the Libyan as much and that if he doesn't toughen up, he'll never make it in this business. He just blinks and grips his reins. But when the stuff is dropped off at Gelon's, the Libyan says he'll pick us up tomorrow and drive us to the quarry.

'Good lad,' says I. 'You've got promise.'

The Libyan's already rolling back towards Alekto's, and we continue our promotion on foot. First, we head to the market, but there are so many people screeching their wares, the details of our show get lost in the price of cheese, salt-fish, and all the other shit that's getting hawked.

'They're not listening,' says I.

Gelon nods but keeps at it. He's shy as fuck, and it's almost a buzz to see him walk up to people with that harrowed look in his eyes and ask if they're a fan of tragedy. He's got no patter, no finesse, but even though I grin and click my heels, I'm not faring much better. Still, on we go. There are a couple of tourists over by the beheading stone. That purple one where they executed Nicias. The same guide is waffling away, and the story has got wilder. This time Nicias didn't just beg for mercy but pissed himself. Next time it will probably be shite, and after that, who knows? Maybe it's frustration at how rough this whole promoting game is; maybe it's something else, but I walk over.

'Absolute bollix.'

The tourists back away.

'Excuse me,' says the guide. 'But this is a private tour.'

'Lampo!' Gelon's calling me over. What am I doing? Who is Nicias to me? He's just some rich cunt who bet on himself and lost.

'Get a refund,' says I. 'Nicias didn't piss himself.'

The tourists look at one another then at the guide. They still seem afraid, but there's a hint of questioning too. Like they want the guide to defend himself.

The guide must notice this, 'cause he stutters, 'He did.'

'Nope.'

He looks at the tourists.

'I'm telling you he did. It wasn't a lot, but still.'

'Why are you lying?'

It's Gelon. He's a good foot taller than the guide, who has to crane his neck up.

'Excuse me?'

'We all watched Nicias die. He died with dignity. What good does it do to taint a man so?'

'But he did!'

'What's wrong with you? You degrade a man's suffering like that for coin. Don't you see it's all of us who lose?'

A funny thing happens then. Just above the guide's eye, the skin starts to twitch, and his voice cracks, and though he's clearly afraid of us, especially Gelon, I don't think it's just fear. There's shame too.

'Okay,' says the guide, shoulders sagging. 'He didn't urinate. I made that up.'

The tourists look furious, and they ask the guide to explain himself, and he whimpers something about him having a family and how it's good for tips. The tourists curse him out and then thank us. They're just over for a couple of days, and what can we recommend to see?

'A play,' says I.

'Really? We haven't heard anything about any new productions.'

They look like they have coin – middle-aged dads just here for a quick break, wife and kids at home.

'It's a new Euripides,' says Gelon. 'Never been seen in Sicily.'

An eager bobbing of heads follows, and they ask where it is.

'The quarries.'

'Eh, pardon?'

'I know,' says I. 'It's out there, but welcome to Syracuse! You know what I mean? Taking risks. This production is using the Athenian prisoners. They're the only ones in all of Sicily who know this new Euripides. Trained actors the lot of them, and I'm telling you, boys. This show is the next big thing. Fuck Nicias' stone. Everyone goes to that. It's like hitting Egypt and only seeing the pyramids, but to catch the Athenians put on the last Euripides, well, man. That's a once-in-a-lifetime thing. This is it.'

The tour guide has slunk off, and now it's just us.

'How much?'

I look over at Gelon and see 'free' form on his lips. Before the sound comes, I cut him off.

'Two drachmae for the lot of you.'

There are six of them, and it's a very high price. I can see the surprise on their faces, but these boys are flush. One look at the boots, kidskin, tells you that.

The money is handed over and I give them the directions. They don't even haggle, and when they shuffle off, they're pleased with themselves, whispering about their luck.

'Shouldn't have charged them,' says Gelon. 'This isn't about money.'

'You're wrong there, though. You give it for free, and rich fellas like that won't bite. I needed to rip them off for them to believe in it.'

He smiles then, a lovely smile.

'Why do you act the fool? You're not a fool.'

'I am. I just know it. I reckon that makes me cleverer than most.'

'Someone said that. Who said that?'

His eyes are furrowed as if trying to remember.

'The great Lampo uttered those words to a gobshite in the Syracusan market, if the tales are true.'

We set off towards Dismas', 'cause promotion is thirsty work.

Chabrias sits on a stool at the door, and I lay a wineskin in his lap, tell him about our play.

'Don't let anyone in without explaining what we're up to. Chorus, full production. Dazzle them, Chabrias. You think you can manage that?'

Chabrias eyes the wine, rubs at his cheek with a ruddy stump of arm, nods.

'We'll have proper music too. Tell them that.'

He takes a long pull of the booze and sighs. 'Back home,' he says, the sag in his posture beginning to tauten, 'Argive music. There's nothing like it here.'

Another moment and he'll be off on one about Argos, so Gelon and I just slip past him and head inside. Whatever buzz selling the show to the tourists gave us dissipates pretty quick under the fishermen's rebuffs in Dismas'. Even seeing Lyra at the bar looking over at me can't take all the sting out of the successive fuck offs I get when I try to pitch the play. Most can't make head or tail out of what we're doing, and the few that do, call us traitors. They say the Athenians should be on spikes, not onstage, and would I ever piss off. Still, I shuffle from table to table, say my piece. Gelon doesn't get quite so much abuse. The fishermen aren't so stupid as that, but no one seems keen.

'Fuck,' he says, when we meet up at the bar. 'Finding it hard to break through.'

'Barbarians,' says I. 'All they understand is booze.'

Gelon starts at that.

'Brilliant.'

'Cheers, man, eh, what?'

Gelon walks over to Homer's chair. There's a fisherman already on it, but at Gelon's approach, he scuttles off as always, and Gelon hops on, and the chair creaks for a moment, the legs bending, and I think to myself, fuck, he's going to break Homer's chair. He coughs and raises his arms. The punters look up from their cups, and a few of the braver ones mutter curses.

'Tomorrow, we're putting on *Medea*, and the newest Euripides play, in the Laurium quarry.'

'Yeah, right,' says someone.

Gelon scowls at him, and the fella finds something particularly interesting to look at on the floor.

'It's happening. If you don't believe it, there's an easy way to find out. Just come to the quarry tomorrow afternoon, and you'll see it. This is a proper production.'

'Yeah. We've got chorus and masks.'

'Music too.'

'We've actually sorted music?'

'Quiet, Lampo.'

Some punters chuckle, and I look away, embarrassed, thankful that Lyra is in the back.

'We have music, but again, you'll see it all yourselves tomorrow.' He stops and fiddles with his purse. 'A jug of Catanian red to each man who pledges that they'll come to the show.'

The room quietens, and people look at one another. Everyone's listening now.

'Bollix.'

'It's not bollix,' says Gelon. He flicks a coin in the air in a jaunty fashion, most unlike him, catches it.

'You pledge to see the play, and you get a jug.'

'I pledge!' slurs a fella in the corner.

'So do I!'

Pretty soon, the whole bar, save a few aristo shits in the corner, have pledged to see our play, and the money I got off those tourists is handed over to pay for it. This hurts, as it would have made a good contribution to the Lyra fund, but this fund is secret, and Gelon just thinks I'm being stingy when I try to keep it.

'To Euripides,' says Gelon, raising a jug to toast. 'To tragedy.'

'To tragedy!' roar the punters, and they clink so hard that some of the jugs shatter, but Gelon buys them another, and so they just cheer the louder.

I want to stay on and talk to Lyra, but Gelon says the evening is young. Dismas' is just one bar, and we have a quarry to fill. He must know those pledges mean nothing. They'll be forgotten in the morning hangover. If a handful show up, we're lucky.

Still, we walk the city shouting about a fabulous new production. How it's the latest Euripides, and the cast are proper Athenians from the big shows back in Greece. Pretty much all we get is the same bewilderment as before. A dark-haired beauty that's the spit of Desma is selling straw petasos hats on the street; I ready myself for Gelon to go into his usual trance, but he just explains to her that we're putting on a play, and she should come. Then he walks on. I'm impressed and am about to tell him as much, but he's already way ahead, and I have to leg it just to catch up. My feet ache; the limp is something comical from all the walking, and I didn't sleep last night, so all in all, the city is taking on that feverish aspect of unreality. It's this, perhaps, that makes me notice it so late.

A chariot is rolling through the streets, drawn by four horses, the frenzied music of the dithyramb rising from it. The fella at the reins is in a mask and flickering robes. There's another at his side playing the lyre and one at the back smashing away at a kithara. They're masked too. The one on the lyre starts to sing. It's a woman's voice and a familiar one at that. She's singing of a brand-new Euripides that will be on tomorrow afternoon at the main quarry. One night only. Miss it at your peril. The people in the streets gape. No one cheers, but no one takes their eyes off them. The chariot thunders past us with a clatter of hooves, swirling dust and music, and there's lingering mist long after it disappears, and the faint echoes of lyre and kithara drifting like smoke above a dark row of houses into the violet sky.

'Was that fucking Alekto?'

Gelon smiles.

'No,' he says. 'That was theatre.'

21.

There's still a bit of light left, and we don't go home but to the quarry. It's strange coming down here without the children. It feels too quiet and lonesome. The closer we get to the pit, the more a creeping sense of dread comes upon me, and it might be a trick of my exhausted mind, but I fancy I can hear the rats scurrying madly down below. If Gelon weren't at my side, I'd turn back, but he is, and so on we go till we reach the little hill that reaches over the pit. It's the same spot where Gelon first proposed we become directors. It's not so black as on that night, and I can still see the Athenians down there, huddled together, or moving slowly about to keep warm. In the gloam, it's hard to tell which are ours, but I reckon it's the ones who move. The ones who shuffle their feet as if their lives were a flame they still want to keep burning.

'What now?'

Gelon takes out a jug of wine. He bought it on the way here from a vintner, and it was the most expensive in the shop.

'Give us a sip.'

He doesn't give me a sip, though. Instead, he pours the wine down into the quarry until the jug is empty, and asks me to take his hand. I don't joke, or curse him for wasting the booze. There's something too eerie about the feel of this place right now; I want the warmth of a friend's hand, and I grip it.

'What now?'

'We pray,' says Gelon.

And for the next few hours, that's what we do.

22.

Morning, still dark, and when I step out the door, Gelon's already waiting for me. In his hands, what looks like a mask and a cloth, and he's rubbing the cloth along the mask, polishing it so that bits of the glossy wood flicker with each movement, cast a cold light like the lonesome star winking out through the navy clouds.

'Early start,' says Gelon, not looking up. 'Best get going.'

I'd wanted to go see Lyra first, and am holding her present: a stylus with a wax tablet. Plus the bone for Dismas' dog. The stylus is in a box under the crook of my arm, but I'm gripping the bone, and I can see Gelon's eyes rest on it, but he doesn't ask any questions. We walk out, and our steps crunch. If the dirt on the road isn't frozen, then it's near, and I can feel the faint chill of the gravel beneath the soles of the crocs. That's right, I'm rocking the crocs, and the lightning-blue chiton, 'cause a director has to look the part, on opening night at least. There's a wagon parked at the end of my street – the horse's breath is steaming against a cracked wall. Alekto's Libyan slave is at the reins. He's wrapped up in wool, but still, his teeth are chattering.

'Morning!'

He nods, and I get in the back. At first, I think the kids are with me 'cause of all the faces, but it's just the masks, their eyes round and mouths gaping. It's a rough ride to start, on account of the gear, wooden swords poking me in the arse, but I use one robe as a cushion and wrap myself in another for warmth, reach a kind of comfort as we roll towards the quarry. Only a couple of birds have started to sing, and their frail song gets drowned out by the wind, the snorting of the horse. I can't see well in the back of the wagon, and it's a curious thing. Not so much seeing the dawn, but hearing it. The birds are tentative to start, like nervous performers before a tough crowd. As we roll along, their confidence grows, and pretty soon they're really going for it, other birds joining from disparate trees, and when I peek out through the canvas, I see a yellowing at the edge of things that in an hour or so will become the sun.

'Today's the day,' says I.

Gelon passes me a wineskin, and we drink in turns, not speaking till we reach the crossroads. There's an old man in a big straw hat waiting. The same fella who sold Gelon the wheelbarrow, and he's here again with another wheelbarrow beside him.

'Is this it?' says the Libyan.

'It is, but wait.'

'For what?'

'The children.'

We don't have to wait long. Can hear their laughter already in the distance, and soon after, we see them marching, military-style, with Dares at the front. The kids get stuck in right away – fill the wheelbarrow to the brim – and Gelon rolls it down towards the quarry entrance. The guard barely sees us, only has eyes for the pouch Gelon gives him, and he steps lazily aside, begins to count the contents.

I whisper, 'Should we tell him about the show? The audience coming?'

'Already done.'

'Grand so.'

We push and weave the wheelbarrow around sleeping Athenians and piles of rocks until we reach the spot. Gelon chose this place a while back because it has a large boulder to lean the sets against, and behind it, the Athenians can change costumes. More than this, it's right at the centre of the quarry, its core, and here you feel encircled by the limestone walls. It's as if you've got something to say, and the very earth is huddling in to listen. Most of the Athenians are still asleep, though some are beginning to stir, and there's the occasional cry or shout as if they're waking from a bad dream or into one.

'Morning.'

'Quiet, Lampo.'

It takes several trips to move it all 'cause today it's not just food, there's the costumes and sets as well, but at last the wagon's empty.

'I'll return in the evening.'

'Thank you.'

'Good luck.'

The Libyan bows, then gives a sharp tug of the reins, and the horse is off, the wheels making an awful racket over the rough gravel. We head back to the quarry, and I notice the old man in the straw hat is walking by my side, something long and thin in his hands.

'Lampo, meet Alcar.'

The old fella removes his hat and nods. His face is full of cracks, like dry soil that's been pounded, and the eyes are narrow slits of blue, but there's humour in them, and though he doesn't smile, it feels like he does.

'Alcar will be doing the music.'

He raises his hand, and I see that he's holding an aulos. The paint on the pipe is chipped and worn away, and the wood underneath is gnarled with the same leather-brown hue as the old man's hand, like it's a piece of it, an especially long finger or something.

'Nice one.'

By this stage, the sun is up, and most of the cast have made their way over to us. The kids are on form. Each of them has a little task, and they set to it. The key to directing is mostly just letting people do their job. Be clear and precise – after that, it's up to them. At least, that's how I run my crew. Some of the kids are responsible for the *Medea* props and costumes, others for *The Trojan Women*, and then there's those whose job it is just to sort out the food. The other prisoners are watching us; a few even crouch forward. Of course, they knew about the play, but we've always tried to keep the rehearsals relatively under wraps, done them behind boulders or in the nooks of the quarry walls. Today we're out and open, and they can all see us. Gelon's brought a couple of extra sacks of meal, and we'll leave it here when the show's over, but right now, we just need to work in peace. No interruptions, and I brandish my club and step forward.

'Good morning, boys. I'm sure you all know what we've been up to. Anyway, today is it. In a few hours, this place is going to be packed with the quality of Syracusan society. They're here to appreciate the only good thing to come out of Athens – Euripides.' I wink. 'You behave, and you might get some booze and a bite to eat when it's all said and done. But you interfere in any way, well, then in the words of the great Homer, I shall cave in your skull.'

I take a couple of wide-angle swings at no one in particular and those who were creeping forward scamper.

'Nice one, I see you know your verse.'

I turn back with a grin, and little Strabo is staring at me, stricken.

'Had to, Strabo. Can't have these poor bastards raiding the supplies.'

He nods, but I don't think he understands, 'cause a little later, he tries to give one of the Athenians a carrot, and Dares has to stop him.

The sets were too big to transport whole, so we had them sawed into three parts that we assemble now. We stack them against the boulder in the order they'll appear; the set for *Medea* up front. That way, when *Medea* is done, we can just pull the set off, revealing the walls of Troy, and be ready to go. Still, we're lucky we got here early 'cause there are countless little things that go wrong in the dress rehearsal. These Athenians haven't worn new clothes in months, and when we hand them the costumes, they just hold them, confused, rubbing them slowly like blind men, and then holding them up, smiles of naive delight, and it strikes me that they've returned to a second childhood. That suffering has stripped away the years in the way carpenters can uncover the youth of a tree by scraping the plane against the old bark. Yes, I think they've found a sort of innocence in their ruin.

'Help,' says Paches, looking over at me, the purple robes of Helen flowing over his arms. He's the first to ask, and I go to him straight away.

'What's the matter?'

'How? Eh, how does it work?'

In truth, the Helen costume is probably the wildest bit of kit that Alekto fashioned for us. It's a mass of glittering fabric, and it takes me some moments to find the holes where Paches' head and arms will fit through, but together we get it on.

'Where's the mask?'

One of the kids hands it to me, and I have to wipe off the chalky quarry dust and untangle the wig's golden knots, but eventually, it's done. Paches puts it on and disappears. The only trace is the green eyes peering out through the holes, but even they are altered, somehow feminine.

'How do I look?'

'Stunning,' says I, and it's true. 'Gelon, check out Paches.'

Gelon and Dares are helping one of the Athenians put on

the fake armour, but Gelon stops what he's doing and pops over.

'What do you think?'

'Magnificent,' says Gelon, and you can see he means it.

'Give us a shake, Helen.'

Paches starts to do one of Helen's set dances, the golden wig swishing a little in the air.

'More hips,' says Gelon. 'Remember, you're dancing for your life. You don't seduce him, Menelaus will kill you.'

'Yeah, Helen, shake it!'

Paches shakes it proper now, and though he trips once on the trailing robes, and the dancing looks awkward 'cause of the lack of music, he's getting there – losing himself and finding Helen. I slap him on the arse.

'Fucking tease. Menelaus doesn't stand a chance.'

The green eyes blink out, and I can hear a breathless thank you.

Repetition is the key. For a good hour or so, the cast do nothing but throw on and off their costumes, get in position. I suggest that we do a full run-through with the words, as there's still time, but Gelon's having none of it. Repetition only goes so far, and he wants them to be a little lost up there too. He says the best theatre isn't about showing something but finding it. Certainty is the way of cowards, and fools – and Euripides is neither. His voice trembles when he says this, and I see he's nervous. I've almost never seen Gelon properly nervous, and at first, I think it must be something else. The cold, or just the quarry mist obscuring my vision, but no, Gelon's tense as fuck, and only now do I notice that everyone is the same. Even the children are quiet, and the few who laugh do so in an exaggerated way, as if they too are actors. The Athenians shuffle about, gripping their costumes for comfort. It seems that they're whispering to one another, but when I get close, I hear that it's only the words of the play, that they're muttering the lines to themselves like a prayer, and each is saying a different part, some at the beginning of *Medea*, others at the end, or in the middle of *The Trojan Women*, and again I feel that creeping sense of the looseness of time in an endless song. Only the old man is at ease. He's over by the wheelbarrow, drinking and humming to himself, and I want some of that calm, and so I walk to him. Paches follows at my side.

'You're on the music so?'

The old man nods and takes a hit of wine.

'Are you decent?'

He pulls back his straw hat so I can see pale blue eyes squinting merrily, and he chuckles to himself.

'What's so funny?' My voice is irritated, but he doesn't seem to notice.

'Too late to be asking that,' he says. 'I'm here, though. That's for certain.'

He offers me some wine, and I say no, and he offers it to Paches, and I decide the old bastard isn't the worst.

The three of us stand there by the wheelbarrow, not talking, just looking about ourselves and occasionally at one another, and smiling, as if it were all just a normal day, and then Paches says, 'Do you think anyone will come?'

'They will,' says I. 'Syracusans are mad for theatre.'

The old man seems about to respond but stops himself. He takes out the aulos and starts playing his fingers along it, not blowing or anything, just moving the fingertips along the holes at a shocking speed. I reckon he's decent.

'The luckiest man who ever lived died in his mother's womb.'

'What's that?'

'An Athenian proverb,' says the old man, fingers still dancing. 'A melancholy people, the Athenians. Fierce melancholy.'

'We're not, though.'

It's Paches, and he takes a long pull from the wineskin.

'No need to defend them, Paches. I know you're different.'

Paches doesn't seem to be satisfied with the compliment, for he frowns and drinks some more.

'Slow down now. Don't want you pissed. A drop to ease the nerves but not so much as to slur the speech.'

'You've never seen a people laugh as much as us Athenians,' says Paches. 'I had a friend who'd make you laugh so hard you felt your ribs would crack.' He grins as if ribs cracking were a wondrous thing. 'The funniest man you could ever meet, and a fine musician too.'

'What was his instrument?' asks Alcar, interested.

'Lyre. He and I would play together.'

He must see the surprise on my face, as he adds quickly, 'I was awful, but he liked me to play with him. He said I made him calm.' Again that smile. 'There's more to Athens than tragedy,' says Paches with feeling. 'We laugh till we cry, and we drink.' Another swig. 'We drink till we fall down, but we're up first thing in the morning to scheme and love and build and do it all again. It's a city of belief, not despair. That proverb has nothing to do with the Athens I knew.'

The old man looks at him, the twinkle gone from his eyes, replaced by something graver, respect even, and he reaches over and pats Paches on the shoulder.

'I meant no offence.'

Paches nods, and for a while longer, we stand there, passing the wine back and forth. Three blokes sharing a drink on a fine morning, and I put my arm around Paches, rub his hair, and am pleased to see that none of it comes away in my fingers.

'This is what it's all about, right?'

'Yeah,' he says, though it's clear his mind's elsewhere.

'Who was your mate, Paches?' I ask. 'Is he back in Athens or what? Where have you been hiding him?'

Paches presses his hands against his temples and seems to squeeze, his eyes shut tight, and the lizard-green disappears. The way his hands are pressing his skull reminds me of when you'd break a pot in the factory, that moment where, on instinct, you'd try to hold the pieces together, even though you knew it was fucked.

'He's here,' he says, numbly, 'in the quarry. I buried him the day we met.'

I feel suddenly wretched, for it strikes me now that I knew this, and only wanted to prise it from him. Why had I done that?

It's almost welcome when I hear voices raised just ahead of us. There's a heated discussion over by the stage sets, and I stroll over, relieved as anything when Paches comes with me. Gelon and Numa are arguing, which is odd, as up until now, it's all been smooth between them. Methinks performance jitters, and I offer both a sip of wine.

'Enough to settle the nerves,' says I again. 'But not so much as to slur the speech.'

'Lampo, tell him it's crazy,' says Numa.

'Think about it,' says Gelon. 'No one's ever done this before.'

'I'm lost.'

Gelon starts explaining. He wants one of the kids to act in *The Trojan Women*. Near the end of the play, Hector's baby son, Astyanax, is murdered, thrown from a tower, 'cause Agamemnon is afraid that if he grows up, he'll come for revenge. This all happens offstage and is described by the chorus, but Gelon wants us to actually act it out. There are no words, so all that's needed is for the Athenian playing the guard to push one of the children off a rock, and we'll set up something to break their fall, so they don't get hurt. Gelon thinks the unexpectedness of it will cause shock and awe, but I'm inclined to agree with Numa, and tell him as much.

'Too risky,' says I. 'It's far too late for new ideas. The audience will be here soon, and we haven't practised it. What if something goes wrong?'

There's the faintest of flickers about Gelon's eyes that makes me think, this isn't a new idea at all.

'It's simple. The wheelbarrow is full of grain, and we throw some cloaks on top, and it will break any fall. It's only a few feet, anyway.'

'But it's not just that,' says Numa. 'We don't have women in plays, let alone children. It's madness.'

'You should, though,' says Gelon. 'That's the way plays need to go. Men, women and children. I believe that.'

Numa shakes his head and seems genuinely upset, for he was an actual pro back in Athens. Theatre is his life. Of course, the final say is with me and Gelon, but till now, Gelon's been playing this like it's a collaboration. Each point being discussed and debated amongst the cast, and I don't think it wise to force bizarre innovation down their throats last thing.

'He's right!' comes a shrill voice.

It's Linar. He's already dressed in the ragged robes of Cassandra, the mask hugged to his chest. If possible, he looks even more agitated than usual, his eyes darting about, stretched wide so you can see a load of the whites.

Numa smiles. 'Thank you, Linar.'

'I meant Gelon. Can't you see, Numa? It's brilliant! The audience won't know what to expect. They'll hear that a child will be executed, and then when one actually appears . . .' He leans forward. 'The boy won't wear a mask, am I correct?'

'That's right,' says Gelon.

'Oh, it will be overwhelming. I think we should do it. It's never been done before, and for all we know this play might never be performed again.'

'Don't say that!' says Numa. 'Of course it will.'

There are murmurs amongst the Athenians. I feel like this could go either way, and I've no clue which. Gelon faces the cast.

'What do you say?'

Nothing at first. It's pretty much impossible to read their faces as a lot of them are covered by the masks, and it's eerie when they all respond at the same time, like a true chorus.

'Use a child.'

Gelon turns to the children. 'What do you think?'

This feels like a formality, like they've already discussed it, and the kids answer immediately.

'Use one of us!'

'Which one?'

'Astyanax is only an infant,' says Linar eagerly. 'It must be the youngest.'

Strabo steps forward, a good head shorter than his mates, and he grins, his crooked teeth looking even more chaotic than usual.

'Am I in the play?'

'You are,' says Dares.

'What do I do?'

'You fall. That's all you need to do is fall, but it's very important, Strabo. Can you do that?'

Strabo nods, and there it is. He's got the role of Astyanax. I ask Gelon why he doesn't just get two of the kids to play Medea's children as well, but he says Medea kills them with knives, and it would be too hard to make that convincing. You'd need blood or some substitute. Besides, the climax of the show is *The Trojan Women*. It's the final play, and he wants to use the effect at the last possible moment.

The afternoon is creeping in, and we spend the next hour just drilling Strabo's fall: pushing him off the boulder so that he drops the few feet down into the wheelbarrow, onto the cushions of grain and cloth. At the start, he keeps squealing with delight when he hits grain, and we have to do it again and again. What we need is a scream of terror at the push, and then nothing. Strabo's confused, but Dares works with him patiently, and in the end, he gets it. On his tenth perfect fall, Gelon picks him up and embraces him, and together they walk, hand in hand, to the centre of the stage.

'Give it up for Strabo,' says Gelon. 'The youngest actor in the world.'

Everyone cheers, the children loudest of all. Gelon pats Strabo on the head, and he shuffles off to his mates, grinning.

'We're doing something new today,' says Gelon. 'Something beyond the normal run of tragedy. I want to thank you all. Everyone here should be proud of themselves and what they've put in. I know I'm proud of you, and so is Lampo.'

'Fierce proud,' says I.

'This is Alcar. He'll be accompanying you on the aulos. The children will also hum.'

Alcar removes his hat and bows.

'Now, I think we're ready, or as ready as we can be. In a little while, people will come down and watch. How many will come? I can't say, but we'll know soon enough. I believe you're going to show them something they'll never forget. When they leave here later today, the few or many will be changed, and whatever happens in the future, Athens will be remembered, and you will be a part of that remembrance. This is what I believe.'

The chorus don't say much, but Gelon's got to them. Logic tells you these bastards are just humouring us out of fear and hunger. It might have started as that, but when I look at the Athenians now, costumed and gripping their props, I see, yes, they're terrified – terrified that people may actually come – but even more than this is another fear: the fear that no one will see it. They want an audience.

Yet, none have come. The cast are in their positions, costumes on and masks clasped in sweaty fingers. The sets are up, and the props at the ready. A fist of sun emits a bruising light, and the quarry has a sombre aspect that fits the opening of *Medea* perfect. Gelon paces back and forth, his neck crooked up towards the path to the pit, searching for someone, anyone.

'I suppose the other prisoners are an audience.'

'Shut up. They'll come.'

But they don't come. The Athenians stay in their positions, trembling slightly with agitation. The children can't keep still, and rush about, whispering, 'Where are they?' and Dares tells them to be quiet.

'We need to start,' says I. 'Wait much longer, and there won't be enough light for the plays.'

'No,' says Gelon, staring up. 'They'll come. They have to.'

More time passes so that even the cast start to whisper that we should just begin.

'Patience,' says Gelon. 'A play without an audience is just rehearsal. We do it proper.'

He sounds certain enough, and the Athenians are comforted, but I know him well, and I can hear the first creep of doubt in his voice. The afternoon is nudging into evening, and still, we stand there waiting, staring up at the winding dark path that leads down into the pits, scouring for movement like a hawk hunting a mouse.

'There,' whispers Gelon, his hand outstretched.

A figure is walking down the path into the quarry and behind that person another.

'Two, well. It's something.'

'Look.'

Another seven or eight follow close behind. To be honest, I thought we'd be lucky to get ten, and I reckon even Gelon will be content now. The main thing is for strangers to see it. People for whom it's all new and puzzling.

'Fellas, get into your positions!'

None of them move. They just stare up – mouths open and eyes wide – so that though they're not yet wearing the masks, they might as well be.

'Get into fucking positions!'

Even the children are frozen. I look back up, and the entire path appears to shiver, like a magnificent snake slithering down into the quarry, and it's no longer dark but made up of countless different colours, and I see what's caused the stir.

There are hundreds of people, and they're all coming our way.

23.

Not since the war have so many Syracusans and Athenians been together in one place. The Syracusans space themselves out in a curve, almost like in a proper theatre. They sit down on rocks, and some of those rocks are the makeshift graves I spoke of. The crowd are silent. Eerily so. They stare with an intensity that unsettles. Many faces, I recognize: potters from the old factory, fishermen from Dismas', women from the markets, and just countless others that I've seen about town but never spoken to. There are even aristos. Not many, but they're here. Conspicuous by the vivid colours of their cloaks and their oily hair that glints in the sun.

My hands are shaking. The fingers look red as cuts, I can feel the pumping of my pulse about the wrists, and my mouth's as dry as the dust at my feet.

'Good afternoon.' The voice that comes out of my gob is a warbling mess, but I press on. 'We have a cracking show for you tonight. I must say you're in for a treat. I –'

'Quiet, Lampo.'

A few chuckle, and though I don't like that it's at my expense, the laughter's welcome.

'Today,' says Gelon, 'you'll see two plays. The first, you know. It's Euripides' *Medea*. The second has never been seen before in Sicily. It's *The Trojan Women* and the latest Euripides. The play he believes to be his greatest.' There are murmurs at this. Gelon raises his hand, and I notice it holds a jug, and he empties it onto the ground so that some of the wine splashes our legs, red like gashes.

'May the gods look favourably upon what we will see and do today.'

Some people in the audience repeat the words, but most don't.

Gelon bows in that way we've seen directors do at shows back in the city, and I follow. In the crowd, a woman is shouting. It grows louder, and when I glance up, I see that she's moving – marching down towards us, her dark hair streaming about crazily, and at that moment, I think the real Cassandra is here.

'Is the world gone mad!' She fairly shrieks the words. 'You're going to sit and watch these bastards dance and sing! My husband's dead, and so is yours!' She points at some woman in the audience. 'And your son is fucking dead!' She lunges for another, when she's lifted off her feet by a big fella with a scar along his throat and carried away, kicking and screaming. No one tries to stop him, but there's murmuring all through the crowd, and I think this is it. A gust of wind in the wrong direction, and we're done.

'What now?'

Gelon's silent. For the first time since this whole thing began, he's as lost as me.

'Women,' says I, forcing a grin. No one laughs. A few even start to hiss. Everything in me is saying leg it. Get the fuck out of here now, but I don't. I just shut my eyes as if darkness is the answer. That's when the music starts. If Alcar is shite, there'll be a riot. If he's pretty good, I still see some rocks coming our way, but he's neither of those things. Alcar plays that aulos in a way I didn't think it could be played, and whatever else happens, we've done the music right. The hissing stops, and, seizing the moment, Gelon leaps on a pile of rocks and faces the crowd, his voice loud and steady.

'Everyone here has lost something in this war. Look a-fucking-round you!'

A few do, and see the skeletal creatures that lie chained about the rocks like animals at the end of things.

'Now look at this stage and don't dare look away. It's not a stage, and this isn't a quarry at all but the palace of Corinth. Look at it. That's all there is now!'

The music drowns out everything, and fifteen Corinthian noblewomen appear. Usually, in the play, this is where the nurse shows up, and the chorus come a little later, but even Numa didn't remember the nurse's lines, and we decided to get straight into the meat of it. Go for the throat and not let go. Sure enough, there's an audible intake of breath, 'cause Alekto did a cracking job, and the chorus look like the real thing.

' "I am sorely fearful," ' they chant in unison. ' "Medea has lost her mind. I'm sorely fearful of what she might do." '

They begin to dance, and it's tentative and awkward. We've done a load of practice to make sure they could move pretty nimbly in their chains, but almost none with the costumes and masks. My heart sinks. Yeah, the costumes are good, brilliant even, as are the sets, but neither costumes, sets nor music will make this play come to life. As if to prove the point, one of the chorus trips mid-spin and snots himself, the mask flying off; another of the chorus, with a tuft of incongruous silver beard stabbing out from his own mask, helps him up. As the actor on the ground fumbles with his mask, you can see his gaunt, panicked face, and the crowd start laughing. Alcar pumps up the volume on the aulos, but the laughter rises higher, and now the audience are pissing themselves. The tension that was so unbearable a few moments ago is gone, and the crowd relax. They turn to one another, grin, nudge and point. Something tells me that this is what they wanted all along. Even if they didn't know it – a shitshow.

I can't bring myself to look at Gelon, and my eyes keep flitting from the stage to the audience so that I'm not really watching the play but its effect. The chorus are falling apart. Their words no longer coming out in unison but in a jumble so that they topple over one another, and it's often a babble. Only Alcar keeps his head, and the music, when you can hear it above the nonsense of the chorus, and the cackling crowd, is perfect, dark and ominous, but you can't always hear it.

Again, one of the chorus trips, but at least his mask doesn't come off, and he's on his feet quick enough, but he's lost the rhythm completely, and he shouts out, solo.

' "Look, there is Medea!" '

Followed immediately by the fourteen others.

' "Look, there is Medea!" '

But there's no sign of Medea, and this too causes laughter.

'Look, there are the Athenians, and they're shite!' calls someone from the crowd. Roars of laughter. I glance over at Gelon, and he's in bits. His face as pale as the limestone he's sitting on, hands balled into fists, but his eyes are still fixed on the stage as if he can't look away. At last, Medea shows up. The robes are scarlet with little pustules of darker fabric at the end that glister like berries. You can't even hear what Numa's saying, the crowd are hooting so much. Numa was meant to begin Medea's entrance with an elaborate dance, but instead, he's deathly still. Then he looks about him very slowly, his words inaudible, but there's a certain menace in these tiny movements, and just watching him, I feel the hairs stand a little on end, and I want to back away. I remember once working my uncle's farm and looking down to see a snake glide past my foot. Well, the feeling I have watching Numa is of that quality in a milder form. Many in the crowd are still laughing, but it's forced – more muscle than mirth. Finally, you can make out Numa's words.

' "Of all creatures given life, us women are the most miserable." '

The crowd shut the fuck up. Numa starts to dance, slowly at first, but the tempo increases with the rhythm of the aulos, and when he spins, the scarlet robes streak the air like gushing wounds.

' "These men speak of the hazards of war. What fools, what utter fools. I would rather face the enemy over and over than bear a child once!" '

Numa fairly snarls these words at the chorus, and though they cower in fear, there's a fluidity to their movement that's new. When they respond, they do so together, fifteen voices as one.

'Back in business,' I whisper to Gelon, but he's deaf to everything but the play.

Don't get me wrong, the chorus don't suddenly turn perfect. There are slip-ups and errors, and the dancing never quite takes off the way it might, but no one laughs, and you can see the audience are losing themselves, forgetting where they are, and that's all you can hope for. One person isn't losing himself, though, and that's Lampo. I'm tense as fuck, because Paches hasn't made his entrance yet. He's up next, and I don't know what to expect. By the last rehearsals, he knew his lines and was a decent Jason. Never anything more. The scenes worked 'cause of Numa, and my eyes are slits when he first steps onto the stage, and I don't see so much as hear him curse Medea out.

I open my eyes, and there he is. It looks a little odd at first 'cause Numa's a good bit taller, but Alekto came through again, and the costume's perfect. Paches is every bit the cocksure Jason, and the green eyes peer out of the eyeholes and look Medea up and down with disdain. Paches told me that he was an aristo back in Athens. His da's minted and even paid for the ship he sailed to Syracuse in. A bad buy, but the point is there was a time when Paches gave the orders, and he must be drawing on that now, 'cause he moves around the stage with an authority I've never seen before.

He struts and tells Medea that though he's leaving her for a woman half her age, it's gratitude he deserves. 'Cause he's doing it all for her and the kids. Medea's not convinced, to say the least. She makes a gesture as if to spring at him, but at the last moment stops and twirls, the scarlet spray of her robes grazing him, and the two just start roaring at each other, going back and forth. The aulos lowering to the faintest hum so that the audience can catch every word, and it's vicious stuff. A proper agon, maybe the best I've seen, and I don't know what to think. One moment I'm with Jason, the next Medea, and it swings this way and that like the battle in the great harbour, but Medea wants it more. She's willing to go all the way, and in the end, it's Jason who scuttles off, muttering something to the effect that all women are cunts, and the stage is left to Medea singing her song of revenge, as the chorus quail in horror.

And then the bodies hit the floor. First, Jason's new wife, then her father, King Creon. All of this happens offstage, but the Athenian who plays the messenger does a cracking job describing their agonizing deaths, and Numa, of course, is brilliant, shrieking with delight at every gruesome detail. Finally, it's time for the children to croak, and I don't know how he does it, but Numa manages to make you feel as sorry for Medea as the kids when Medea walks off to do the deed.

The rest happens quickly. Jason weeping when he finds his children's bodies. We've no crane for the deus ex when Medea escapes in the chariot of dragons, so we get the chorus to describe it. They dance around the weeping Jason, point at the sun, and howl about how Medea is getting away, carried off to her grandfather, the sun god, and though it can't be true, perhaps the gods condone even this. As luck would have it, just then, a couple of rooks swoop through the quarry and up, glide darkly towards the sun, and that's it. The music stops. The play is over. The audience is silent. From the faces closest, I see nothing but haunted gazes. It's better than I'd hoped, and I feel a loosening in my muscles. I didn't realize how tense I'd been. How afraid. Gelon isn't beside me, and I hear movement at the stage, but I'm too dazed to care. Suddenly he's back and has leapt up onto an even taller rock. There's a wild innocence to his stare; like a child's eyes have been plopped in his sockets and are seeing everything for the first time.

'You're no longer in Corinth,' he shouts. 'You're outside the walls of Troy after it's been sacked. Hector is dead. Achilles too. The Greeks have won. Don't you dare look away!'

The lush backdrop of the Corinthian palace is gone, replaced by white walls streaked with blood, and cracked towers. Even I'm exhausted. There's no way Numa and the others can go straight into this, but they do.

24.

They're wrecked. You can see it by the way they take the stage, trudging like they're stepping through mud and not dry quarry stone. The flowing robes of the Corinthian women are gone, replaced by raggedy chitons cut to bits so that you can see the Athenians' bony legs, the chains on their ankles, and pale arcs of rib. It's perfect, really. Everything about them that's fucked and broken fits with this play. They're meant to be Trojan women who've lost all, sifting through the ruins of their city as they wait for the boat to Greece.

There's no story. Or if there is, I can't explain it. It's more like a dream watched through a stranger's eyes. Everything's misty and obscure, not helped by the wind that's picked up and filled the air with quarry dust, so that at times you can't see the actors, only hear their singing, the clinking chains and the haunting music of Alcar. If I didn't know for a fact that Numa was Hecuba, I wouldn't believe it. There's not a trace of the proud princess in the crooked figure who stares out at the audience and chants softly that everything she's ever loved has died or will soon be taken away. And once all the love is gone, when each piece of attachment is burnt and disperses like smoke on the wind, will she even exist?

We started late. The evening is galloping in. Lucky this is a short play; otherwise, they'd soon be singing in darkness. For now, the stage pulses with a cindery glow. So far, it's just been the chorus and Hecuba singing to one another, teetering on shaky legs, and you can see the exhaustion in each, but suddenly the energy shifts, and there's a piercing cry from behind.

' "It's beautiful Cassandra!" ' sing the chorus.

' "Oh, my poor, clever daughter. Suffering has shredded her wits, and she has become a child." '

Linar bounds onto the stage and trips. A few in the audience laugh. He doesn't get to his feet; he just lies there on his belly, face planted, and begins scratching away at the ground like an animal burrowing for safety. I don't know if it's stagecraft, but when he gets up and raises his hands, there's blood trickling from cracked nails, down through the fingers, and he starts to dance. After the sluggish moves of Hecuba and the chorus, there's shocking vitality to Linar's jig, and pretty soon I'm just watching Cassandra. It's a prophecy of doom, certainly, but there are flickers of hope I hadn't noticed in the rehearsal. Her mother thinks she's mental. The chorus do too, and she probably is, but beneath the mania, there's a point she's trying to make – just 'cause their lives are fucked, it doesn't mean they've nothing left. There's always something left for the person who remembers. And Hecuba and her go back and forth, and it seems just an agon between madness and reason, but it's not only that. It's despair and meaning that are being pitted against one another, and it's asking, if meaning departs from reason, might there not be wisdom in a faith-filled lunacy? Before there's an answer, the Greek guards show up and take her away to the boat to Argos. The bed of Agamemnon. Cassandra is dragged off the stage, and the clinking of her chains finds an echo, a counterpoint all around us. The audience for this play has more than doubled, though not with Syracusans. There's still the same number of them. It's the Athenians: those prisoners who were never part of our production. They're huddling forward, careful to keep a safe distance from the Syracusans, while getting as close to the stage as they can. I thought that these fellas didn't give a shit about anything. That they'd reached a point beyond desire, but the withered faces that stare at the stage are rapt.

It's the next scene. Andromache, the wife of Hector and mother of Astyanax, shows up. Kallias, the Athenian who plays her, is decent, but he forgets some of his lines, and I can see by the way Numa is leaning in that he must be whispering prompts. Listening to Linar, I'd lost myself in the spectacle, but I'm back out of it again and nail-biting nervous. This is the scene where they kill Astyanax, and the true innovation of our production comes in. I can see some movement behind the stage, and once or twice, the children's heads pop out. Astyanax is meant to be here by now, and I wonder if Strabo is acting up or having second thoughts. Then he shuffles out. The audience gasp. They've never seen anything like this. They'd expected the usual fare of a short bloke, with a squeaky voice, playing the kid, but no. We're going all the way. The sight of Strabo seems to have inspired Kallias, 'cause he settles into the role now, and when he hugs Strabo to him and starts to weep, for the briefest of moments, it's a mother and son I'm watching. The fella playing the guard takes Strabo by the hand and improvs something brilliant. He kneels and asks Strabo if he'd like to go up to the tower and look at the city he'll one day rule, and Strabo laughs with delight, and that innocent laugh cuts through the audience. You can almost watch them recoil and then loosen when the boy and man walk off the stage. Loosen, 'cause there's relief in knowing that at least they won't have to see the killing.

No play shows that.

But then man and boy appear on a boulder above the stage, still holding hands, and the guard points out to a spot on the horizon and says, ' "Would you like to fly over your city?" '

Strabo says something, but his voice, as ever, is a croak, and I can't make it out.

' "Then fly!" '

He pushes Strabo, and there's a squeal of terror, and the child disappears. I know that it's just a few feet down and onto a bed of grain and cloth, but I forget this in the moment and cry out like the rest.

'The child!' someone shouts. 'That was a real child!'

This person gets hushed. Concern for the kid is lost in the need to see what happens next. There are muffled sobs scattered about the audience. The show goes on. Next comes Paches as Helen. It's good, not quite as good as the last scene, but the last was the best of the night. Still, Paches knows his lines, and the Helen costume dazzles. In the scene, Helen pleads with Menelaus for her life and Hecuba for her death. Paches dances away seductively, swinging his hips in the tight-fitting glittering dress, and there's something unspeakably horrible about it, coming just after the child's murder. I join the rest and hiss and curse Helen out, so that you can't hear a lot of Paches' speech, just see him swing his hips and laugh triumphantly as the guards lead him off, and everyone knows that Helen has won. It's to Menelaus' bed she's headed, not the executioner.

It's the end soon, and lucky for us, 'cause there's not much light left in the sky, barely enough to get the lines out, but Numa's a pro and doesn't rush. If anything, he slows down, teasing out every drop of sorrow from the words like it's the most precious of juices. They carry out Astyanax's body on a wooden shield. He's streaked with crimson and reeks of booze. The kids squeezed a skin of Catanian red on to mimic blood. I'm close enough to see Strabo's foot twitch and the little curve of a smile on his lips. Here fading light is our friend, and the audience can't see the details, just a dead boy on a shield. I can hear sobbing now. Fishermen with faces craggy as the quarry rocks are snivelling. Aristos too. Even the prisoners weep. It's the maddest thing. 'Cause for the briefest moment, Syracusans and Athenians have blended into a single chorus of grief for this make-believe. Numa stands over Strabo and touches his face.

' "Oh, the child of my child. The soft cheeks that should have been the comfort of my old age." '

The chorus chant.

' "Your old age. The comfort of your old age!" '

' "The sweet laugh that was to me finer than any music." '

' "Music! The boy's laugh was music!" '

' "Stories I would tell you of your father. Oh, your –" '

Numa never finishes these words. Instead, the chorus scream. The last while, I've mostly been looking at the audience, gauging what was happening from their reactions, but I turn around now, and Numa's on the ground. The Hecuba mask is shattered so that only the lower part with the mouth is attached, and there's blood pouring from it. He's crawling away, and Biton's walking behind him. He raises the club, and Numa puts up a hand and says something I can't make out, and then his face disappears beneath the dark wallop of wood, and the next time I see it, the head's caved in. Another wallop, and it's matted hair, yellow bits of skull, a flap of skin with a single brown eye. Biton stands over what's left and prods it with the tip of his boot. There are tears pouring down his cheeks. He's not alone. A bunch of fellas are with him – a few I recognize from the audience. They all have weapons of some sort, and they're going for the chorus.

It's like a battle, though a battle where the other side has surrendered. The chorus might have a chance to get away, if it weren't for the chains or if their costumes were lighter, but the combination of both means they're fucked, and they trip over each other as they try to run.

Gelon's already in there, trying to stop it, but it's ten to one,

and alone it's suicide. The audience watch, most look horri-
fied, but they don't move.

'Help!' I scream at them. 'Would you please fucking help us!'

No help is coming from them. I left my own club in the
wheelbarrow and run in with nothing but my hands.

'Stop it, lads! Fucking stop!'

Gelon's on the ground and bleeding. Biton is kicking him,
and a kid is crying. I think it's Dares, and he's scratching at
Biton. Someone grabs me from behind. I turn around and see
a handsome young aristo with familiar long-lashed grey eyes.

'You care more for these Athenians than your own people,
citizen?'

He spits in my face, and there follows a cudgel against my
nose, and the bone splits, then another blow to the back of the
head, and my knees buckle. The quarry is wet and salty, and I
feel like I'm drowning in a stony sea.

25.

Night-time. A hand on my cheek and a voice in the darkness, the words indistinct. I gasp. Try to gulp in air, but it's thick and syrupy with blood and broken things. The voice again and a person-shaped thing hovering above. The world is wobbly, unstable. Probably, I'm on the ferry through the Styx and the shadowy figure the ferryman. It's death indeed, and I'm Hades bound. But fuck, it hurts. My head most of all, and when you're dead, you don't feel pain, or so the priests say. The thought's a comfort, and I try to speak. The words are muffled and wet, but I make out, 'Where am I?'

'With us,' says a familiar voice.

'Who's us?'

'The Athenians.'

There's a loosening, and I'm gone again. Drifting in and out. If it's a dream I'm having, then it's a shit one. I dream of rats, an uncommon number of rats, the sound of their scurrying in my ears, and someone kicking them away. Then I'm at Troy, a gleaming tower in the distance from which a child keeps falling. Beyond the tower, a huge red sun that takes up half the sky. There's a chariot riding across it, a woman at the reins, her black hair fluttering behind her like crows, and other dreams, I don't recall, but all of them feverish. It's brighter now, though still dark. A man leans over me, rubbing what feels like a damp cloth against my forehead. His eyes are a weird green, lizard-green.

'Paches?'

He smiles.

'You recognize me? That's good. Drink.'

He squeezes something, and liquid sprays into my mouth. It stings the cuts on my tongue and gums, but I swallow it along with what feels like a tooth. When I speak next, my words are clearer.

'Gelon? Is he okay?'

There's hesitation, and I try to get up, but he stops me.

'Rest.'

'For fucksake. Answer me. How's Gelon?'

'Not good, but he's alive. He's lucky. So are you.'

This time I sit up and look around. The roof is low, with slender white points of stone like fangs. It feels like we're in the maw of some giant animal, and I'm confused, to say the least.

'Where are we?'

'One of the caves near the wall. It wasn't safe out there.'

'And Gelon, where the fuck is he?'

'Close. I'll take you to him soon. But drink, you have a fever.'

I am shivering, but with the pain, I hadn't noticed so much, and I drink the wine he sprays at me, feel its warmth spreading, and the pounding in the skull eases a little.

'Tell me then. What the fuck happened?'

Paches puts his face in his hands and scratches his cheeks, a kind of low moan through the fingers, but when the hands come away, there are no tears, and his voice is steady. Biton and the others killed almost all the cast. He only survived by pretending to be dead. Gelon would have been killed if it weren't for the kids who huddled around him, and in a sense, you could say they saved us all because it was only when Biton struck Dares, not with a club but with his hand, that some in the audience intervened. It was one thing hitting Athenians, but Syracusan children were another matter.

'The kids are okay?'

'A few bruises, but yes.'

'Thank fuck for that. Well, I'll have to get them some sweets.'

'You know, it was Alcar and Linar who saved you.'

'Alcar? A drink then. I owe him a drink. Linar will get triple rations.'

Paches shakes his head and looks at the ground.

'Eh, when Linar pulled them off you, they went for him. Then Alcar tried to save you both, and I'm sorry, but they kicked him to death. Linar too.'

'Oh.'

Paches makes me take a bit of food. He'd been saving some of the bread from the rehearsal feedings, and he removes a chunk from his stash beneath a rock. It's stale, and my teeth are loose, so I have to soak it in the wine before I chew it. I don't know what to say or think of this news. I didn't know Alcar at all. And Linar I thought was a weirdo. They saved my life and lost their own. Would I have done the same? Not at all. I went in there 'cause of Gelon. Maybe I'd have tried to help Paches, but otherwise, I'd have legged it. What made them risk themselves for the likes of me boggles the mind, and I tell myself that Alcar, at least, didn't know the true danger when he helped. He would have thought being a Syracusan protected him. Yet somehow, I know this isn't the case. Why, I can't rightly say, but I feel it, and the idea that someone would act like that unsettles more than it comforts.

Paches helps me to my feet, and we head out into the quarry proper. It's the edge of the night – the sky more bruised than black – and the ground is shivering with rats. The thickness of the crocs gives decent protection, but there are so many that you still feel the feathery swish of their tails on your ankles. Paches can see better than me, or else he just knows the quarry so well he can navigate by instinct, and often he'll say watch out when all I see is just a different shade of darkness. I'm trembling proper now, and Paches tells me to stop. He takes off what he's wearing and puts it on me. It's Helen's robe and a flowing thing; I huddle into the folds of fabric, and the shakes ease. On we go, and the morning whispers of its coming. An orange kindling amongst the navy clouds; above the screeching rats is a scattering of birdsong. It's like we're gaining light with every step, and Paches doesn't need to hold my arm, but he does. There's a wheelbarrow just ahead, something or someone in it.

'Gelon?'

The thing in the wheelbarrow moves, but there's no answer. I try to run now, but it's too much, and I'm reeling, my legs bandy, and I'm stepping on rats. They squeak madly, and I feel their tiny teeth sink into the crocs, and if I fall, this will be bad, but again it's Paches to the rescue, and he holds me up as he kicks them away. It is Gelon in the wheelbarrow. He looks absolutely fucked. His skin is like the sky: violet and navy, with fiery-red flashes where the cuts haven't scabbed over. His lip's busted, and when he breathes, he winces, so I reckon a rib or two are cracked.

'You awake, man?'

Only one eye opens. His right eye is swollen completely shut, and the left's a glob of piercing blue.

'Dares?'

'He's okay. All the kids are okay.'

The single eye blinks rapidly, water trickling down into the open cuts, and he whispers what I think is a prayer of thanks.

'And the others?'

I tell him what Paches told me, and his face crumples, tightens. Under pressure, the few scabs start to crack and open like red eyes and the weeping blood mixes with his tears. He asks for my hand, and I give it to him, but his right arm doesn't move; it just hangs there, limp, from his shoulder.

'That might be broken, man.'

Gelon nods and throws up his left, and I pull him to his feet and then help him down. Paches and I both support him as we walk. I want to get out of here, but Gelon insists on going back to the spot where we did the play. He wants to make sure we haven't missed anyone, and so we stumble from the edge of things towards the heart of the quarry. The backdrop of Troy is still there. The bodies of the chorus strewn around. A lot of them have their masks on, and those who don't, have heads that are smashed in. I wouldn't know who the fuck is who, but Paches points from the masked corpses to the ones that are just bits of skull and, crying, says, 'That's Laches,' or, 'There's Meno.' Gelon is crying too. I'm not. I just feel empty, and wrecked, and I want to go home.

Gelon checks the pulse of each, and only when he's certain that they're all dead does he agree to go.

'Linar,' says Paches, kneeling over a twisted body we missed. A pale horn of bone curves out of dark curls, and the Cassandra mask is still attached, though the wood's cracked. It must have protected the skin, for when I peel it off, the face is remarkably undamaged, and his doe eyes are wide and lovely. Alcar lies a few feet away from him. The grey hair is matted with blood and sunken, the face a glistening ruin. It's almost like they went worse on him 'cause he was Syracusan.

'Has Alcar got any family?'

'No,' says Gelon. 'He lived alone. He has a dog, though.'

'Oh.'

Gelon bends down and picks something up. It's Alcar's aulos, chipped but still intact.

'Can I have it?'

I don't know why I want it. I've no training in music and can't play, but just then, it seems very important to have the thing. Gelon hands it over and, satisfied that everyone is dead, we walk up to the quarry exit. The guard doesn't know what to make of us, all in bits and me in the Helen costume, and it takes a while to convince him we're Syracusan. In the end, he lets us out. Paches waves and shouts something that might be goodbye. I don't know how I'm going to make it back to the city in this state. Gelon's worse, and the two of us wheeze like old men, hock up blood, and clinging to each other for support, reel up the hill and stumble onto the empty road. Only the road's not empty. There's a wagon parked on it, and Alekto's Libyan slave is at the reins.

'Get in the back,' he says.

We get in the back.

'I've been instructed to take you home or, if you wish, to Alekto's. Which do you prefer?'

Neither. Instead, we ride a few miles out to a shack by the beach. Nothing in it but a straw bed, a jug of flowers, and a little sandy terrier on a rope. It whines when I pick it up, then wags its tail when I take out the aulos and put it to its nose. I untie the dog and wrap it in my cloak, and we get in the wagon and drive back to the city.

26.

The big news in the city is the decree. The quarries are going to be opened back up for stoneworks at the end of the month, and the Athenians need to be gone. Where will they go? There are still hundreds of them, and though they don't have much left, they exist, sleeping on good limestone that could be used for building and beautifying the great city of Syracuse, which is too full of wood, a real paucity of stone structures. I didn't see this debate, just heard about it from Ma, who heard about it from the fella she gets her bread from, and at the end of it all came the decree, chilling in its simplicity. Stop feeding the Athenians. Cut their rations completely, and in a couple of weeks, they'll be gone, and we can open the quarries back up and build. Build something that will get the whole world talking. Build a city that's so beautiful it will make all Greece howl with envy, and the Carthaginians cry. It's time to move on. Athens is done. But we're here to stay, and what stays when all else has withered? Stone: stone assemblies, stone courts, stone houses, and yes, the jewel on top of it all, a stone theatre. Not like the wooden shite we have now that splinters in the sun and rots in the rain. A theatre to last a thousand years – and the first step in all of this, the first stone in the foundation of eternity, is simple: stop feeding the Athenians.

Apparently, I'm famous. People are talking about what we did. Two unemployed potters who put on *Medea* in the quarry and a new Euripides that had never been seen before. Surprisingly good, they say, proper strange but not bad considering. Did you see what happened at the end? Biton took it too far, of course, went and killed a Syracusan. If they find him, it will be execution, and that's a shame, 'cause everyone knows Biton's a good fella, just twisted with grief, and he did what he did out of love. Love for his son and Syracuse. I hear all this in dribs and drabs from Ma, who gets it in the market. She tells me in those lucid snatches between dream and delirium, 'cause for near on a week after the show, I'm in bed and only get up to piss or feed Alcar's dog.

Then one morning, something is different. The shakes are gone; the fever too. The dog watches me from the corner. I don't even know its name, so I just call it dog. When I say Alcar, its ear twitches and there's a faint fluttering of the tail. I get out of bed, and it hurts to walk, but at least my legs move, and I limp into the kitchen, clean the fetid tang from my mouth with wine, and then into Ma's room. She must be at work 'cause the bed's empty, and I check out the damage in the bronze mirror she keeps in the corner. The bruises on my cheeks are greenish, but the cuts have healed well. The nose is fucked, though. I always had a dainty, straight little nose, and now it's flat and round as a beach stone. I look like a boxer – a shit boxer but a boxer nonetheless – and I smile at this, note the absence of a tooth in the bottom row. There's character in this face. I hope.

People stare at me on the street, and there are whispers. It's not the face, 'cause there are loads in Syracuse with far worse scars than these. No, it's what I did. What Gelon and I did. The mad bastards who put on a show in the quarry with fucking Athenians. Did you hear what happened at the end?

I've always wanted to be famous. To be watched and discussed. Now it's come, and I want to go back to what I was. The Lampo who blended in with the city and was a piece unnoticed, and I feel the wet leak of blood from my nose, and it falls on the road as I walk, moistens the dust. The dog whines beside me, goes to lick it, and I push on till I get to Gelon's.

He's still in bed, and the room has the same fever-reek as my own but more intense. I ask him how he is, and he tells me that he'll live.

Then I say, 'You hear about the decree?'

He hasn't, and I tell him.

'What do we do now?'

The dog barks and licks Gelon's wrist, but still no answer.

'Come on, man. What should we do?'

'Nothing,' he says. 'There's nothing we can do.'

I don't know what I'd expected, but this isn't it, and I tell him as much. He looks at me; the sun through the window illumi-nates his face, and it's a wreck. The right eye is still swollen shut, and his cheeks are gaudy with colourful bruises, the lips cracked, and there's a crooked tilt to his jaw as if the hinge of the bone is loose. You'd need a proper imagination to recog-nize the face was once beautiful. Still, all of this is nothing to the desolation in that one open blue eye. It blinks rapidly. Gelon was never what you'd call jolly, but I haven't seen an expression like this since the days after his Helios died. There's nothing in that eye but its colour, and I reach out and take his hand.

'Come on, man. We get things done. We're directors. Remem-ber?'

A grimace.

'Never mind how it ended. Those plays were cracking, and we did something that should have been impossible. We can do this.'

'Do what?' There's no curiosity in his voice, just exhaustion.

'Save them,' I says. 'Save Paches. We have to try.'

A laugh now. A hollow, bitter laugh, unpleasant as meat on the turn, and it clearly hurts him 'cause he holds his ribs.

'Fucking Paches. It's over, Lampo. You think the guards will just let you take him out? That's a capital offence. No one cared what we did with them as long as they stayed in the quarry, but try to bring one with you, and you'll see what happens. They'll kill you this time.'

'You won't help?'

The single blue eye moistens, and I think this is it. Of course he'll help: Gelon and Lampo, liberators of the Athenians, known from song and story.

'No, I won't. I'm sorry, Lampo. But I can't.'

'Grand so.'

I go to leave but halt at the door. Gelon's watching. He wants me to say it's alright and that I understand. Reckon that's what I'll do, and I open my mouth to oblige. All the sourness that's been festering pops like a blister and oozes out, the words salty from the cuts in my gums. I tell him it's his fault Numa, Linar, Alcar and the others were killed. It's probably even his fault they're scrapping the Athenians' rations and opening up the quarry. The show got everyone talking about them again. It was a stupid fucking idea and could only end one way. We're just lucky the children made it out alive. He's a selfish prick and always has been, and I'm glad he's not going to help, 'cause everything he touches dies, and would he ever fuck off and do the same?

Gelon says nothing. The wet blue eye blinks, then shuts, and he rolls onto his side.

27.

It's still in the docks. Moored in the merchants' quarter, right at the end, with the battering ram twinkling like some greenish star and the dodgy-looking crew sat about the deck doing fuck all. I climb the ladder, and immediately they're on their feet, tense as fists – no sailors' knots in their hands, just glinting blades, and I think I might have made a serious error of judgement, but then one of them laughs and slaps me hard on the back.

'Ah, the director. Don't worry, boys. He's harmless.'

It's the tall fella with the scar on his throat like a scarlet mouth.

'Listen, I need to speak with him.'

The tall fella pulls out a wineskin and offers it to me. I take a bare sip 'cause I want my wits about me. Behind him, the hatch that leads below deck is open.

'It's important,' says I. 'Please.'

He shakes his head with sorrowful patience.

'Got strict instructions not to disturb him. Now, if I go down there, he's liable to be mean.'

'I'll pay.'

He frowns at the silver in my extended palm and looks at the others.

'Think I accept bribes? Fuck off now.'

I turn as if to leave but don't. Instead, I leg it past him and jump down the hole into the bowels of the ship, tumbling into darkness and smacking my shoulder against wood. The pain is blinding, and I curse and crawl to the first door, pull it open. It's empty. The second door. Empty. I scramble for the third, but someone grabs me, and I'm smashed against the wall. It's the fella with the throat scar, and he's shouting in some tongue incomprehensible, spittle on my cheeks, but I get the gist, and I shut my eyes, too wrecked to fight back, resigned for whatever is coming, when I hear a familiar voice behind.

'Leave him.'

Tuireann's standing at the third door – the one where Gelon saw the god. He closes that door carefully and takes a step in our direction. I tell him I need to talk. That it's a matter of the utmost importance; he places his finger to his lips, says hush. His hair is loose about his shoulders. It's not the same glossy black but streaked with iron grey, and there's a weariness in his eyes that's new. He opens the second door and beckons me into a dark room, the floor soft with rugs.

'I can't see much.'

'Oh.'

A rap of knuckles on a wall, and I hear a click, followed by wheezing and fumbling in the corner. A lamp bursts into life, its orange flame sputtering smoke and sinewy light around the room, and I see all the things I saw the last time: the plush couches, scarlet rugs, wall paintings. I see the ancient servant, too, standing there, holding a tray in trembling arms as the cups on it rattle.

'Wine, sir?'

'No, thanks.'

'Leave us.'

The old servant and the fella with the sliced throat get out, and it's just the two of us, alone, and I think this is not a great idea.

'Your production was incredible.'

I start at that. He's not reclining like last time but leaning forward, earnest, hands clasped together.

'You saw it?'

'Of course. What kind of a producer do you take me for?'

'Then you saw the end.'

'Shocking, my condolences.' His voice lowers. 'That second play, what was it called?'

'*The Trojan Women.*'

'*The Trojan Women*? The finest I've ever seen . . .' He hesitates. 'Once, something very much like that happened.'

'War, sure it happens all the time.'

He smiles sadly and nods.

'Yes, it does. It truly does. But this happened in another world entirely. Not the dusty plains of Ilium, nor Syracuse. No, it was in a land of rain and woods, a green-growing world, but yet it happened in almost exactly the same way. The hearts of men are alike wherever you go. The rest is scenery.' He stands up and then sits right back down. 'What did they call the boy? The one thrown from the tower?'

'Astyanax.'

'A haunting piece. I knew a boy like Astyanax once. Only he didn't die. His father died. His brothers and sisters too. Everyone he ever loved died, except his mother. She was taken away, probably to be fucked by the very men who killed her children. But the boy survived. He sometimes wished that he hadn't, but for some reason, the life in him was persistent, like those weeds that grow in the most inhospitable of places. The boy grew rich, and they say the things he's seen and done, well, they are beyond belief. They say he still lives.'

'Reckon they're right about that.'

Tuireann smiles.

'Now, what is it you want to talk about?'

I tell him everything. About the decree and how the quarry will be open by the end of the month, and I have a mate, an Athenian mate, who I'm going to save. Him and more, if I can.

'What does Gelon think of this?'

My first instinct is to lie, but I see the intelligence in the dark eyes, and of course I know that will do no good. The only way with this fella is to lay it out straight, come what may.

'He thinks I'm nuts. He won't help.'

Tuireann nods, and again I'm struck by the sense that nothing I've told him is news. Still, his face is earnest. No trace of the usual irony. Whether it's an act or not, he seems to actually give a shit, and I think to myself, he might just help you, and only then do I say it plainly. 'Please fucking help me.'

'How? How exactly am I to help?'

The words tumble out. Hearing them, I see that it's not a plan at all so much as desperate hope, a bit of delirium concocted in those nights of fever after the show. Tuireann doesn't laugh; he just listens, and for that, I'm grateful. When it's all out, he raps his knuckles on the wall, and out of the mouth of the Hydra emerges the old man, gripping his rattling tray.

'Drink.'

'Not thirsty.'

'Please drink with me.'

The old man fills two goblets with dark ooze. It's the stuff we had that night in Dismas'. Tuireann proposes a toast and then whispers something in a language I don't recognize.

'If one of my directors were to come and ask me this, I'd have bet it would be Gelon. You surprise me. What's your name again?'

'Lampo.'

'I want to help you, Lampo. Do you believe that?'

'Yeah.'

'Good, because it's the truth. I misjudged you. I see that now, so believe me when I say this, I want to help, but what you suggest is impossible.'

I take a long pull of the black stuff, and the heat of it brings tears to my eyes, and there's a salty sting on my scabs; the little cuts in my mouth burn. His eyes don't leave my face.

'This ship has – how shall we say? – things on it. Things that would make its being searched most inconvenient. I simply cannot take the risk. You know your city. These docks are busy at all hours. Let us imagine that you get your friends out. What will people think when they see you and your chained comrades strolling through the docks and onto this ship?'

'Please. They'll die if we don't.'

'They'll die if we do. Just a little later.'

He stands up and rubs his hands through his hair, and there are black stains on his fingers. He sees me see them, and the smile returns.

'Vanity, I know. My original hair wasn't even black, but red. It is hard to dye convincing red hair, though. And now, I must ask you to leave. See, it is a particularly inconvenient time. Our ship is sailing tomorrow morning. My work here is done.'

'What work?'

He winks and puts his fingers to his lips, and says hush. The irony is back, and I see that he's laughing at me again. Perhaps he always was.

'Fuck you.'

I drain the goblet and drop it to the floor, get up to go, but he's a quick bastard, and he's already up and has slid in front of the door, blocking my path.

'Hyccara.'

'What?'

'Hyccara,' he whispers again. 'That's where our ship will be, two nights from now. From there, we leave Sicily and sail for Carthage. After that, it's mainland Greece. I can't let them board this ship in Syracuse, but if you can get them to Hyccara, I promise you I will.'

Hyccara's fucking ages away. It would take a week just to

walk it, and I tell him as much. He shrugs and sits back down, leans against the wall, and there's something dark and wispy nailed there. It hangs down past his ear like a snake's tail, but it's not a snake. It's a bit of rope, and I recognize it.

'The old man sold it in the end?'

Tuireann doesn't answer. He just drinks and looks up, surprised that I'm still there.

'Good luck,' he says. 'I don't think I'll see you in Hyccara, but I hope I do. Do you believe that?'

'I don't know.'

He gestures for me to leave, and I go. No sooner am I out the door than he starts to sing. The words are familiar. It's a song from *The Trojan Women*, the one Andromache sings to Astyanax just before they throw him off the tower. He knows all the words – or at least he seems to – and sings it well, except for the fact that he's crying. I halt, and some instinct makes me step out of the lamplight and huddle in the shadows as I listen.

Not long after, there's the creaking of hinges, and Tuireann emerges. He's taken off his chiton, and the pallor of his arms and chest don't prepare me for the gaudy madness of his back. Almost every patch of the skin there is lurid with scars; some with the clear puckering of countless brandings, as if he's been bought and sold aplenty. Mostly, though, they're lash marks. I've never seen the like of it. Tuireann's still singing Astyanax's song and fumbling with the lock of the final door. Finally, it opens, and there's a faint pulse of light, almost greenish in hue, like the sun passing through well water, and he steps inside and is gone.

28.

Hyccara's a place I haven't heard mentioned in a long time. Right over at the other end of the island, a fort town the Athenians sacked and razed to the ground. This was in the early days of the invasion, when it seemed they could do no wrong, and the towns fell, one by one, and all Sicily said we should cut a deal before it was too late. The assembly was aching with the need to cut that deal, save the city. And then, whether the gods fancied a change or it was just our time, the Athenians started to lose. Small skirmishes at first, of no real consequence, but each loss, each near-miss took a little bit of their faith away, unspooled a thread of soul so that when the real battles came, the ones that would decide it all, they no longer believed, and you could taste their doubt in the air, like fetid rain on the wind, and the only deal we were interested in was hawking their possessions after total and utter surrender.

What people expect rarely happens. Things which seem impossible come to pass. It's always been the way. The gods have the best seats in town, and we're their favourite show. This view is liable to ruin your buzz if you like what you have, but I don't. Common sense says I'll never get Paches or any other Athenian out of that quarry without being caught, and if by some stretch I do, Hyccara's the other side of the island, a week's walk under wind and rain over shitty roads. They'll die before we make it, and even if we get there, it will be too late, 'cause Tuireann won't wait long, a few days, and he's off to Carthage. But common sense said we should have surrendered two years ago. Common sense is common, has no imagination, and only works by precedent. It leaves the man who follows it poorer, if not in pocket, then in his heart. Fuck common sense.

I'm at Alekto's, scouring the courtyard for the horses and wagon. There's horse shit all around me in dark buzzing heaps, but no sign of the animals. Not a good beginning. If this is to work, the first thing needed is transport. As I said, Hyccara by foot is as good as death. This leaves boat or horse. After leaving Tuireann, I asked a few fishermen how much to sail to Hyccara, but their skiffs are slender and not built for long distance, and anyway, why the fuck would I want to go to Hyccara? It's a ruin. Everybody knows that. 'And look at the sky,' said one, jabbing a finger up at the dark mass roiling above. 'Not a chance.'

Between the weather, my lack of coin, and the weirdness of the destination, none will take me. This is probably for the best 'cause these fishermen are simple folk, and there's every chance, if I succeed and rock up later with Athenians, they'll get spooked and rat me out, and it will be in prison, not Hyccara, I'll end up. Horses it is, and so I walk around Alekto's garden, following a trail of nag shit, in circles.

'Lampo?'

It's the Libyan slave, his head peeking out of the window above me.

'Hey, man, how are things?'

'Good,' he says. 'What are you doing?'

I smile. 'Ah, you know how it is. A bit of this, a bit of that.'

'Yeah, I'll get Alekto.'

'No, don't bother her. Just say I said hello.'

He frowns, then disappears from the window. Fuck that. I go to leave, but Alekto must have been watching from somewhere, 'cause the front door opens, and she steps out and asks me what exactly I find so stimulating about horse manure.

I start waffling about how Ma needs it for her garden. She can't get anything to grow with all this rain, and I catch Alekto's eye and understand that, like with Tuireann, if there's any hope, it's with the truth. She's too clever by half, and I'll need to spill it all, but that will place us both in a bind. When she hears what I say, by law, she must report me. Even telling her is to implicate her. Ma and Alekto were real close when they were young, but they're not young now. Maybe her age will help. Maybe Alekto will figure she's not long left, and it's best to do the right thing, but this is just a wish. Some people don't believe they'll die, not really, and no amount of years and wrinkles will convince them otherwise. I think Alekto is one of those people, and with her, I can't count on whim or impulse. I start to tell her my plan.

'Shut up.'

'Eh?'

Alekto scans the courtyard.

'Get in.'

I get in. There are feathers everywhere, the air throbbing with the heady reek of glue, and on the workbench is an enormous wing, like some dismembered Pegasus, and Alekto's crew are taking feathers from a pile and sliding them into the wing.

'New commission,' says Alekto, 'Aristophanes' *The Birds*. I think your show satiated whatever appetite was left in the city for tragedy. There's going to be a comedy festival all winter. The passion now is for laughter.'

I don't know what to say to this and mutter something even I can't understand. Alekto sits me down and takes out a jug, and pours two cups of cold white.

'Never speak your business in public. That was incredibly stupid.'

'Fair enough.'

'Now, tell me exactly what you want. And don't lie. If you lie, I'll know.'

She would indeed. I tell her the plan, if that's what you'd call it, and she listens, not just with her ears; you get the sense with Alekto that she's listening with every part of her being, noting the movement of your eyes, the way you rest your hands, the little hesitations, or shifts in voice, it's fucking invasive, but I continue till it's all out, and Alekto shakes her head, almost pityingly.

'That won't work.'

'It has to.'

A sigh.

'You think those men will be able to climb up the quarry walls on a rope?'

'No, we'll pull them up. Tie the rope to the wagon and have the horses –'

'My wagon? Correct. My horses?'

'Yeah.'

'And let's say you pull them up, what state do you think they'll be in after being dragged along jagged rock by horses. If the rope doesn't break, their bones will.'

'Then, they die.'

She looks at me then, surprised.

'And that's okay with you?'

It is, and I tell her so. See, if it doesn't work, it's a quick death, and a quick death is better than this slow starving. Yet if, somehow, we make it, then it's life. Maybe years of it, and so I think the risk is pretty low.

Alekto smiles.

'The wagon fits but a few.'

'A few's enough. A few is everything.'

She stands up and walks to the workbench, plucks a feather from the wing, lets it fall.

'The glue mixture is wrong. We'll need to start again . . .'
Then to me, 'Come back tonight. The wagon will be ready.'

'It will? Why?'

A silly response, but I didn't expect a yes. Not really.

'Because you are so very persuasive.' She takes a drink.
'Because I'm an old woman, and I'm bored. Because the quarry
is an evil place, and maybe you're right, a few is everything.'
Another drink. 'Mostly, because you will do it anyway, and
without horses, you'll die, and your mother would be upset.'

I try to hug her, but she pushes me away and tells me to
make myself scarce – they've a wing to finish.

Rope I get in the docks, and it's a rip-off, and back-breaking
heavy, and with all the stops and starts, it takes near on an hour
just to lug it to Alekto's and fling it into the courtyard. I slip
away and head straight for the quarry. The walk is hard-going,
and the pressure of each step makes the welts and bruises on
my legs throb, and I notice that I'm limping on both feet. If this
keeps up, I'll need a stick, a proper old man I'll be, and I sit on
the road a couple of times, wheezing and feeling sorry for
myself.

At the crossroads, I stop and pour some wine on the ground
and say a prayer for Alcar. Then on to the quarry proper, but I
don't go in. Yet. Instead, I walk around the edges, scouting a
good spot for a rope throw. A place where the quarry wall is
relatively smooth, so Paches – and whoever else joins him –
won't get cut to bits when I pull them up. What quickly
becomes abundantly clear is that there's no good spot. The
porousness of the limestone means it's all eroded away, uneven,
with holes and jutting shards. It's not all limestone either.
There's a yellow and blackish stone that blends into the white
like rotten teeth, and I know from a summer stint in the quarry,
years back, that the yellow stone is hard as fuck, wrecks your

pickaxe, never mind your skin. I do a couple of laps, scooting on my belly and carefully examining each stretch of wall, once, twice, but it's no good. I just don't see them making it. I believed what I said to Alekto: yeah, the Athenians might die, but given their current prospects, that seems fairly low risk. The thing is, there's a big difference between might and will. I'm not coming out here in the dead of night just to bash my mate to death and then drive home.

Another lap of the quarry, and still no luck. Then I notice something so big it was easy to miss. The fence. See, the reason we put the Athenians in the quarry, apart from bragging rights, was just that there were so fucking many of them. Nowhere in Sicily, never mind Syracuse, was there a prison big enough to fit the bastards, and to build one would have cost a fortune. The quarries with their deep pits were a ready-made prison, walls of solid rock. The bare minimum of guards would hold it, and absolutely nothing needed to be constructed. Almost. The pits are cavern-deep, except for a little stretch of no more than a few stadia, along the west side of the quarry's edge. Here it wasn't a sheer drop but more of a slope, a gradual incline that a daring prisoner could conceivably make their way up. To cover this, the city built a fence along that stretch, about twenty feet high, a dark wall of trees peeled and sharpened at the top to spikes, fixed into the ground. Really the fence was overkill, more than enough to do the job, and on my laps, I'd only given it a cursory glance. Now, seeing that the cliff climb was death, I decided to examine it properly – take my time, and check out each individual stake. If I'm to kill Paches, then I need to know that I've done my best not to.

I kneel down and begin, and it's as I feared. Each wooden spike must be dug a man's height into the ground 'cause they don't budge even a little. They're packed together, with only a few fingers' width of distance between them. The Athenians have slimmed down during their ordeal, but not that fucking much. Still, I keep checking, more for my conscience than in hope. One by one, I go through those stakes, pushing against them with my shoulder, prodding them for weaknesses, like some carpenter checking out the woodsman's wares. A waste of time, and then the rain starts to fall – and fall hard and heavy. My blue chiton turns black with water, plastered against the skin so close you can see my fucking nipples. A bit of dizziness now, and I have to stop again, take a few bracing sips of the red that I'd brought for Paches. My boots are soggy, the hard soil dissolving to mud, and they sink into it like wet carpet, and I'm sliding now, having to grip and claw at the fence for balance. I go on checking, my teeth chattering so hard I'm expecting one to crack, but they hold up, and then near the end of the fence, something wonderful happens. One of the stakes gives a little as I shoulder it. The rain has loosened the soil, transformed hard earth into squishy clay, and the wood budges a tad. I push at it with everything I have till the veins in my hands are wriggling blue worms, and it moves some more – about a palm's worth of distance between it and the next stake. Not enough. More pushing, and I think one of those worms in my skin will surely burst. No use. It won't go any farther, and a palm is all I'll get. You'd need a fucking horse. Horses. A few strong horses, and you might just be able to widen that gap enough for a starving bastard to squeeze through. It's the longest of shots but better than scaling the quarry walls. If this doesn't work, then at least I won't have killed him.

I take out a pot of olives, also intended for Paches, chuck as many as I can into my gob, and then smash the pot against the stake. It's a terracotta pot, and it leaves a rust-coloured heap of shards so that I'll be able to recognize this spot later on.

A new guard's at the entrance, and he's no interest in wine, only silver, and he fairly cleans me out. Still, I get in, and I'm back down in the quarry for the first time since the show. Once or twice during rehearsal, it had rained, but never like this. This is a storm, and the centre – being wide open – is fairly empty, with most of the Athenians seeking cover over by the walls, in those parts where the rock juts out, giving a bit of shelter. But in others, the quarry walls act more as a kind of waterfall, the rain gushing down, and still, you see Athenians huddling in these spots; they're so drenched and cadaverous, they put you in mind of the Styx and the poor bastards drifting under the ferryman's boat. Starvation has stripped away their ability to improvise, react to what is. The walls should offer protection, and so they remain there, even when reality sings a contrary song. This image of the Athenians, drowning and immobile, disturbs me more than I can account for. I start to shake and ramble around for a while, looking at everything, reaching over and touching the rock piles that house their graves. If all goes well, this is the last time I'll come here. If all goes badly, this is the last time I'll come here. I suck it in. Sentimental and shivering, I walk, and stare, wanting to remember this moment. I feel a hand on my ankle, and I look down, and it's a dying Athenian, pregnant belly, eyes wet and bright with antic colour.

'Mother?' he whispers.

'Nope,' says I.

He doesn't hear me. He's much too far gone.

'Mother,' he says again. 'I'm sorry. I'm so sorry.'

I don't say no this time, just wait and listen, and he starts talking to me like I'm his ma. All this stuff about a farm and how he didn't want to be a farmer. It just wasn't him. He was useless at it, but he'll come and get me. See, he's made good and has a place in Piraeus with a sea view and I'll love it there. He never meant to be away so long, and would I forgive him and come to Piraeus?

'Yeah, I'll come.'

This doesn't satisfy him, though. He wants more, and he's asking me if he's no good, if I still love him.

'Of course I love you,' says I, sobbing. 'Always have. You're my son.'

He smiles at this, squeezes my hand, shocking strength in this vice of bones, and I hold it until it loosens, and he's gone, wherever it is we go. I lean over and kiss him on the head, and some of his hairs are left on my lips. Then I get back up and walk on.

The backdrop for *The Trojan Women* is still there where we left it, propped against the boulder, and the rain streaming down the painted towers and sky gives the scene a dreamlike quality. Other prisoners must have buried the dead 'cause the bodies are gone. The only trace of what happened is the masks scattered around, mostly broken, the wood and paint lambent in the storm so that the mouths and eyes shimmer on the ground, and I feel not at all myself, and call out Paches' name, but no one answers.

He always preferred the quarry walls, the protection of the tunnels, and that's where I go. I peek my head into these tunnels and say his name, and there are Athenians crouching, and they stare out from the dark with wet, bright eyes, but none are green. There are fuckloads of blues, browns and even greys, but none are green. Until one pair is. Slits of green like blades of grass glinting in the rain.

'Paches!'

A twitch and a groan.

'It's me, man. Don't you recognize me? It's Lampo.'

'Eh, Lampo?'

I crawl in, and at first, it's so dark I can barely make out his features, but my eyes adjust fairly quick, and it's a shocking sight. In the week since the show, with the extra rations gone, he's deteriorated fast. The cheeks are hollow again, the eyes sunken, the black hair is flecked with silver, though on closer inspection, this is a cobweb, and I remove it and blow it away. I thought I'd launch straight into it, but he's too fucked for that, and I just pass him the drop of red that's left. The bread in my satchel is mush from the rain, but he tucks in straight away, only stopping to suck the wine and catch his breath; then he starts to puke, and I hold him and pat his back.

'Slow down. Plenty of time.'

He rinses his mouth with booze and goes at the bread again, keeps it down this time, and when he looks at me, his eyes aren't quite so glazed.

'Lampo?' he says again. 'You came back.'

'Of course. We're doing *Oedipus Rex*. Rehearsals start tomorrow. Considering you for the role of Jocasta. A meaty part. What do you say?'

A bad joke and I don't know why I made it. Paches looks like he'll burst into tears, and I tell him, don't worry, was only messing, and he should bear with me as I'm not in great shape either.

'Please, no more plays,' he mutters to himself.

'Told you. Was pulling your leg. Alright?'

He nods and then goes to puke, but doesn't. Outside, the quarry stone is cindery, and it's odd that. The sun was nowhere to be seen all day, just shrouded in clouds, and now that it's setting, all is glistening with a falling glow. I've got to explain the plan now. Make sure he knows before it gets too dark. I tell him everything. About the fence with the loose stake and Alekto's wagon, the ship waiting in Hyccara. A ship that will sail to Athens.

'Stop joking,' he says.

'No jest. It's all true.'

'Stop it!' He sounds angry now, and if he weren't so fucked, I'd be afraid the fella might hit me.

'I won't stop it, man. This is it. I swear on my ma's life. We're going to spring you tonight, so shut up and listen, 'cause there isn't much time.'

I pull him out from the tunnel, and he's reeling. We walk on, and he moves so slow, I seem like a runner from the Olympics in comparison. I point up at the fence, the stakes like tongues of orange flame.

'That's it, man. That's your deus ex fucking machina. You're going to disappear.'

He stumbles, and I have to catch him.

'Paches, you okay?'

He nods and coughs. I twist his head in the direction of the hill, the fence at the summit. Suddenly that hill looks like Mount Olympus, way too high.

'You think you can make it?'

'I don't know.'

'You can. Of course you fucking can. That's nothing. You'll jog up there easy. Right?'

'Yeah.'

I'm starting to feel desperate, and I shout at him. He's going to make it up that hill. But he's got to do it at night so the guards won't notice. I can't help him. I need to head back for the wagon, and I'll be up there on the other side of that fence when the sun goes down, waiting, 'cause he's out of here, Athens bound, and all he needs to do is get his arse up that hill. Do whatever you need to do. Tell a few mates – ones with the strength to help you. We can take as many as the wagon will fit, but we're not leaving without you. Tell them that. He's listening. I think he believes me now, at least.

'How will I know where you are?'

'What?'

'That fence is long. How will I know which part you're behind? I can't be shouting your name.'

This is good. He's reasoning. I've no answer for him, and I reach in my pocket to give him some food instead. There's no food, but in my hand is Alcar's aulos.

'This!' I say desperately.

'I don't understand.'

'See, I'll show you where I am with this. Listen out for this.'

I blow into the pipe and twiddle my fingers, and the din that comes out is a screeching whistle. Shit music, but it's the kind of sound a guard might mistake for a bird, and is certainly better than screaming, 'Over here!'

'You listen for this. Right?'

He nods.

'Remember, get help if you need to. Don't go up until dark, and wait and listen. This is going to happen, alright?'

'Okay.'

I put my arm around him, tousle his hair.

'If I don't make it,' he says, 'I want you to know that I –'

'None of that negativity! You're making it. You're out of here. Now I've got to go. You just get up that hill!'

He tries to say something, but I'm off. Legging it as best I can with two bad legs, back up to the exit and the guard, who's squeezing rain out of his sopping cloak. When he sees me, he grins and says I'm welcome any time.

'Fuck that,' I say. 'You'll never see me again.'

I don't go straight to Alekto's. I should, as the sun has set and the lamps are out, swinging arcs of flame on their hooks, and the bluish stars above. I'm standing outside Dismas'. It's been ages since I've seen her, and the reason is simple and maybe daft, but I might as well say it. What I want to do is a long shot, and it would be of great help to have a god or two on my side.

232

I've poured jugs of wine and prayed till my mouth got dry with pleading. I even toyed with robbing a calf and having a priest kill it in the name of Zeus or whoever the fuck is listening, but I didn't. It struck me that the biggest sacrifice I could make wasn't coin, but not seeing her. To stay away till the job was done. I walk a little closer to the door. The shutters are open, the windows yellow and warm, music and chatter seep out with the light. Someone is singing. I decide I can take a peek. When I said 'see her', I meant to not talk with her, or touch her; to be so close that I could feel the heat and get the spicy scent of her skin. I didn't literally mean I wouldn't see her. The gods aren't pricks. They didn't begrudge Odysseus a glimpse of Penelope before setting out for Troy.

I go in. It's jammed, and the air is hot and soupy. I have to rub my eyes to adjust to the dim, wet lantern light that oozes about the bar; faces glisten with sweat and booze. Everyone's staring in the same direction. At the stage. Lyra is on it, her smock dishevelled so you can see a tanned slope of shoulder. She's singing a song about a girl whose da disappears and her quest to find him. The girl searches all across the city, in every tavern, hotel and alley, but there's no sight or sound of him. And this is where most little girls would give up, but she's not like most, and heads out the main gates into the dark hinterland beyond the city walls, looking for her da, bursting into smoky hovels asking if anyone has seen him, describing him down to his bushy eyebrows, and his orange shoes with the curled toes, but none have seen him. On she goes, farther from the city, exhausted and unsure about the way back. She stumbles on and down to the beach as the sun sinks lower, disappearing into a violet sea, and a ship is moored on the shore, and an old man with a kind grey face explains gently that, yes, her father is on the ship, if she'd just step on and say hello. She steps on. When she steps off, she has a chain about her neck, and everything has switched, the smells in the air, the people's clothes, the language out of their gobs a babble, and the man whispers in her ear as he licks it. This is your new home. You have no home.

Lyra finishes, and most are stunned into silence, save one fella near the stage who stamps his feet and smashes his hands together. She looks about her as if coming out of a trance, says thank you, and then our eyes meet, just a moment, and she puts her hand to her mouth, in shock, and when it comes away, there's this big grin on her face, and her eyes are shining, and I think to myself, yes, fucking yes, that's unmistakable, she's not pretending. I whisper, 'I love you.' Whether she understands or not, I can't say, but she steps off the stage and moves towards me with urgency, squeezing through the crush of bodies, and it takes every bit of will I have to pull myself away 'cause I swore to the gods. Not till this is done. That's the sacrifice, and I wince as I back away from her and out of the bar.

'Lampo!'

It's Lyra. She's gone and followed me out. I keep going, but each step I take feels like someone is cutting into me, and I've half turned around before I stop myself. If I see her now, I know I'll break the promise, and I fairly leg it away, kicking up the sand and pounding the dirt road back to the city proper and Alekto's.

The house is black and shuttered, no lanterns or any other light. Still, the air is rich with the scent of fresh horse shit, and when I step through the gate, it's there, at the back of the courtyard, the wagon all hooked up, nags at the ready, their breath steaming into the night. The Libyan slave's at the reins, rubbing his hands together and blowing on them.

'Chilly,' says I.

'If we get stopped,' he says, 'you kidnapped me and stole the wagon. Is that clear?'

'Of course. Sure, that's the plan anyway.'

I wink and get in the back. The horses set off at a canter, the wagon rattling along. It's dark as an arse in here, and I shut my eyes, and think through the plan again, try to visualize each step, but the blood goes full-on percussion in my skull, and my guts are slithering snakes. I need a fucking drink, badly.

'Any wine, man?' I call out.

Immediately something gets placed in my hands, a goatskin by the feel of it, and I look around. There's another person in here with me, and I let out a cry of fright.

'Alekto?'

'Get that into you,' says Gelon. 'You're shaking.'

I can't see him, on account of the darkness, just make out his general shape, and I reach my hand over, and another hand squeezes it, shocking strong, and I wince.

'I'm sorry,' says I. 'I didn't mean that shit I said. You know?'

'Drink,' he says.

I drink, and we pass it back and forth, not speaking. Gradually my eyes adjust to the darkness, and I can make out his face, and it's still wrecked, encrusted with purplish jewels of bruise and scab, but the eyes are unmistakably his, and I didn't realize till now how fucking alone I felt, how desperate, and I tell him as much, but he says nothing, just listens, and takes a sip from the skin and passes it back.

The wagon stops.

'This is it.'

We step out into the mud. The rain has eased, and it's drizzle now. The sky's bleak. The moon, like a yellow bone being gnawed by jaws of cloud, drips insipid light, and the stars aren't much better.

'Another storm's coming. We need a lantern.'

'Too risky,' says Gelon, and he's right, but I can barely see a thing.

The fence is just a more substantive stretch of dark, and I move towards it, laughing at myself for marking the loose stake with a broken pot. I thought that was clever, but you can see fuck all, and I just plop on my knees and start gripping a random stake and shaking, desperate for a bit of give. The mud here is harder than I'd expected, and the first ten or so that I check don't budge. When one finally does, I have to bite my tongue to stop from yelling out. It's not as loose as the one I'd marked, and there's barely a two fingers' width between this and the next stake, but it will have to do. I whisper and wave, and Gelon joins me. We get right down to it – start digging around the stake, scooping out the muddy soil with little spades like what you'd use gardening, making the hole bigger so that the stake has room to move. Then Gelon begins to push. Even with his injuries, he's way stronger than me, and the wood actually jerks; the gap widens a bit, but not enough.

'Horses.'

'Right.'

I get the rope I bought at the docks. We tie one end around the stake and then the other to an iron join at the back of the wagon, and the Libyan tugs the reins, and the horses move, and the stake totters in the hole, but it's still not enough, and I go over and give the horses a clatter. The Libyan curses me out and says not to touch them; then he starts speaking to the nags, gentle as anything, squeezing the reins at a steady pressure, all the time talking to them, and they pull. They pull till their muscles pump and shine like slugs in rain.

'Just a bit more,' says Gelon.

They're snorting now, and I can see white foam on the gums of one. Not a good sign.

'More.'

The rope is wearing thin, and the horses are snorting madly, and I think this was a stupid plan, and Gelon says, 'Enough.'

I head over to the fence, and there's near a foot gap now. Not enough for a healthy man to get through, but a starving bastard would just about make it.

'Cheers.'

The Libyan doesn't say anything. He's checking on the horses, rubbing the spit from their mouths, and trying to get them to drink from his own waterskin, cooing at them like a mother with her child.

I stick my head through the gap for a peek. It's too dark, and I can't really make out anything, just the general crescent shape of the quarry whose white stone picks up the scant light in the sky better than anything living. There are hundreds of Athenians in there, probably snoozing, but I can neither see nor hear them, though the scurrying of rats is loud as ever. I blow into Alcar's aulos – a low whistling sound follows, like a sick bird, and Gelon grabs it out of my hand.

'What the fuck are you doing?'

I explain, and he shakes his head as if it's the stupidest thing he's ever heard, but he blows into it anyway. If mine was a sick bird, his one is Hades bound, and what comes out is the frailest of squeaks.

'My ribs are cracked,' he says, handing it back.

I take a drowning man's gulp of air and blow into the fucker with everything I've got. The aulos rings out across the quarry, properly loud now, louder than any real bird, but with the wind and the rain, it might pass. I play – though, of course, you couldn't really call what I'm doing playing – but it clashes with the scurrying of rats, their awful screeching, and in my mind, those rats aren't just rats, they're everything in the world that's broken. They're things falling apart, and the part of you that wants them to. They're the Athenians burning Hyccara, and the Syracusans chucking those Athenians into the quarry. They're the invisible disease that ate away at the insides of little Helios till he couldn't walk or, in the end, even speak, just cry with the pain. Those rats are the worst of everything under an indifferent sky, but the sound coming from the aulos, frail as it might be in comparison, well, that's us, I say to myself, that's us giving it a go, it's us building shit, and singing songs, and cooking food, it's kisses, and stories told over a winter fire, it's decency, and all we'll ever have to give, I say to myself, as my lungs burn and my eyes water, 'cause I don't have much left, but I keep blowing away at the aulos, playing my song, but the rats are as loud as ever, and this is madness, I'm pouring water in the desert, hoping flowers grow, what does it even matter if a few do, we're fucked, and the music stops. Gelon's taken the aulos, and I'm too spent to protest. I feel hollowed. He's pointing at the gap in the fence, or really, a pale arm reaching out of that gap, followed by a head.

'Paches?'

The head doesn't answer, just grunts, and the pale arms clutch at the ground, try to pull the body through. I go over to help.

'You made it.'

'Thank you!' says a strange voice.

'Who the fuck are you?'

'Cephalus,' he says. 'Thank you so much.'

'Where's Paches?'

The fella shakes his head and coughs.

'He collapsed . . .' another cough. 'Halfway up the hill.'

I grab him by the throat, and he's gasping.

'Listen, you prick. I'm here for Paches. You want to come with us, you've got to bring him with you. Get the fuck back in there.'

I push his head back through the fence, and he moans and

starts begging to be let out. He says Paches and him are mates, and Paches wanted me to take him. There's no way he'll be able to get him up that hill. It will be both of them who die, and what good is that?

'He's right,' says Gelon. 'Let him out.'

Of all the ways I saw this going, this is not it. If we get caught by the city patrol, we're fucked, and I'm not risking prison for some random Athenian prick. Am I?

I give him my hand and pull him out. He's on his knees thanking me, then Gelon. This is the right thing. Surely. I'm saving lives. It doesn't feel right. It feels like absolute shit. I push him away and go to the fence.

'Lampo?'

'Fuck off.'

I try to squeeze through the gap. I'm a skinny bastard, and I push and squeeze till the wood tears the skin from my belly and ribs like peel from a fruit, and I can feel the hot slickness of my own blood, but there's no way I'm getting through. A child would barely do it. These Athenians are skinnier than children.

'For fucksake. We can't go without him.'

'We have to,' says Gelon. 'The guards could come.'

Another pale arm reaches out, and I grab it.

'Paches?'

'Eh, no, but Paches wanted you to take me.'

This is too much, and I push the bastard back through the gap, hear him tumbling a bit.

'No, these pricks have to try. I'm not saving randomers and leaving him to die. I'm not doing it, man.'

'How? They're half dead. They can't carry a man.'

I untie the rope from the stake. For extra length, I tell the Libyan to do the same on the wagon side. A hand is reaching out, and like with the other fella, its owner is begging to be let out. Talking about his family back in Athens and how close he and Paches were.

'I'll get you back to Athens,' says I.

He starts sputtering thanks and again goes to pull himself out, but I push him back in and throw the rope after him.

'You can't carry him. Fair enough, but if he's halfway up the hill, you tie a knot around his fucking waist and come back up here, and we'll do the pulling.'

The Athenian is crying now, naming all the gods, and swearing by each that he's a pious man and a father.

'Good stuff. Now get back down there and find me Paches.'

He disappears. While we're waiting, other heads pop out through the gap and plead. To them all, I say the same thing. They will get out with Paches, or not at all. Gelon's not impressed. I can't see his face, but I can hear it in his short, sharp disapproving breaths. The next fella insists he was in the chorus: Antikles, surely we remember? All I make out is the silvery glint of his beard. Gelon reefs him out, and I step back in, quick, to block the rest. We've been waiting for a long fucking time now. I blow at the aulos in case they got lost, but still nothing. Then something. The rope stretching through the gap twitches, and a panting Athenian stutters that he's done his best and thinks the knot is tight. I let him pass, and he collapses on the ground, kissing it.

I pull, and there's definitely something at the end of that rope, fairly heavy.

'A bit of help.'

Gelon takes hold of it too, and together we pull. You wouldn't think this would be hard, given how starved Paches is, but Gelon's busted up, and I'm not much better, and it's very fucking hard and takes a long time, but at last, all the rope has been pulled up and something thuds against the fence. I rush over, and grab a head through the gap. It's still too dark to see the face clearly, and anyway, it's covered in mud.

'Paches?'

No answer.

'Paches, it's Lampo. Is that you, man?'

Still nothing. The body is pretty cold, but it's a cold, wet night, so maybe. I pull him out, gently as I can.

'Is that him?'

'Don't know.'

Gelon picks him up and carries him over to the wagon, puts him in the back. It's just some randomer. I know it. The Athenian probably grabbed the first dead body he found on the hill. I feel sick. More of them are coming through the fence, clawing at the soil when they spill out, as if to check that it's real, then they crawl over to the wagon. I don't help them, but I don't try to stop them either. The wagon is packed now, no room for anyone else, and it's time to leave. I move about in a daze, and I can see Athenians still squeezing out, pale hands bursting through the darkness.

'We have to go,' says Gelon. 'We have to fucking go.'

'Alright, alright.'

I walk up to the gap in the fence. Hands are clutching at me, heads pleading.

'Are you Paches?' I ask them all.

They say no. That's not true. One fella swears he is, but it's not Paches, and I push him away, tell the rest that I'm sorry, but our wagon is full, and I hope they find a way home, and they lunge at me, but weak as they are I push them off easy, and leg it into the wagon. The fella who's meant to be Paches still isn't moving. I hold his head in my arms and listen out for a breath. The wagon sets off, and the Athenians by the fence are begging us to stop, wailing about wives and children, but we don't stop.

We won't stop again till Hyccara.

29.

We take the exit through Victory Gate. It's still so dark in here that I can't make out the features of the face I'm touching. The nose feels small, straight and dainty, like Paches', and the hair is about the right length, and tufts come away in my fingers, but that would be the same with any of the Athenians. They're all in bits. I can feel their spindly bones jabbing into my back, taste the moist deathly tang of their breath. I try to push them away so that whoever it is I'm holding has space to breathe. He's alive. I think. I've got my hand where I reckon his heart should be, and there seems to be something fluttering un-evenly beneath ribs, like a bird with broken wings flapping through a storm, but it's there.

'Paches?'

Nothing. I pour some wine on his forehead and cheeks, and it just rolls off him, not even a twitch. It sounds like one of the Athenians is licking the spilt red from the wagon floor, lapping like a parched dog. We're outside the city limits now, into proper farmland. You can hear the braying of sheep, the low-ing of a cow, but no human din. Thank fuck. This is still technically Syracuse, but we're in the hinterland now, just a bit farther, and we're out. The safest way is to take the back roads and stay out of sight, but we don't have time for that. Two days to make it to Hyccara before Tuireann sets sail. It flits across my mind that it's all a load of bollix. He was just toying with me, and we'll find nothing there but the ruin of a town and the empty sea. I push this thought away, and grin in the darkness.

'All set for Athens, lads?'

'Yeah,' croaks an Athenian beside me.

'In a week or two, you boys will be sipping cool white in the agora, listening to speeches in the Pnyx. Maybe catching a show. Right?'

'My daughter,' says one tearfully, 'I hope she's okay. I'm so worried about her.'

'Liven up!' I don't know why, but him saying 'I hope' just pissed me off. 'Of course she's fucking okay. She's great. Your daughter's a stunner, and all the lads are smitten. She's just waiting for you to come back so she can pick one.'

'She's nine.'

'Going on twenty.'

'Lampo, be quiet.'

'No, man. We're saving their skins, and it feels like a funeral. Where's the buzz? We're –'

Gelon covers my mouth, hisses into my ear.

'Hear that?'

I hear nothing but his question, and I'd tell him as much if he'd take his hand away.

'Listen.'

This time I hear it. The sound of horses' hooves ahead, a man's voice calling out.

'Border patrol,' says the Libyan from the reins. 'What should I do?'

'Stop right there,' says a man's voice, closer now.

The Libyan doesn't ask us again. He stops, and the wagon screeches to a halt; the horses kick out and neigh. The patrolman must be carrying a lantern, as the canvas of the wagon glows with a yellow light that edges towards the back with the squelching of the patrolman's boots, and I see the Athenians, men that till this moment had remained hidden, gaunt and ragged, eyes blind with terror, and I look down at the face I hold in my hands, and it's Paches. I pull back the lids to be sure,

244

and the eyes are lizard-green. It's him. Thank fuck, but the relief is short-lived. The flap at the back opens, and the patrolman stands in front of us. The naked flame in the lantern seems impossibly bright after all the darkness, and I rub my eyes. The patrolman takes a step back. I can see him now, and he's a middle-aged fella with a tired face, a greying beard that sparkles from the drizzle. He holds the lantern up in a fist lively with scars, and in his other hand, he grips a sword. His eyes take us in: the Athenians with chains still around their ankles. Gelon and me in normal clothes but busted up.

'We're slavers,' says Gelon.

'Yeah,' says I, 'delivering these cunts to Catana.'

The patrolman says nothing, just stares. The grip on his sword tightens, and I see that this is the end. He understands exactly what's happening.

'I know you,' he says to Gelon.

'Don't think so.'

The patrolman raises the lantern, so the full weight of its light pounds Gelon's face like a hammer.

'You were the one at the play. That play in the quarry. You introduced it.'

Gelon says nothing. The patrolman looks around, tilting the lantern to the Athenians cowering, at me holding Paches in my arms.

'Did these act in it? Are these the ones that survived?'

'What play?' says I. 'We're slavers and –'

'They did,' says Gelon.

The patrolman shakes his head, and it seems to me that he doesn't know what it is he will say and do, and then he sighs, looks up at the sky.

'A bad night for travelling. You best be on your way.'

With that, he closes the flap of the wagon and walks off. We listen to the wet crunch of his boots and then the galloping hoof music of his horse over the hills, and I turn to Gelon. Maybe it's the creep of morning, or I'm just getting used to the dark, but I can see his bruised cheeks, and I says, 'What was up with him?'

Gelon frowns, but it's like the guard's lantern has left a bit of its light in Gelon's eyes; his cheeks, though still dark and bruised, are brighter than before. The wagon starts to move at a cracking pace so that the spokes rattle and the horses gasp, but it does the trick, and in no time at all, we've left Syracuse behind us, are out in no-man's-land on a road that I hope leads to Hyccara.

But there's no direct road, nor any clear, defined route. Why would there be? Hyccara was never more than a fort town at the top of the island. People didn't talk about it much until it disappeared, and even then, it wasn't really Hyccara they were talking about, but the Athenians – what they were capable of and what was at stake if we lost this war. It was a warning and nothing else. When I tell the lads in the wagon where it is we're going, they all look frightened, confused. Is it some cruel joke I'm playing on them? I press them for details of what exactly happened in Hyccara, but they won't talk about it.

We stop off at taverns for supplies and directions. The supplies are available for coin, but no one seems very sure about which way to go – the best we can come up with is from a cobbler who tells us to take the road to Catana and then ask from there, and that's what we do. The rest all passes in a kind of fever dream, and though the journey is only the guts of two days, it feels like we're in that wagon for weeks. Time loosens, and the sweltering darkness, the stench, it all gets too much, and in the end, I have to cut a hole in the canvas to let some air in. This is a risk, of course, as the weather is shite; drizzle and freezing winds come in through that hole, but my mind clears, and it means a great deal to be able to look out and see the landscape change. I've never been but a couple of miles from Syracuse before, and am now traversing the island, and it's mad to see how much lusher things get in the centre. There are forests, and wheatfields of shivering gold, gleaming temples on cliffs so close to the edge they almost hover above the sea, and mountains too, blue snow on their peaks. Shocking variety to this island, and I drink it in with my eyes and promise that I'll take Lyra to see this stuff, 'cause it's fucking beautiful.

Paches wakes up near Centoripa. He's out of it at first, just saying the same name, 'Philo', over and over.

'Anyone called Philo in here?'

They all say no. Then the fella with the silver beard mutters something. He's not Antikles from the chorus. I see that now; the face is different, more angular, the beard still has blond in it. He was lying to save his skin. Biton and the rest must have killed them all.

'What was that?' I ask.

'Ah, don't mind him,' croaks the fella. 'Philo's long dead. He and Paches shared a tent in the war. Even in the quarry, they found a tunnel and wanted it all to themselves. You'd hear them laughing away, as if there could be anything funny in those pits.'

I feel Paches move beneath me, and when I look down, the eyelids are fluttering. I give him some water. He's so weak he can only take little tiny sips, and it's almost like feeding a child, and I think if he's going to make it, I need to get some food in him, but he's barely able to chew, and I soak the bread in wine till it softens to mush and feed it to him in soggy violet crumbs. I spend so much time in the nursing of Paches that I'm no help at all when it comes to navigating the route, and it's Gelon and the Libyan who do the real work. If we make it to Hyccara and the Athenians are saved, it will be them that do it. On the second morning, I get out to stretch my legs and take a piss.

We're on a dirt road surrounded by woods in the middle of nowhere. There's not even a shack, or any sheep, nothing to give the sense that men have made a dent here, save the road, which is silvery with frosted grass sprouting through the soil, and probably won't be a road for long, just a frailer part of the woods. The horses are in terrible shape. The hoof of one is cracked, with blood weeping from it, and the eyes of both are infected, their lips sudsy with froth that the Libyan wipes away with his sleeve, then cleans the gunk from their eyes, and kisses each on the head.

'How much farther?' I ask.

He doesn't know.

'Will we make it? Today's the final day.'

He doesn't know that either. We give the Athenians their rations, take them out to do their business, but apart from one fella, none of them can go. It's like their bodies are sucking everything we give them in, holding it there in case the supply ends, and their skin has a weird swollen look, and it's unsettling how they manage to look starved yet ready to burst.

The dirt road leads up a hill, and rising above it, in the distance, is a mountain, black and gold, and the peak is shrouded in mist.

Gelon points at it with a stick of bread and says, 'We're close. Behind that mountain are the sea and Hyccara.'

'Best be going, so.'

We hop back in, and it's a furious pace from then on. Everyone is gripped with it, and even the Athenians urge the Libyan to go faster, push harder, and he listens, 'cause this is it. The horses are whinnying madly. They sound terrified, and someone mutters about wolves, but something tells me it's not what's out there that frightens them. It's what's inside. They're dying and know it. The pace slackens, and the wagon swerves a little. You can tell the poor bastards are stumbling, and it seems any moment now they're going to collapse and leave us stranded on a desolate road, but they don't. The horses keep going, drag us up a hill of ridiculous steepness, and the Libyan lets out a yell of triumph.

The wagon halts. Gelon gets out, and I follow with Paches leaning on me. One of the horses takes a knee and is shaking its head from side to side as if to ward off flies, but there are no flies. The Libyan's not yelling any more. He's tending to the sick horse, stroking its ears, and trying to get it to drink. Below us is the sea, and it glows gorily in the sinking sun. The mist around it gives the impression of steam rising from winter wounds, and it's freezing, and I have to stamp my feet to get sensation back in the toes.

'There!'

The sea fog obscures much, but I squint and gradually see what looks like a walled town with towers and battlements at the very edge of things, almost unto the sea itself. The town is black. Even in the giddy evening light, it's no other colour, a hole in the world, and behind me, I hear the clinking of chains as the Athenians step out, and though I know the answer, I ask Paches if this is Hyccara, and he says it is and turns away.

30.

The horses collapsed, and the rest of the journey is on foot, not long at all really, and it's downhill, and though once or twice Gelon and I have to stop and pick up a toppling Athenian or wait for them to catch their breath, they make it okay. The Libyan stayed at the wagon with the horses, but he gave us a lantern, and the fire is welcome as much for the heat as the light. We're right down by the walls now, at the gates of the town, but we haven't entered yet. The walls are stone and not very tall. Nowhere near tall enough for their purpose, and all charred black. The gates, what little remain, are black, and the streets visible through those shattered gates are black too. This makes the thing in front of us all the more startling. A plinth about ten feet high heaped with glittering shields, helmets, spear points, and at its top a bronze dish with the head of a goddess – I reckon Athena. There's an inscription at the base.

'What's it say?'

'Hard to make out,' says Paches.

I know he's lying, so I ask again.

'It reads –' he looks about him – 'it reads, "This trophy is to commemorate the Athenians' great victory over the barbarians of Hyccara. The first step in the liberation of Sicily."'

'Do you remember it?'

Paches nods.

I want to ask more, but night is almost here – the moon thickening above us – and there's no time to reminisce, so we press on past the trophy, through the hole in the gates, and into Hyccara.

'You boys weren't messing around.'

The Athenians say nothing.

Everything is charred to a crisp blackness yet, oddly, you can still make out the general shape of things, the streets and houses; they're all still there. You look in through burnt windows and see, amongst the piles of ash: beds, chairs, and even a kid's doll. If someone wanted to, they could rebuild this place and know exactly what to do. The streets are narrow, and walking on through them stains your clothes and boots with ash. The smell in the air is curious. It's still smoky. Hyccara was sacked more than two years ago now, and somehow that odour lingers, overwhelming the salty scent of the sea, which must be close, 'cause I can hear it, waves crashing not far in the distance, but all I can smell is the reek of a long-dead fire. It gives me the creeps, and I want to get out of here. The Athenians are the same, almost jogging in their chains, setting a pace I didn't think them capable of, and strangely, they seem to know the way. When I go to make a turn, one of them grabs my arm and says, 'No, the harbour is up there.' He fucking remembers. We head up there, and he's right, 'cause after squeezing through an alley of ash, we spill onto a wide-open space, and I can breathe again, my nose filled with sea air, and it's night-time now, and the water is black too, but a glistering black like ringlets in dark flowing hair. Steps lead down to a tiny harbour, a tenth the size of the one back home, and moored there is a single ship.

The Athenians start cheering and beating their breasts, and even I join in a little, 'cause it's only seeing it now, docked and undeniable, that I realize I didn't think he'd be here. I never believed. I just needed to, which isn't the same. I take Paches' arm and help him down the steps, which are slimy and treacherous with seaweed, and we make our way towards the ship. The deck glows with the wobbly light of lanterns, and there's music rising from the ship. Within it, I think I hear a woman's voice, then the wind starts to howl, and one of the lanterns swings from its hook and cracks, and the music stops. There are men up there, not lounging like usual but busy, tossing rope and scrubbing the deck. So focused on their toil, they don't notice us till we're right below them, and I'm shouting up that we've come and need to speak to their master.

Straight away, one of the sailors stops what he's doing and slides down the ladder. It's the fella with the wounded throat. He's all smiles today and claps me on the back as if we're mates, looks at the Athenians and shakes his head in disbelief.

'Poor bastards,' he says in that ruined voice. 'They don't look like they should be standing.'

'They'll need food,' says I. 'Rest.'

'Rations and work duties aren't my decision.' He shouts up. 'Get the master! Tell him they made it.'

We wait. The planks of the harbour are packed thick with sheaths of glossy ice, and I know that it's fucking cold, but somehow I can't feel it. All I feel is the blood bubbling in me and a sense that this is it, whatever it is. Tuireann has come out, wrapped tightly in furs, and he's looking down at us, at the Athenians. He's definitely surprised, but not so much as the crew, and he tells me to start getting them on board, 'cause they need to be going.

Getting them on board is not as simple as it sounds and takes a long time, as the Athenians keep falling off the ladder, and Gelon and I have to go behind them, pushing them up by the arse, with the ship's crew on top pulling. Paches can't manage at all, and has to be hoisted up with ropes. When we're all on deck, the Athenians pretty much collapse. Amidst the crew, there's a fella with one arm, struggling to tie a knot. When he looks up I see a horse branded on his head.

'You bought Chabrias?'

Tuireann doesn't seem to hear me – is too busy giving orders. 'Boil some stew,' he says quickly. 'Cloaks for every one of them.' He turns to Gelon. 'You came? Well, this is a pleasant surprise.'

Gelon mumbles something and keeps his distance.

'And you,' he turns to me. 'I must say, I did not think you would be here.'

'Fancied a change of scenery.'

His eyes widen at this, and he reaches over and takes my hand.

'Do you? Really.'

'Eh.'

'You know you are welcome on this ship. I will pay you very well. Would you like to see the world?'

This is a shock, as I didn't think Tuireann liked me very much, but it's an easy decision.

'No, thanks.'

That should settle it, but he grips tighter and asks again, an odd intensity this time.

'Are you sure? I believe you would be happy with us. I really do. Think of it, the world: Carthage, the pyramids of Egypt, Babylon, Lydia, Athens?'

At the mention of Lydia, I start, but the answer remains the same, and I thank him, tell him he's sound, but Syracuse is my home, and I have work to do, a life to build.

Tuireann looks genuinely disappointed, but he shrugs as if that's all he can do.

'Well, remember that I asked. Now, we really must be on our way.' He turns and walks to the hatch that leads below deck, but stops. 'I do not think we shall ever see each other again. I feel that with a strange certainty. You have refused my offer of employment, that is your decision, but if there is anything that I might do for you, say it now.'

The words fly out.

'Money,' I say. 'I need money.'

'How much?' And again, I think he's disappointed.

'Three hundred drachmae,' I say, just as quick.

Tuireann sighs, removes a few of the many pouches hooked to his belt, and tosses them at me.

'Say your goodbyes now. I wish you all the best in your life, but I worry about you. Take care.' He bows and disappears below deck.

Everything happens very quickly. The crew are bustling about, unfixing the moorings and getting ready to set sail. I kneel beside Paches. When I got him on deck, he nearly fainted with exhaustion, and he's half asleep now, wrapped up in a thick wool cloak one of the crew gave him. I have to shake him, but when he understands this is the end, he gets to his feet.

'Look after yourself.'

He kisses me on both cheeks.

'In Athens, this is how friends part.'

I don't know why this moves me so much, but I find myself choking up, and I grin and kiss him on both cheeks too. Paches goes to say something else, but it gets drowned out by the crew shouting at us to get the fuck off or stay till Carthage.

Gelon tugs my cloak, and next thing I'm back on steady ground, standing on the harbour's frosted planks, and the ship is gliding away. A single Athenian is waving at us, his chains jingling, and I think I hear my name called out, and I start to cry. Gelon asks me what's wrong? We did it, and I say, I say it's just that I'm so fucking happy, and then I sit on the ice and watch the ship disappear.

31.

We're walking back through the charred ruins, and I find myself mouthing a question that's been on my mind for ages. I've asked Gelon a few times before, but he's never answered. Maybe now, I think, and I wipe my eyes with a tattered sleeve, feel some of the town's ashes streak across my cheeks.

'What did you really see on Tuireann's ship? Was it a god, or were you only taking the piss?'

Gelon stops. His chest is heaving, though our gait has been slow, and his steaming breath makes weird shapes in the air like grey flowers are bursting from his lips and wilting on the wind.

'Desma,' he says, at last, 'I saw Desma, and Helios too. They were in the water.'

I shiver, though of course it's impossible, and I tell him as much. For I was at the funeral when they burned Helios' body on the pyre, and Desma's in Italy, if the rumours are true.

'She's dead, Lampo. I understood all that on the ship. Maybe I didn't see it, maybe I just felt it. It was like a song playing through the water, I don't know, but I'll meet them again. The god told me that. I'll be with her and Helios again.' He whispers with conviction. 'There were other things too. You should have looked,' and it might be in my head, but for a moment, I fancy I detect a waver in his voice, and I wonder if he saw anything at all, and perhaps he spots the doubt in my eyes, for his glance turns quizzical.

'Do you know what your problem is, Lampo?'

'I'm too good-looking.'

Gelon smiles and shakes his head. 'Apart from that. It's that you've no imagination.' He puts his arm around me and starts into the first book of *The Odyssey*, and though I've no memory for poetry, I recall bits and pieces and join in when I can, and like that we walk out of Hyccara.

The journey there took two days – the way back weeks. The horses are in bits, will most likely die, but the Libyan's a softy, and he pays to have the nags cared for at a stable this old couple run, and the rest we do on foot. We sleep in woods and fields, drink from wells when we can, but they're scarce, and more often, it's rivers, streams and sometimes even puddles. We pick berries till our fingers bleed, and we can taste the salt and the sweetness blending. Near Inessa, we see a black mountain that roars like sky in a storm, a smoky red river flowing down it, like no river I've ever seen, and Gelon says it's Etna, and best avoided, and we do. We see a lot of shit, and I think I'm happy, but more 'cause of what we're going to than through. Really, I'm just desperate to get home.

The day we walk into Syracuse, it's sunny, and my crocs have worn away to nothing, just a greenish tinge to the soles, and I'm barefoot, my feet hard as boiled leather. People stare at us and whisper, and I clutch the coin and hold my head up high. Gelon and I agree to catch up later for a celebratory drink. We've had many such drinks on the way back, but this is the real one, 'cause tonight I buy Lyra's freedom. Some nights, sleeping in the woods on a bed of frosted leaves, I was in a fever, and saw mad things and often woke in a panic, my skull buzzing with midnight visions, and I felt sure the three hundred drachmae were just one of these – Tuireann had never given it. I was still broke and years away from doing what I said, but then I'd touch the coin, press its soothing coolness against my burning temples, bite the gold and taste the yellow wealth, and know it was real, and what it meant.

I head to the sea for a bath, and though it's freezing, it cleans off the worst of the dirt, and brine does its work on the cuts and bruises so that when I get out, the exhaustion's gone, and the blood is pulsing. I'm very alive. After that, it's back home for a change of clothes, and a peek in the mirror. I'm leaner than before, more hollow-cheeked, and there are a few greys in my beard and about the temples that I never saw before. It's not a handsome face, but I can look at it without the usual wincing, and I put some oil in my hair and part it in the way Lyra said suits, feed the dog, and then set out again for Gelon's. I find him in clean clothes, spruced up like myself.

'Looking good,' says I. 'All set?'

He eyes me guiltily, then says, 'Sorry, Lampo. I can't do drinks. See, I'm –'

A giddy laugh behind him, and a boy steps out with a fishing rod. It's Dares.

'Oh,' says I.

Dares smiles and claps me on the back.

'We're going fishing,' he says. 'And then when we catch a nice one, Gelon is coming back to mine, and my mother will cook it up. She is the best cook in Syracuse, you know.'

He says it with such conviction that I can't help laughing, and Dares frowns.

'It's not a boast. I never lie about such things. You can come, if you don't believe me?'

'Yeah, it would be fun,' says Gelon.

'Maybe some other time.'

They both nod, as if a little relieved, and they set out with me. We walk together part of the way, with them turning off at the beach in the direction of the rock pools and me sticking along the sandy part, down to Dismas'. Long after we split up, I can hear their chatter and laughter in the distance. I rattle my coin pouches and force a smile. It's a fine day. The finest in a long time, and the sea's that summer blue which makes you want to drink it, and soon I'm standing outside Dismas'. It's unrecognizable. They've given it a paint job, a soft buttery colour, heightened by the sun so that the place looks like a lamp, and is much bigger than before with extensions on both sides. There's a new bouncer too – a tall fella who's better dressed than I am, and at first, he won't let me in, but when he sees the gold, he bows, and the door's flung open. Inside's as much of a shock, and I'm walking on rugs. Soggy rugs from the spilt booze, but rugs all the same, and there's not the usual fishy whiff but the sweet jangle of different perfumes fusing, and the faces that turn to me are as smooth as sea stones. They're all aristos, or near enough, and I feel their eyes drill into me with disapproval, but fuck them, and I strut up to the bar, try to hide my limp, and ask for a jug of Catanian.

A young fella is serving, pale and pretty as a girl, and he says that they don't serve Catanian any more. It's swill.

'A jug of the finest, then,' says I, winking.

He nods and comes back with a honeyed red that's sickly sweet.

'Where's Lyra?'

He shrugs as if he doesn't know what I'm talking about.

'Lyra, she works here?'

A yawn, and the kid makes to take another order, and when he goes to walk past me, I grip his cloak.

'Where the fuck's Lyra?'

'I don't know. I'm new.'

The sweats start, but my voice is calm enough.

I say, 'Get me Dismas. I need to talk to Dismas.'

I grab his arm, ram some silver in the palm and push him roughly back.

'Okay, okay.'

He scampers up the stairs. People are looking at me now, muttering and shaking their heads, and I grin and drink, but the jug slips along my fingers 'cause of all the sweat, and I spill half on the countertop. The boy comes back.

'Dismas is out. Come back tomorrow.'

'Bollix.'

'N-no,' he stammers. 'I swear. He's out.'

I hop over the bar, shoulder past the boy, send him banging into a shelf of jugs that sound like they smash, but I'm already up the stairs, stamping down the hall to Dismas' room. I kick the door open for no reason, just to kick something, and sure enough, Dismas is sitting down reading. He fairly shrieks when he sees me, then smiles and puts up his hands.

'Lampo, how are things?'

'Fantastic,' says I, throwing the pouches at him; he catches the first two but the last smacks him on the temple, leaves a red mark like an egg.

'That's three hundred drachmae. All of it, you can count. I'm here for Lyra.'

He smiles again, a twisted one, and won't look me in the eye.

'I'm sorry, Lampo. I really am.'

'Sorry for what? Is she okay?'

'She's fine. Oh, she is fine, but –' he stops. 'The thing is, I sold her.'

I reef him to his feet. He won't look at me. He's scared, and so am I.

'What the fuck are you talking about? You didn't sell her.'

'It was a crazy offer, Lampo. I had to take it. Anyone would. I'm sorry, I mean, I really am, but seven hundred drachmae! It was mad money, and I know I look like I'm doing well, but I've debts, Lampo, I've got debts coming up to my eyeballs.'

There's a pain in my skull like a needle pushed slowly through my ear.

'Who did you sell her to, then? What's their name? I'll speak to them.'

'They're long gone, Lampo. It was a foreigner, a funny name I can't remember, but he said he was from the tin islands. I'm telling you, he was nuts about her, Lampo, came here every night just to hear her sing. He said she'd be a sensation. It was a crazy offer.'

I just stand there, shaking, trying to suck breath into me – it's like I'm drowning, and the more air I gulp, the worse it gets, and I crumple to the floor and can taste the dust on the floorboards and hear Dismas sputtering over me about how he's awful sorry, but he has new girls coming in who are much lovelier, and he'd be happy to let me choose one at the agreed three hundred, even two fifty. Lyra had those ugly scars, and her teeth were crooked. He'll sort me out, and I close my eyes, and the sound out of my mouth is like some animal, and Dismas shuts up and gets out of the room.

32.

Evening, a soft rain of surprising warmth is falling, and I'm sitting on the crest of a hill – the spot where the quarry fence used to be, and the soil is rutted from where the stakes have been pulled up. There's no need for a fence any more. I take a swig from a jug and look down, and I see, I see nothing. That is, no Athenians. In the weeks we've been away, they've disappeared. How many escaped through the hole we made, and how many just withered, I don't know, but the quarry is empty. Even the rats have moved on, looking for food, meat, and the place is unsettling quiet. There isn't even a wind, no inkling of a breeze. You can't hear the sea, or the city. The only sound is the wine swishing around my gums, and my breathing. I'm it. I take out the money pouches. I haven't spent a single coin of it, and the sum remains the same: three hundred drachmae.

I throw one down, and there's a soft clink when it hits the rock below. A stone-worker might find that tomorrow and wonder how it came to be there. It will be a mystery, and it might change his life, yet he'll never know. I throw down another, and it's a lovely sound – separate from myself and that ragged breath. Like a man who's run a race, but I've done nothing to merit it, just sat on my hole drinking. I keep throwing and swigging. And I wonder which will empty first, the jug or the pouches. It's the jug. There's still quite a bit of coin left, and I flick the rest down, scatter it like golden rain from a sacred sky till the last pouch is empty. I imagine three hundred different men finding these coins over the years, three hundred different mysteries, and I get up and stumble, more 'cause of my foot than the booze, and I promise myself that I'll never come here again, take a piss, and then head back towards the city, humming a tune.

I think about stopping off for another. The tavernas are packed, their windows glowing like kilns; laughter and music spill onto the streets in a way that entices, but I go straight home. Ma is up. Her door is partly open, and I can see the reddish flame of the lamp and smell the oil burning, and I stop at the threshold and take a little peek. She's seated with her hands clasped, and a woman is standing over her. It's Alekto. Ma's grey hair is down below her shoulders, and Alekto is cutting it, the curls falling away like silver birds. They're both smiling, though they don't say a word, and I step away and walk as softly as I can to my room. I was born in this room, and apart from the trip to Hyccara and that time in the quarry, I've slept here every night of my life. The straw is coming out of the bed, and I stuff a few clumps back in and take a look around – at my stuff. It's not much. A toy soldier from when I was a kid, a slingshot and dagger from the war, a few chitons and old tools from the pottery days. The dog's in the corner, and it barks as if to say, I'm yours too. I rub its ears; the tail wags, and it licks my fingers. I go back to counting my possessions, adding in the dog and Alcar's aulos, and just when I think it's all done and the pile meagre, I find a stylus and wax tablet. It was hidden in a boot along with the money I'd been saving from the market work. I take it out. This was the last gift I bought Lyra, but I never gave it to her. It was a selfish gift, really, as the hope was that she might teach me how to write. All she managed was that time on the beach when she'd shown me my own name on the wet sand, drawn the letters with a stone. Since that day, I'd practised it when I could, mostly with stones in the mud. I take up the stylus and begin to make the markings, my hand shakes so that the word looks crooked and frail, but it's there on the wax:

Lampo

I touch the letters and curse myself for not having learnt how to write her name. I'd have loved to have written that, and I could have put them together, hers and mine, joined the letters so that they made one word. That would have been something. It gets me thinking that I should learn it. It's not too late. I could find someone in the city who can show me how to write 'Lyra'. But then I think this isn't enough. I want to learn it all. I want to know all those different symbols by which a whole world is created – like those aristo kids in school who are given all the letters and all the words. And when I've learnt, I'll put it on wax or clay or whatever I can get my hands on. I'll set it down so that I always remember what we did, and yet I might as well say it, now that I've reached the end. All this happened years and years ago, and I'm an old bastard. I never learnt to read or write. I certainly tried, but I couldn't seem to make it stick, and so I have to trust that clever Strabo has set it down, for he's a man, grown now, and often stops in to see me. I've told it to him a piece at a time, and he says he's writing it on great big rolls of papyrus. Really, I've no clue 'cause my eyesight's gone, and Strabo jokes that I'm like the blind bard, a second Homer.

Not to end on a downer, but the word is that Syracuse is doomed. We're under siege, and the Carthaginians are meant to sack the city any day now. Make us slaves. People are getting out, and Strabo wants me to go too, but I won't. It's mad; I've always wanted to leave Syracuse, ditch this house, but now that I have a perfect excuse, I don't know, I can't seem to do it. Stubborn, I guess. There's Gelon's grave, too, and that needs tending. It's up past Epipolae, and I make my way there most weeks and tell him what I've been up to, which usually isn't much. Sometimes I'll play a tune on the aulos, and though I won't win any prizes, I've been practising for a while now and reckon I'm decent. The odd time, I'll see old students paying their respects. Gelon set up a little school, teaching kids *The Iliad* and whatnot. The plan was I'd join him and be a teacher too, but sure, the kids knew more than me.

Apparently, there are six hundred ships in the great harbour. Even more than when the Athenians came, but it doesn't feel real, because I can't see them. The world outside has gone bleary like it's glimpsed through mist.

Only when I close my eyes are things clear. Eyes closed, I see it: the quarry theatre. Gelon, the Athenians, the kids, and even Biton, all of us as we were back then, and though she never came, I see Lyra too, and we're moving about tinily beneath the staring sky, shivering with want, and mad with the conviction that this is it, cold ground below, eternity winking above, as we whisper our parts, and it seems to me a soft and delicate thing.

Athens

408 BC

On the last night, there was a storm of the kind that made the dogs howl, the children weep, and the tiles scatter off the roofs so that they mingled with the fallen leaves, and the people said this was auspicious. A man who had written such words could not be sent on his way with anything so humdrum as good weather. His possessions had been packed in boxes, and the house, stripped of every personal effect, was eerily bare. Four wagons were required for all of it, and two of those were just for the books. Papyrus rolls as long as carpets. No man could have a use for so many words, and yet the guests, when they arrived to say farewell, their gifts clasped in nervous fingers, what did most of them bring? Not anything so useful as furs for the harsh northern winter, nor jewels, nor gold. They brought books, and knew that he would not have wanted it any other way.

The taller boxes served as tables. The smaller ones sufficed as chairs, and it was a strange sight because the men seated on these boxes awaiting their dinner were amongst the richest and most esteemed of the city, fellows used to reclining on sofas as slaves glided about anticipating their every whim. Tonight there was only one servant. An old man with a thick head of iron-grey hair and dark watchful eyes. The servant's name was Amphitryon, and he was furious.

For years he had done his best to run a good house. It was he who had first suggested his master give symposiums. What had begun as a tentative bid to make his master more respectable transformed itself into the most sought-after event in the city. Noblemen would accost him in the street and implore him to put in a good word – please, might there not still be space? These gatherings had been Amphitryon's life's work. What his master had put into his plays, he had given to parties. He wrestled with the problem of what pastry to choose the way a philosopher might with the issue of first causes. The correct wine to accompany each dish kept him awake. Of course, he hired the best musicians, singers whose voices and skill would make Orpheus blush, and profess himself a dabbler, but more than anything, it was the conversation. That peculiar kindling that happened when good wine, music and minds came together. And yet now, on their final night in Athens, it had come to this: men seated on boxes as their stomachs growled, and still his master had not deigned to make an appearance.

A hand touched his wrist, and he looked down and saw a young man, unnervingly handsome, tousled blond hair in the latest style, and his cheeks still bare save for down on his chin. He was the son of some politician people were talking about. There was a time when Amphitryon would not only have known his name but been able to draw his family tree. He was out of touch. The young man was smiling in that way of the very good-looking – confident that its reception will be warm – yet when he spoke, there was a breathy apprehension to his speech that the lad took evident pains to hide.

'Pardon. Do you think he will be down soon?'

'Yes, sir. He is just finishing an important dispatch, but he will join us shortly.'

A lie, but you could not very well say the truth. That the farewell dinner was his idea, and his master had wanted to sneak out of the city in the night, telling no one. That he was most likely reading and would come down at the last possible moment. No, important dispatches were infinitely preferable.

'Oh, I imagine he has much correspondence,' said the young man eagerly. 'Kings and queens, no less.'

'It has been known to happen.' This was true, and it felt good to stop lying.

'But does Macedonia count?'

This was Kritias. Also a politician, but one so influential that even Amphitryon could not remain ignorant. A fine athlete in his youth, in middle age he had run to corpulence, and there had been a flattening of his features till they became indistinct. Whether it was hunger or malice, he had been passing sniping remarks since his arrival.

'I mean,' said Kritias, 'it seems we demean royalty by taking every petty chief at his word. There's a fellow in the Kerameikos just now. A cutpurse who styles himself the king of the beggars. Is he really a monarch?'

A few guests tittered. Amphitryon offered Kritias more wine.

'I don't quite see your point,' said the young man.

'Evidently, your father's son. Need to have things explained slowly, eh?'

More laughter and the young man blushed; his ears, in particular, became very red.

'As we are guests, I will pretend I did not hear that.'

'Pretend if you like. I admire imagination in the young.'

'However, I must object to what you have said about Macedonia. It is a powerful land, and its strength grows every day.' He looked about him, blinking rapidly. 'And I think the man whose guests we are, one of the finest minds our city has ever produced, I think if he should choose to leave us and take his art to Macedonia, then from that fact alone, it would be a great kingdom.'

Before Kritias could reply, Amphitryon excused himself and went upstairs to his master's quarters because, really, this was too much. He found him much as expected, with a book on his lap, reading.

'You have to go down. They're becoming restless.'

His master looked up.

'So, he didn't come?'

'I'm afraid not. He is very ill and cannot leave his bed. The doctors do not think he will live out the winter.'

A nod, as if it were expected.

'Yet, I think he will pull through. If only to outlast me. He must win at everything.' He smiled, but there was bitterness in it, melancholy too.

Amphitryon brought him his stick. They both had sticks, though the handle of his master's was tipped with silver. He got to his feet – a tall man. There had once been near a head of height between them, but his master's back was bad, and he stooped so much they had become equals. Only the limbs showed the discrepancy. Amphitryon's were short and stumpy; the master's long and slender, with fingers delicate as reeds, and there were stains about the tips from the constant scribbling. They made their way slowly down the creaking stairs.

When the guests saw him, they stood and cheered.

'Apologies for the state of this place.' His master addressed no one in particular. 'We leave tomorrow morning, you see. The only thing I have not packed is my bed. Does anyone want a bed?'

No one, it seemed, did.

'It's a fine bed. Oak frame.'

The young man raised his hand.

'I write poetry,' he stammered. 'Or really, I try to. Perhaps it will bring me luck.'

Kritias chortled, and Amphitryon braced himself for the worst. His master had a wicked tongue and might very well lash out at such foolishness.

'You shall have it then, though I warn you I was never much of a poet.'

Amphitryon smiled and laid out the supper. The soup was rather cold, the cooking fire down to its embers, and he padded the meal by bringing out various cheeses. The men ate greedily and gave excessive compliments. The master said little and seemed ill at ease. The conversation moved inevitably to the subject of the war. The guests were of different factions and did not trust each other. They talked around things rather than about them, and it was a welcome respite when there was a knock on the door.

Kritias slapped his knee and grinned.

'Dancing girls? Really, you shouldn't have.'

'No, sir,' said Amphitryon icily. 'This is not that kind of house.'

The knocking grew louder, and he bowed and went to answer it. He felt that old throb of expectation, so common in the past, when a door knock meant another splendid arrival. He unhooked the latch and found a man on the threshold, sopping wet. A stranger. For if they had met, he would certainly have remembered this man. He was of middle height, and his hair was tangled and black as rook feathers. The wrinkles embedded so deeply into his cheeks they resembled scars, and his eyes were the vivid green of serpent scales. The face of a tramp, yet his clothes were exquisite, rich purple and gold, and of a fashionable cut.

'Is this the home of the playwright Euripides?' came a youthful voice.

Amphitryon was so startled by the incongruity of the voice that he hesitated.

'It is.'

'Oh, thank goodness. May I please come in? I wish very much to speak to him.'

'I'm afraid that will not be possible. You see . . .'

The stranger raised his hands in supplication.

'I know he is leaving tomorrow. That's why I'm here. I should have come before, but I didn't. I think I was afraid.'

Amphitryon's first instinct was to shut the door in his face, but he checked the impulse. Why, he couldn't quite say. Perhaps it was the storm. The rain was falling from the stranger as if he were some cloud. No, he had turned men away on stormy nights before. It was something else. The voice, maybe. The youth of it emanating from this ruined figure. Whatever it was, he sighed and wondered what the guests would think.

'Come in, but I warn you to be quick. He is entertaining.'

The stranger clasped his hand.

'You are kind. You are kind.'

'Enough of that. Get in before you drown.'

The stranger followed a few feet behind, the water dripping loudly on the tiled floor. The men on the boxes craned their necks to get a better look at the arrival, and when they did, they were disappointed, to say the least.

'I am sorry, but this man. Eh, he says he . . .' Amphitryon's voice trailed off. Standing before his master and some of the most eminent men in Athens, he realized he had nothing to say. Could not think of any reasonable introduction.

'Pardon,' said the stranger. 'But may I ask which one of you is Euripides?'

Laughter, awkward and forced. In truth, the room was more tense than amused.

'I am he,' said his master. 'Welcome to my home. Excuse its sorry appearance.'

The stranger walked to him and knelt at his feet.

'I think you have a fan,' said Kritias.

Amphitryon was suddenly frightened. What if he'd let in a madman who meant violence? Still kneeling, the stranger pressed the master's hand and kissed it, and the knuckles glistened. He had begun to cry.

'I am sorry, so sorry. I had a speech prepared, but it's gone now.'

'Get up,' said the master gently. 'It can't be so bad as all that. There is another box just there.'

The stranger sat down.

'Now, would you like some wine? You must be chilled to the bone.'

'Yes, please. I think I am rather.'

Wine was brought, and the stranger sipped it; tears made his wrinkles glimmer in the lamplight, and he wiped his eyes with the hem of his cloak, muttered something under his breath.

'What is your name, good fellow? Have we met before?'

'Paches, son of Croton,' he stammered. 'Once, briefly, when I was a child. You gave me a sweet, but I cannot imagine you remember.'

The master furrowed his brow and then shook his head.

'I'm afraid I don't, but it still counts. We are not strangers, then. Is there anything I can do for you, Paches? Tell me.'

The stranger put his hand inside his cloak and removed a scroll.

'This is for you.' He unrolled it. 'An original Heraclitus, written in his own hand. I am told it is rare.'

His master smiled.

'I thank you, but truly it is too much. I give you a sweet, and in exchange receive this.'

The stranger shook his head vehemently and again gripped the master's hands.

'I owe my life to you. My debt could not be repaid with a thousand books!'

Kritias whispered something that made the others laugh.

'Syracuse,' said the stranger. 'I was a prisoner there.'

The laughter ceased immediately.

Even now, more than four years after the fact, the mention

of Syracuse was enough to make the air in the room feel chill and malevolent. Yes, soldiers had made it back from the disaster, but these men had escaped after the final battle. Of those who had been imprisoned, none had returned. At least no one in this room had seen them. Even Kritias was solemn, gripping his cup and straining to hear what would come next.

When the stranger spoke, his tone was altered. It held the confidence of resignation. His words came fluently. It was a curious tale. Too improbable to be believed. All about a theatre in a quarry, run by potters and children, and how he and many other prisoners were given food in exchange for the master's words. These lines were life to them, and that was why he'd come here, and please excuse his interruption and his ragged face, but he had not always looked like this, and he had to come. His master had begun to weep during the telling, in that silent way of his, and he took the stranger's head in his hands and pressed it against his own as if he wanted their very thoughts to join. For the remainder of the night, he ignored the other guests and spoke only to this man.

Amphitryon wondered how it had come to this. How, on their final night, he should choose to spend it listening to the imaginings of this broken fellow. Yet, he reasoned, perhaps in the end, it was fitting, for his master was ever in love with misfortune and believed the world a wounded thing that can only be healed by story.

Acknowledgements

This book took a long time for me to write – about seven years from the first line to the last. On many occasions, I lost my faith in the thing. I thought to myself that it would be best to do something else entirely, and I would try that for a while, but in the end, I always came back to this novel. Somehow I needed to finish it. Yet no amount of needing would have got me to the end, were it not for the help of so many people along the way.

Firstly, thank you to my family: my brothers, Anthony and David, for their constant support, encouragement and laughs. Thank you to my mother, Anne. It's a rare parent who phones up their unpublished son to tell him that he must, on no account, let his job distract him from his writing. Our house was always full of books, and you taught me there were things more important than making money and that they often came bound.

Thank you to the two Rebeccas: thank you, Rebecca Stott; without your initial support and encouragement, this novel would most likely have ended as a vignette. Thank you to my wonderful agent, Rebecca Carter, for seeing the promise in the work, sticking with me, and for your keen editorial eye. Thank you, Chris Clemans, my fantastic US agent. I feel incredibly lucky to have both you and Rebecca representing me. Thank you to the outstanding team at Janklow & Nesbit.

I have been fortunate enough to have not one but two amazing editors: Helen Garnons-Williams and Caroline Zancan. Thank you both for caring so much about this novel and for elevating it with your insights, questions and edits. Thank you for making this process so surprisingly fun and enjoyable. A huge thanks to Ella Harold, Ellie Smith, Charlotte Faber, Shan Morley Jones, Jon Gray, Chloe Davies,

Jasmin Lindenmeir, and everyone at Fig Tree and Penguin for your fantastic work on this book. Likewise, my thanks to all at Henry Holt.

Thank you to Shane Mac an Bhaird. For years you have been one of my first readers; because I trust your judgement, and you never let me down. This time was no exception.

Thank you to my friends and writers at DWG Paris. Thank you Albert Alla, Peter Brown, Helen Cusack O'Keeffe, Amanda Dennis, Nina Marie Gardner, Rachel Kapelke-Dale, Rafael Herrero, Matt Jones, Corinne LaBalme, Samuel Leader, Reine Arcache Melvin, Dina Nayeri, Chris Newens, Tasha Ong, Alberto Rigettini, Jonathan Schiffman and Nafkote Tamirat. Thank you to Nicolas Padamsee, John Patrick McHugh and Rory Gleeson for the friendship, book talk and support.

Thank you to the teaching staff at UEA and the many terrific writers I met there. Thanks to Elizabeth Reapy for publishing my first short stories and seeing there was potential.

A special thanks to Sarah Bannan and all of the team at Arts Council Ireland. During the writing of this novel, I was often very broke, and the two bursaries I received at crucial times allowed me to keep amassing words and paying rent.

Thanks to the Kildare Arts Service for supporting my residency at Annaghmakerrig. Thank you to the staff there who looked after us and created that rarest of things: a place where the only thing we needed to do was write.

Thank you to Carol McGuire, the brilliant teacher who first introduced me to Thucydides and *The History of The Peloponnesian War*. For that, I am forever grateful. Thanks to the Classics Department at University College Dublin, where I did my degree.

Thank you to my son, Aaron, who, being four months old during the final revisions, was limited in his editorial feedback, and yet I think he helped and is continuing to help me on my way.

Most of all, thank you to my first reader and wife, Emma Durrant-Lennon. This book is dedicated to you, and so it should be. Your belief in my writing and this story kept me going. Everything has been better since you showed up in The Stag's Head that night. I love you more than Gelon loves Euripides.